OPEN

MW01061358

New York City, Spring/Summer 2007

Number Twenty-Three

OPEN CITY

Actual Air
Poems by David Berman

"David Berman's poems are beautiful, strange, intelligent, and funny. They are narratives that freeze life in impossible contortions. They take the familiar and make it new, so new the reader is stunned and will not soon forget. I found much to savor on every page of *Actual Air*. It's a book for everyone."
—James Tate

"This is the voice I have been waiting so long to hear . . . Any reader who tunes in to his snappy, offbeat meditations is in for a steady infusion of surprises and delights."
—Billy Collins

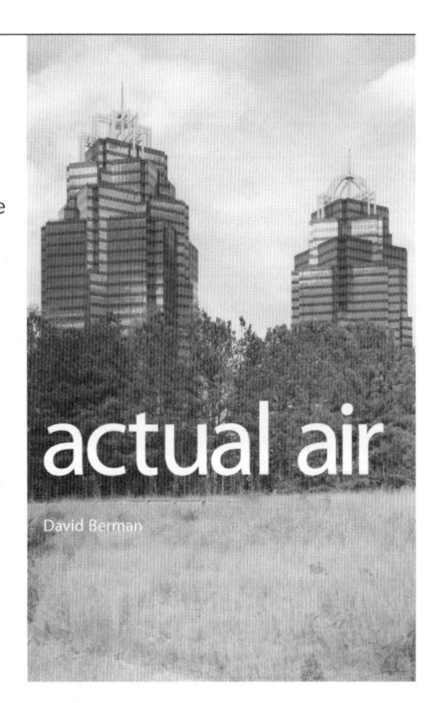

My Misspent Youth
Essays by Meghan Daum

"An empathic reporter and a provacative autobiographer . . . I finished it in a single afternoon, mesmerized and sputtering."
—*The Nation*

"Meghan Daum articulates the only secret left in the culture: discreet but powerful fantasies of romance, elegance, and ease that survive in our uncomfortable world of striving. These essays are very smart and very witty and just heartbreaking enough to be deeply pleasurable."
—Marcelle Clements

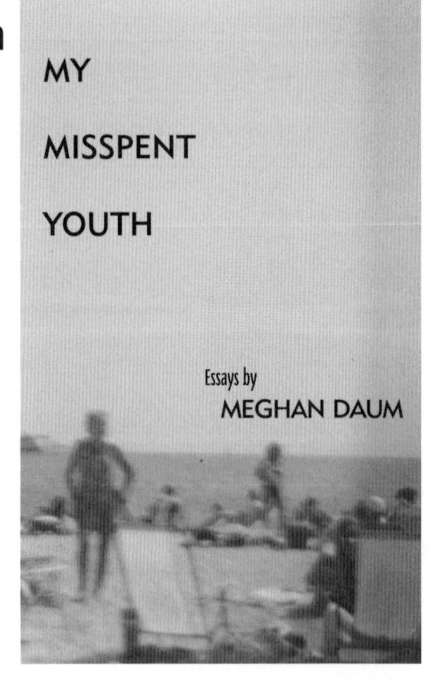

Open City Books are available at fine bookstores or at **www.opencity.org**, and are distributed to the trade by Publishers Group West.

Venus Drive

Stories by Sam Lipsyte

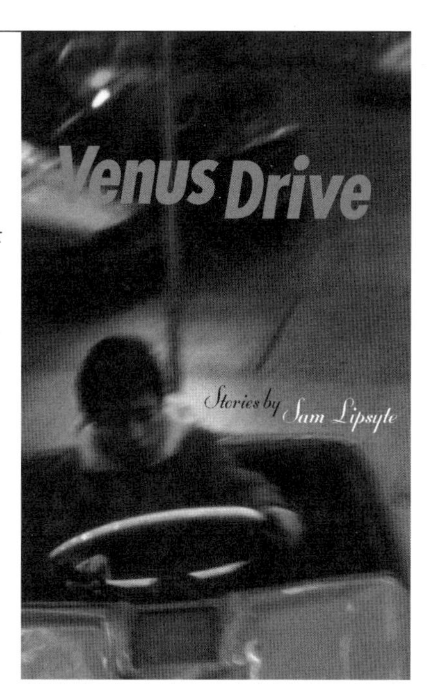

"Sam Lipsyte is a wickedly gifted writer. *Venus Drive* is filled with grimly satisfying fractured insights and hardcore humor. But it also displays some inspired sympathy for the daze and confusion of its characters. Above all it's wonderfully written and compulsively readable with brilliant and funny dialogue, a collection that represents the emergence of a very strong talent."
—Robert Stone

"Sam Lipsyte can get blood out of a stone—rich, red human blood from the stony sterility of contemporary life. His writing is gripping—at least I gripped this book so hard my knuckles turned white."
—Edmund White

Karoo

A Novel by Steve Tesich

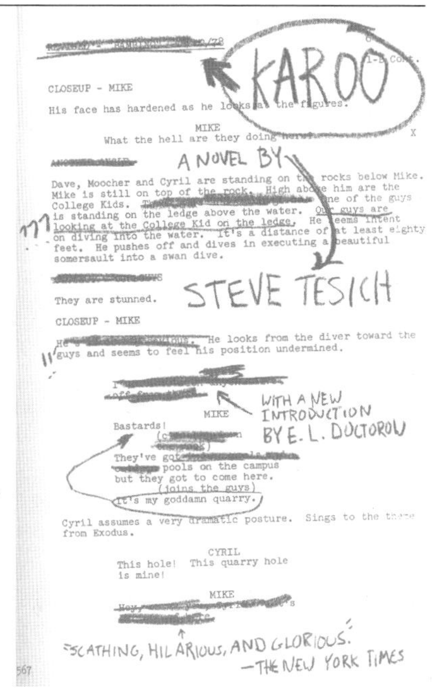

"Fascinating—a real satiric invention full of wise outrage."
—Arthur Miller

"A powerful and deeply disturbing portrait of a flawed, self-destructive, and compulsively fascinating figure."
—*Kirkus Reviews* (starred)

"Saul Karoo is a new kind of wild man, the sane maniac. Larger than life and all too human, his out-of-control odyssey through sex, death, and show business is extreme, and so is the pleasure of reading it. Steve Tesich created a fabulously Gargantuan comic character."
—Michael Herr

OPEN CITY

Some Hope
A Trilogy by Edward St. Aubyn

"Tantalizing . . . A memorable tour de force."
—*The New York Times Book Review*

"Hilarious and harrowing by turns, sophisticated, reflective, and brooding."
—*The New York Review of Books*

"Feverishly good writing . . . Full of Algonquin wit on the surface while roiling underneath. *Some Hope* is a hell of a brew, as crisp and dry as a good English cider and as worth savoring as any of Waugh's most savage volleys."
—*The Ruminator Review*

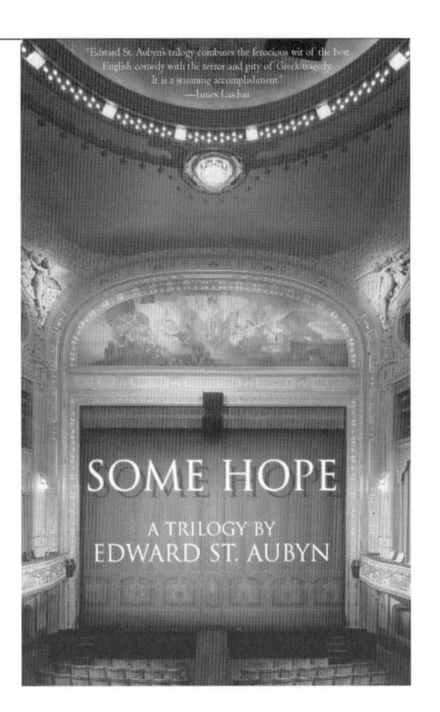

Mother's Milk
A Novel by Edward St. Aubyn

"St. Aubyn's caustic, splendid novel probes the slow violence of blood ties—a superbly realized agenda hinted at in the novel's arresting first sentence: 'Why had they pretended to kill him when he was born?'"
—*The Village Voice*

"Postpartum depression, assisted suicide, adultery, alcoholism—it's all here in St. Aubyn's keenly observed, perversely funny novel about an illustrious cosmopolitan family and the mercurial matriarch who rules them all."
—*People*

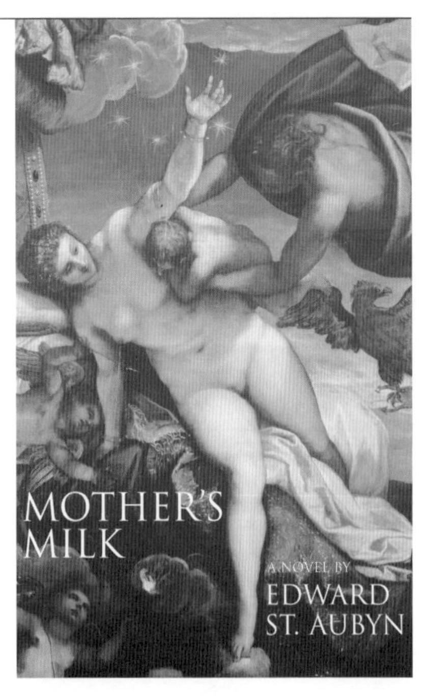

BOOKS

Goodbye, Goodness
A Novel by Sam Brumbaugh

"*Goodbye, Goodness* is the rock n' roll *Great Gatsby*."
—*New City Chicago*

"Sam Brumbaugh's debut novel couldn't be more timely. *Goodbye, Goodness* boasts just enough sea air and action to make an appealing summer read without coming anywhere near fluffsville."
—*Time Out New York*

"Beautifully captures the wrung-out feel of a depleted American century."
—*Baltimore City Paper*

The First Hurt
Stories by Rachel Sherman

"Sherman's writing is sharp, hard, and honest; there's a fearlessness in her work, an I'm-not-afraid-to-say-this quality. Because she knows that most of us have thought the same but didn't have the guts to say it."
—*Boston Phoenix*

"Rachel Sherman writes stories like splinters: they get under your skin and stay with you long after you've closed the book. These haunting stories are both wonderfully, deeply weird and unsettlingly familiar."
—Judy Budnitz.

TWO SUMMER TITLES

LONG LIVE A HUNGER TO FEED EACH OTHER

POEMS BY JEROME BADANES

INTRODUCTION BY NANCY WILLARD

"Reading Jerome Badanes' poems is not so much reading a voice from the heartfelt past as reading a poet whose work is very much alive and yet reflects a lost—and meaningful—age. He is one of our good souls; he is one of our poets. I treasure his work."
—*Gerald Stern*

OM OPEN CITY BOOKS

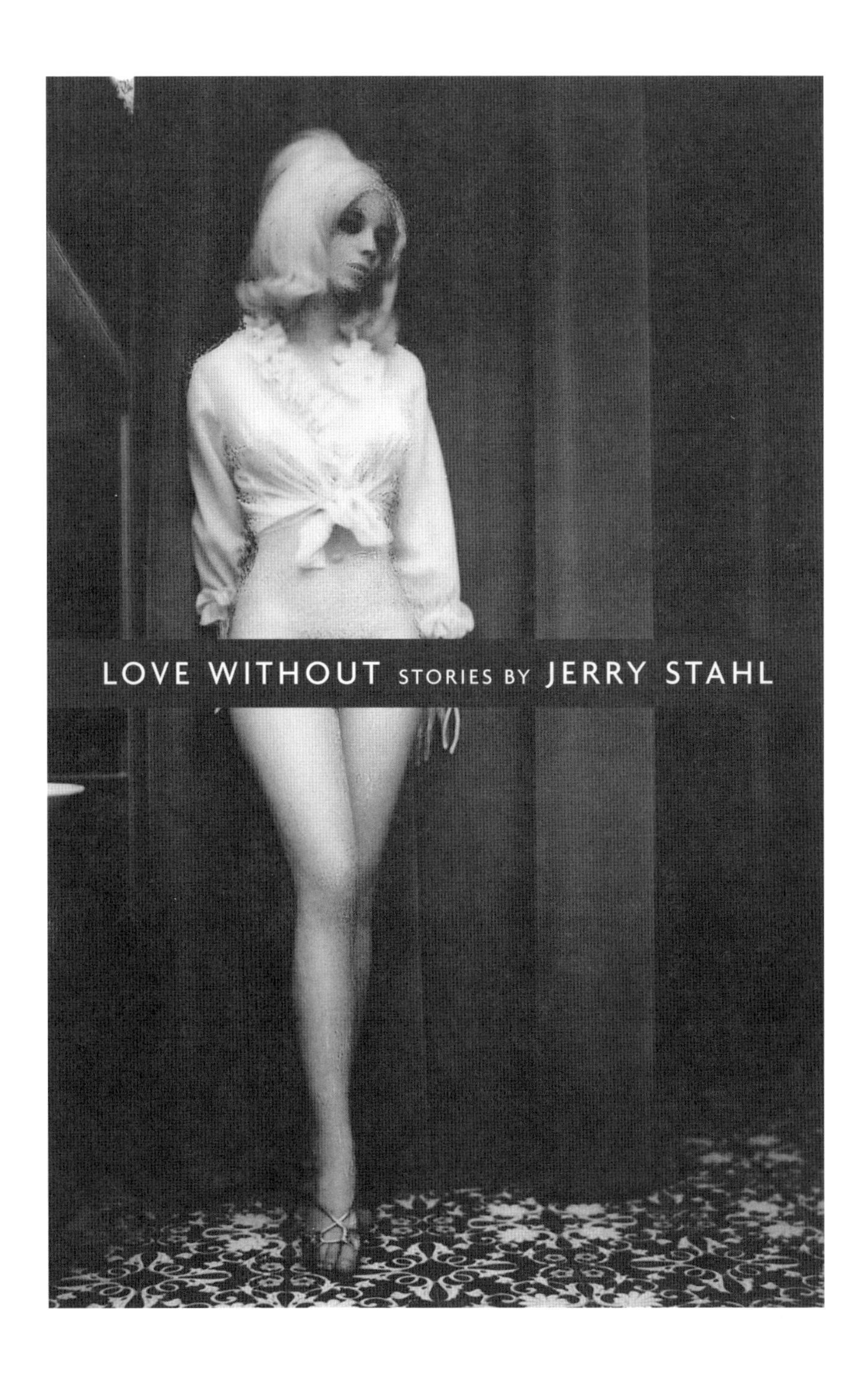

OPEN CITY

NOON

NOON

A LITERARY ANNUAL

1324 LEXINGTON AVENUE PMB 298 NEW YORK NEW YORK 10128

EDITION PRICE $9 DOMESTIC $14 FOREIGN

150 East 3rd Street at Avenue A
New York City
212.358.0195
www.annanyc.com

OPEN CITY

Open City is published by Open City, Inc., a nonprofit corporation. Donations are tax-deductible to the extent allowed by the law. A one-year subscription (3 issues) is $30; a two-year subscription (6 issues) is $55. Make checks payable to: Open City, Inc., 270 Lafayette Street, Suite 1412, New York, NY 10012. For credit-card orders, see our Web site: www.opencity.org. E-mail: editors@opencity.org.

Open City is a member of the Council of Literary Magazines and Presses and is indexed by the American Humanities Index.

Open City gratefully acknowledges the generous support of the family of Robert Bingham. We also thank the National Endowment for the Arts and the Council of Literary Magazines & Presses for a regrant from the New York State Council on the Arts.

Printed in Canada.
Copyright © 2007 by Open City, Inc.
All rights reserved.

ISBN-13: 978-1-890447-43-4
ISBN-10: 1-890447-43-9
ISSN: 1089-5523

OPEN CITY

EDITORS
Thomas Beller
Joanna Yas

ART DIRECTOR
Nick Stone

EDITOR-AT-LARGE
Adrian Dannatt

CONTRIBUTING EDITORS
Jonathan Ames
Elizabeth Beller
David Berman
Aimée Bianca
Will Blythe
Sam Brumbaugh
Amanda Gersh
Laura Hoffmann
Kip Kotzen
Anthony Lacavaro
Alix Lambert
Vanessa Lilly
Sam Lipsyte
Jim Merlis
Honor Moore
Robert Nedelkoff
Parker Posey
Beatrice von Rezzori
Elizabeth Schmidt
Lee Smith
Alexandra Tager
Tony Torn
Jocko Weyland

INTERNS
Ruth Baron
Hilary Metcalf Costa
Rebecca Green

READERS
Terra Chalberg
Catherine Griffiths
Michael Hornburg
Jessa Lingel
Aaron Rich
Ben Turner

FOUNDING EDITORS
Thomas Beller
Daniel Pinchbeck

FOUNDING PUBLISHER
Robert Bingham

SOUTHWEST REVIEW

The David Nathan Meyerson Prize for Fiction

The *Southwest Review* is pleased to announce a new prize, beginning in 2008, for fiction writers who have not published a first book. Named for the late David Nathan Meyerson (1967-1998), a therapist and talented writer who died before he was able to show to the greater world the full fruits of his literary potential, the prize will consist of $1,000 and publication in *Southwest Review*. With the generous support of Marlene, Marti, and Morton Meyerson, the award will continue to honor David Meyerson's memory by encouraging and taking notice of other writers of great promise.

The David Nathan Meyerson
Prize for Fiction guidelines
to be announced.

~

— www.southwestreview.org —

PETE'S CANDY STORE

Pete's Reading Series

HOSTED BY MIRA JACOB AND ALISON HART

For seven years running, Pete's has earned a reputation as Brooklyn's premier reading series, where today's literary icons and tomorrow's stars take the stage regularly.

Every other Thursday, September-June

Pete's Candy Store
709 Lorimer Street,
Brooklyn, NY

www.petescandystore.com

NICK STONE DESIGN

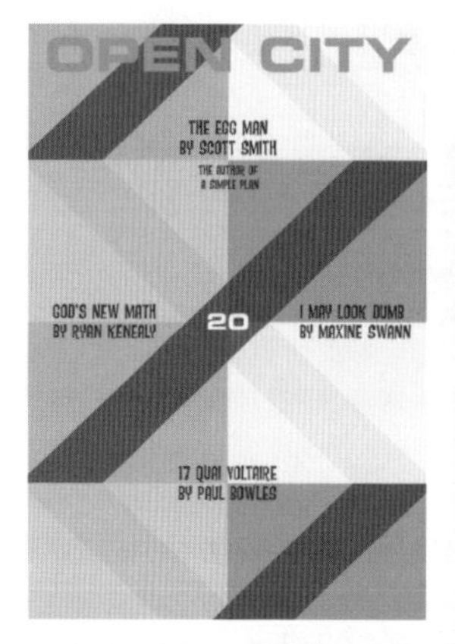

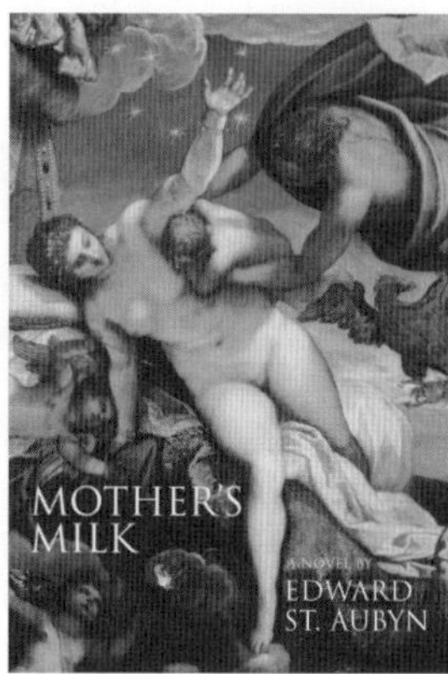

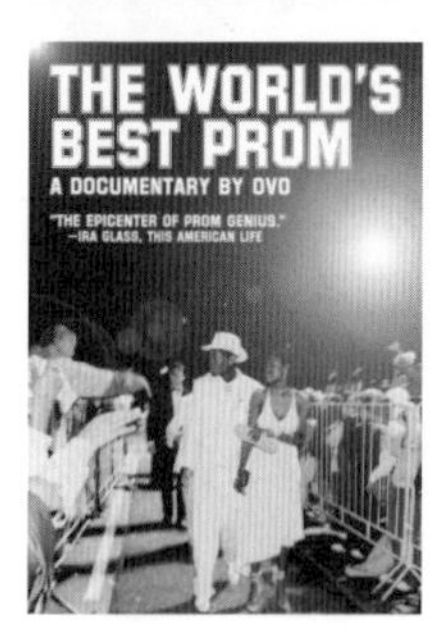

www.nickstonedesign.com
stone@nickstonedesign.com
tel: 212.995.1863

HOUSING WORKS
BOOKSTORE
CAFE

READ WORK
YOUR
DONATE BOOKS

RENT SPACE
OUR
IMPROVE WORLD

www.housingworksbookstore.org

anderbo.com "Best New Online Journal"
—storySouth Million Writers Award

anderbo.com

fiction poetry "fact" photography

Out now: Elk #13
Now I Hate Summer catalog with an essay by Craig Stecyk, poems by Francis Picabia, and artwork by Judy Chicago, Rick Griffin, John McCracken, Von Dutch, Robert Irwin, Ed Roth, and others.

Forthcoming: Rick Charnoski *Sleepers*
www.elkzine.com

Installation of "Now I Hate Summer" with Mott.January 2007.
Photography: Genevieve Hanson courtesy of Blood, New York.

LINCOLN PLAZA CINEMAS

Six Screens

63RD STREET & BROADWAY
OPPOSITE LINCOLN CENTER
212-757-2280

Alex Abramovich
Benjamin Anastas
Emily Barton
Franklin Bruno
John Darnielle
Jim Dickinson
Geoff Dyer
Will Eno
Samantha Gillison
Robert Gordon
Ahmet Ertegun
Brian Howe
Shelly Jackson
David Knowles
Jonathan Lethem
Sam Lipsyte
Gary Lutz
Megan Matthews
Lydia Millet
Jason Moran
Rick Moody
James Morris
Jenny Offil
Aesop Rock
Christpher Sorrentino
Dana Spiotta
Blake Schwarzenbach
Nick Tosches
Tony Tost
Joanna Yas

moistworks.com

an mp3 boombox

CONTRIBUTORS' NOTES

JEROME BADANES was a novelist, poet, and screenwriter who died in 1995 at age fifty-eight. Also a professor at Vassar, Sarah Lawrence, and SUNY Purchase, Badanes was born and raised in Brooklyn. His cult novel, *The Final Opus of Leon Solomon,* was published in 1989, and his posthumous poetry collection, *Long Live a Hunger to Feed Each Other*, is forthcoming from Open City Books in June.

HADARA BAR-NADAV's poems appear or are forthcoming in *Beloit Poetry Journal*, *Chelsea*, *Indiana Review*, *The Journal, Quarterly West*, *TriQuarterly*, *Verse*, and other journals. Her poetry collection, *A Glass of Milk to Kiss Goodnight*, was chosen by Kim Addonizio for the *Margie* First Book Prize and will be published this spring.

JILL BIALOSKY is the author of two collections of poetry, *The End of Desire* and *Subterranean,* and a novel, *House Under Snow*. Her new novel, *The Life Room*, from which this excerpt is drawn, is forthcoming from Harcourt in August. She is an editor at W. W. Norton and lives in New York City.

MAX BLAGG was born in England and has lived in New York City since 1971. He is the author of several books of poetry, most recently *Pink Instrument*, and is co-editor of the literary magazine *Bald Ego*. This story is from a libelous forthcoming "novel" entitled *101 Nights*.

NICK FLYNN's *Another Bullshit Night in Suck City* won the PEN/Martha Albrand Award for the Art of the Memoir, and has been translated into thirteen languages. He is also the author of two books of poetry, *SomeEther,* winner of the PEN/Joyce Osterweil Award, and *Blind Huber*. His poems, essays and non-fiction have appeared in such publications as *The New Yorker*, *The Paris Review*, and *The New York Times Book Review*. He teaches at the University of Houston one semester a year, and spends the remaning months elsewhere.

DEBORAH GARRISON is the poetry editor at Knopf and a senior editor at Pantheon Books. She is the author of the collections *A Working Girl Can't Win and Other Poems* and *The Second Child*. Her poetry and prose have appeared in *The New Yorker*, *The New York Times*, *Poets & Writers*, *The Yale Review*, and other publications.

JIM HARRISON, whose most recent novel is *Returning to Earth,* spends the year in Montana and on the Mexican border. This excerpt is the first appearance of *The English Major*, his novel in progress.

RODNEY JACK lives in rural North Carolina and is currently working through a collection of intermediate torch songs and big band standards for piano.

WAYNE KOESTENBAUM has published five books of poetry: *Best-Selling Jewish Porn Films, Model Homes, The Milk of Inquiry, Rhapsodies of a Repeat Offender,* and *Ode to Anna Moffo and Other Poems*. He has also published a novel, *Moira Orfei in Aigues-Mortes*, and five books of nonfiction: *Andy Warhol*, *Cleavage, Jackie Under My Skin, The Queen's Throat* (a National Book Critics Circle Award finalist), and *Double Talk.* His contribution to this issue is an excerpt from his book, *Hotel Theory*, forthcoming from Soft Skull Press.

CYNTHIA KRAMAN a.k.a. Cynthia Genser a.k.a. Chinas Comidas is the author of four collections of poetry, including the recently reissued *Taking on the Local Color* (Wesleyan University Press). Her band's CD, *Chinas Comidas 1977–80 Live and Studio Recordings,* came out in 2006 on Exquisite Corpse Records; a band reunion will kick off in Seattle this summer. She lives in New York City.

Born in Hertfordshire, England, GLYN MAXWELL is the author of ten books of poetry, including *The Breakage*, *The Nerve*, and *The Sugar Mile*. His plays, which have been widely published and produced, include *The Lifeblood* and *Wolfpit*, which was staged at Theater Three in New York City in 2006. His novel, *The Girl Who Was Going to Die* (excerpted herein), as well as his next poetry collection, are forthcoming in 2008. He currently lives in London and is the poetry editor of *The New Republic*.

THORPE MOECKEL is the author of *Odd Botany*, a collection of poems, and several chapbooks. He works a small farm with his wife and daughter in western Virginia, and teaches at Hollins University.

GREG PURCELL works at St. Mark's Bookshop in New York City's East Village. His poetry and prose have appeared in *Fence*, *McSweeney's* and the *Denver Quarterly*.

ANNE SEXTON, born in 1928 in Newton, Massachusetts, published eight collections of poetry during her lifetime, including *To Bedlam and Part Way Back, All My Pretty Ones*, *The Book of Folly*, and *Live or Die*, which won a Pulitzer in 1966. She also formed a chamber rock group called Anne Sexton and Her Kind, which backed her at readings. "All God's Children Need Radios" was originally published in *Ms.* magazine in 1973. She committed suicide in 1974.

VIJAY SESHADRI is the author of two books of poems, *Wild Kingdom* and *The Long Meadow,* as well as many essays, articles, and reviews. He teaches at Sarah Lawrence College.

JOE WENDEROTH grew up in and around Baltimore. He is the author of the poetry collections *Disfortune* and *It Is if I Speak*; *Letters to Wendy's*, a novel in verse; and *The Holy Spirit of Life: Essays Written for John Ashcroft's Secret Self*. His new book of poems, *No Real Light*, is forthcoming from Wave Books later this year. He also teaches in the creative writing graduate program at the University of California, Davis.

NANCY WILLARD's most recent book of poems is *In the Salt Marsh* (Knopf). Her book of essays on writing, *The Left-Handed Story,* is forthcoming from the University of Michigan Press. She teaches at Vassar College.

REBECCA WOLFF is the author of two books of poems, *Manderley* and *Figment.* She is the founding editor and publisher of Fence and Fence Books. Her essays have been anthologized by Soft Skull Press and Iowa University Press, among others. Wolff lives in Athens, New York with her family, including novelist Ira Sher. Her story in this issue is excerpted from *The Beginners,* a novel-in-progress.

“*Returning to Earth* [is] quietly magnificent.”

—Will Blythe, *The New York Times Book Review* (Front-Page Review)

“[A] moving meditation on life and afterlife . . . Admirably unsentimental . . . Harrison gradually illuminates the often traumatic past, throwing up shadows that signify the vast spaces of his imagined world.”

—*THE NEW YORKER*

“A prodigious achievement . . . Raucous, literary, bawdy, goofy, and wise. It is heartbreakingly sad. And it registers the redemption of love, the power of the word to speak the truth, the peace that comes to those who live even when it is time to die.”

—BART THURBER, *THE SAN DIEGO UNION-TRIBUNE*

“A force of nature in American letters . . . *Returning to Earth* is a watershed work for Harrison.”—*THE SEATTLE TIMES*

GROVE PRESS
www.groveatlantic.com

OPEN

"The Crazy Person" by Mary Gaitskill, "La Vie en Rose" by Hubert Selby Jr., "Cathedral Parkway" by Vince Passaro. Art by Jeff Koons and Devon Dikeou. Cover by Ken Schles, whose *Invisible City* sells for thousands on Ebay. Stan Friedman's poems about baldness and astronomy, Robert Polito on Lester Bangs, Jon Tower's real life letters to astronauts. (Vastly underpriced at $300. Only three copies left.)

ISSUE # 1

A first glimpse of Martha McPhee; a late burst from Terry Southern. Jaime Manrique's "Twilight at the Equator." Art by Paul Ramirez-Jonas, Kate Milford, Richard Serra. Kip Kotzen's "Skate Dogs," Richard Foreman's "Poetry City" with playful illustrations by Daniel Pinchbeck, David Shields' "Sports" and his own brutal youth. (Ken Schles found the negative of our cover girl on Thirteenth Street and Avenue B. We're still looking for the girl. $25)

ISSUE # 2

Irvine Welsh's "Eurotrash" (his American debut), Richard Yates (from his last, unfinished novel), Patrick McCabe (years before *The Butcher Boy*). Art by Francesca Woodman (with an essay by Betsy Berne), Jacqueline Humphries, Allen Ginsberg, Alix Lambert. A short shot of Lipsyte—"Shed"—not available anywhere else. Plus Alfred Chester's letters to Paul Bowles. Chip Kidd riffs on the Fab Four. (Very few copies left! $25)

ISSUE # 3

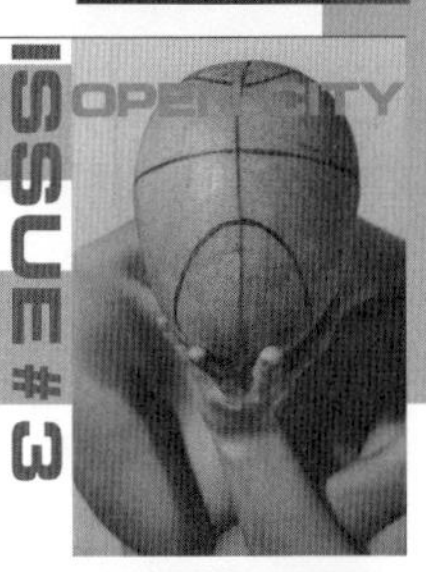

Stories by the always cheerful Cyril Connolly ("Happy Deathbeds"), Thomas McGuane, Jim Thompson, Samantha Gillison, Michael Brownstein, and Emily Carter, whose "Glory Goes and Gets Some" was reprinted in *Best American Short Stories.* Art by Julianne Swartz and Peter Nadin. Poems by David Berman and Nick Tosches. Plus Denis Johnson in Somalia. (A monster issue, sales undercut by slightly rash choice of cover art by editors. Get it while you can! $15)

ISSUE # 4

Change or Die

Stories by David Foster Wallace, Siobhan Reagan, Irvine Welsh. Jerome Badanes' brilliant novella, "Change or Die" (film rights still available). Poems by David Berman and Vito Acconci. Plus Helen Thorpe on the murder of Ireland's most famous female journalist, and Delmore Schwartz on T. S. Eliot's squint. (Still sold-out! Wait for e-books to catch on or band together and demand a reprint.)

CITY back issues

Make an investment in your future...
In today's volatile marketplace
you could do worse.

The Only Woman He's Ever Left
Stories by James Purdy, Jocko Weyland, Strawberry Saroyan. Michael Cunningham's "The Slap of Love." Poems by Rick Moody, Deborah Garrison, Monica Lewinsky, Charlie Smith. Art by Matthew Ritchie, Ellen Harvey, Cindy Stefans. Rem Koolhaas project. With a beautiful cover by Adam Fuss. (Only $10 for this blockbuster.)

ISSUE # 6

The Rubbed Away Girl
Stories by Mary Gaitskill, Bliss Broyard, and Sam Lipsyte. Art by Jimmy Raskin, Laura Larson, and Jeff Burton. Poems by David Berman, Elizabeth Macklin, Stephen Malkmus, and Will Oldham. (We found some copies in the back of the closet so were able to lower the price! $25 (it *was* $50))

ISSUE # 7

Beautiful to Strangers
Stories by Caitlin O'Connor Creevy, Joyce Johnson, and Amine Wefali, back when her byline was Zaitzeff (now the name her organic sandwich store at Nassau & John Streets—go there for lunch!). Poems by Harvey Shapiro, Jeffrey Skinner, and Daniil Kharms. Art by David Robbins, Liam Gillick, and Elliott Puckette. Piotr Uklanski's cover is a panoramic view of Queens, shot from the top of the World Trade Center in 1998. ($10)

ISSUE # 8

Bewitched
Stories by Jonathan Ames, Said Shirazi, and Sam Lipsyte. Essays by Geoff Dyer and Alexander Chancellor, who hates rabbit. Poems by Chan Marshall, Lucy Anderson, and Edvard Munch on intimate and sensitive subjects. Art by Karen Kilimnick, Giuseppe Penone, Mark Leckey, Maurizio Cattelan, and M.I.M.E. (Oddly enough, our bestselling issue. ($10))

ISSUE # 9

Editors' Issue
Previously demure editors publish themselves. Enormous changes at the last minute. Stories by Robert Bingham, Thomas Beller, Daniel Pinchbeck, Joanna Yas, Adrian Dannatt, Kip Kotzen, Geoffrey O' Brien, Lee Smith, Amanda Gersh, and Jocko Weyland. Poems by Tony Torn. Art by Nick Stone, Meghan Gerety, and Alix Lambert. (Years later, Ken Schles's cover photo appears on a Richard Price novel.) ($10)

ISSUE # 10

OPEN

ISSUE # 11

Octo Ate Them All
Vestal McIntyre emerges from the slush pile like aphrodite with a brilliant story that corresponds to the tattoo that covers his entire back. Siobhan Reagan thinks about strangulation. Fiction by Melissa Pritchard and Bill Broun. Anthropologist Michael Taussig's Cocaine Museum. Gregor von Rezzori's meditation on solitude, sex, and raw meat. Art by Joanna Kirk, Sebastien de Ganay, and Ena Swansea. ($10)

ISSUE # 12

Equivocal Landscape
Sam Brumbaugh, author of *Goodbye, Goodness*, debuts with a story set in Kenya, Daphne Beal and Swamiji, Paula Bomer sees red on a plane, Heather Larimer hits a dog, and Hunter Kennedy on the sexual possibilties of Charlottesville versus West Texas. Ford Madox Ford on the end of fun. Poetry by Jill Bialosky and Rachel Wetzsteon. Art by Miranda Lichtenstein and Pieter Schoolwerth; a love scene by Toru Hayashi. Mungo Thomson passes notes. ($10)

ISSUE # 13

Hi-fi
Sam Lipsyte introduces Steve. Nick Tosches smokes with God. Jack Walls remembers the gangs of Chicago. Vince Passaro ponders adult content. Poetry by Honor Moore, Sarah Gorham, and Melissa Holbrook Pierson. Mini-screenplay by Terry Southern. Art by Luisa Kazanas, Peter Pinchbeck, and Julianne Swartz. Special playwrighting section guest edited by Tony Torn. ($10)

ISSUE # 14

Something Like Ten Million
The defacto life and death issue. Amazing debut stories from Nico Baumbach, Michiko Okubo, and Sarah Porter; Craig Chester writes on why he has the face he deserves; a bushy, funny, and phallic art project from Louise Belcourt. Special poetry section guest edited by Lee Ann Brown. A photo essay of fleeing Manhattanites by Ken Schles. The cover is beautiful and weird, a bright hole in downtown Manhattan. ($10)

ISSUE # 15

That Russian Question
Another excerpt from Amine Wefali's *Westchester Burning (see Open City #8)*. Alicia Erian in *Jeopardy*. Jocko Weyland does handplants for an audience of elk. James Lasdun on travel and infidelity. Lara Vapnyar's debut publication. Poetry by Steve Healy, Daniel Nester, Lev Rubinshtein, and Daniel Greene. ($10)

Please send a check or money order payable to:

Open City, Inc.
270 Lafayette Street, Suite 1412
New York, NY 10012

For credit-card orders, see www.opencity.org.

ISSUE # 16

I wait, I wait.
A brilliant outtake from Robert Bingham's *Lightning on the Sun*. Ryan Kenealy on the girl who ran off with the circus; Nick Tosches on Proust. Art by Allen Ruppersberg, David Bunn, Nina Katchadourian, Matthew Higgs, and Matthew Brannon. Stories by Evan Harris, Lewis Robinson, Michael Sledge, and Bruce Jay Friedman. Rick Rofihe feels Marlene. Poetry by Dana Goodyear, Nathaniel Bellows, and Kevin Young. ($10)

ISSUE # 17

They're at it again.
Lara Vapnyar's "There Are Jews in My House," Chuck Kinder on Dagmar. Special poetry section guest edited by Honor Moore, including C. K. Williams, Victoria Redel, Eamon Grennan, and Carolyn Forché. Art by Stu Mead, Christoph Heemann, Jason Fox, Herzog film star Bruno S., and Sophie Toulouse, whose "Sexy Clowns" project has become a "character note for [our] intentions" (says the *Literary Magazine Review*). See what all the fuss is about. ($10)

ISSUE # 18

I Want to Be Your Shoebox
Susan Chamandy on Hannibal's elephants and hockey, Mike Newirth's noirish "Semiprecious." Rachel Blake's "Elephants" (an unintentional elephant theme emerges). Poetry by Catherine Bowman and Rodney Jack. Art by Viggo Mortensen, Alix Lambert, Marcellus Hall, Mark Solotroff, and Alaskan Pipeline polar bear cover by Jason Middlebrook (we're still trying to figure out what the bear had for lunch). ($10)

ISSUE # 19

Post Hoc Ergo Propter Hoc
Stories by Jason Brown, Bryan Charles, Amber Dermont, Luis Jaramillo, Dawn Raffel, Bryan Charles, Nina Shope, and Alicia Erian. Robert Olen Butler's severed heads. Poetry by Jim Harrison, Sarah Gorham, Trevor Dannatt, Matthew Rohrer & Joshua Beckman, and Harvey Shapiro. Art by Bill Adams, Julana Ellman, Sally Ross, and George Rush. Eerie, illustrated children's story by Rick Rofihe and Thomas Roberston. Saucy cover by Wayne Gonzales. ($10)

ISSUE # 20

Homecoming
"The Egg Man" a novella by Scott Smith, author of *A Simple Plan* (screenplay and book); Ryan Kenealy does God's math; an unpublished essay by Paul Bowles. Stories by Rachel Sherman, Sam Shaw, and Maxine Swann. Art by Shelter Serra, William McCurtin (of *Story of My Scab* and *Elk* fame). Poems by Anthony Roberts, Honor Moore, and David Lehman. ($10)

OPEN CITY

back issues

ISSUE #21

Ballast
Matthew Zapruder's "The Pajamaist," David Nutt's "Melancholera," fiction by Rachel Sherman, a Nick Tosches poem, Phillip Lopate's "Tea at the Plaza," David A. Fitschen on life on tour as a roadie. Poetry by Matt Miller and Alex Phillips. Art by Molly Smith, Robert Selwyn, Miranda Lichtenstein, Lorenzo Petrantoni, Billy Malone, and M Blash. ($10)

ISSUE #22

Fiction/Nonfiction
A special double-sided issue featuring fiction by Sam Lipsyte, Jerry Stahl, Herbert Gold, Leni Zumas, Matthew Kirby, Jonathan Baumbach, Ann Hillesland, Manuel Gonzales, and Leland Pitts-Gonzales. Nonfiction by Priscilla Becker, Vestal McIntyre, Eric Pape, Jocko Weyland, and Vince Passaro. ($10)

SUBSCRIBE

One year (3 issues) for $30; two years (6 issues) for $55.
Add $10/year for Canada & Mexico; $20/year for all other countries.

Please send a check or money order payable to:
Open City, Inc.
270 Lafayette Street, Suite 1412
New York, NY 10012
For credit-card orders, see www.opencity.org

The city has a thousand stories...What's yours?
Tell your New York stories

www.mrbellersneighborhood.com

Attention Teachers:

Mapsites.net is a web based teaching tool that allows students to post historical presentations, personal essays, and creative writing onto an interactive map of their neighborhood.

Mapsites.net is ideal for American History and Urban history courses, as well as English courses in which creative writing or personal essay composition, or even photography, play a role. Any class which encourages students to think about their physical environment in terms of the past or the present could make excellent use of Mapsites.

www.mapsites.net

RICE

NEW LOCATION

292 ELIZABETH ST

N O H O

212-226-5775

RICENY.COM

33 crosby street nyc 10013

www.bloodboards.com

The Man in the Twelve Thousand Rooms

Jerome Badanes

MY FATHER WAS NOT A HERO, NO PRESIDENT OF AN ORGANIZATION, no wealthy contributor to important causes. He was someone considerably more rare: a man who harmed no one. Literally. He never asked for more than his own portion, and he had a powerful sense that other people needed their portions too.

For forty years he was a house painter. I once figured out that he must have painted at least twelve thousand rooms. At work he was called Louie; at home, he was Leo, Leybl, Leybele, daddy, and later, to his grandchildren, papa.

Each morning he would wake at 5:30. Then he would walk four-and-a-half blocks to Sixty-fifth Street in Brooklyn, to the bakery, for fresh rolls—the same bakery, Prussacks, that he would be called in to paint every four or five years. After he brought home the rolls, he would make a pot of fresh coffee. Then he would cut and squeeze eight oranges to make fresh juice, and leave all of this waiting for my mother, Reyzl, who by that time was dressing for work, and for my sister Estelle and me, who were just waking up. Then he went off to work.

I imagine these twelve thousand rooms—the people who lived in them, who argued and dreamed, who died in them, the infants conceived in freshly painted eggshell bedrooms, and who came into the world with little blue or pink rooms all sparkling and ready to receive them.

Our apartment was upstairs front at 6118 Twenty-third Avenue. I remember the bedroom Estelle and I shared when we were small—and the smell of paint as my father stirs it in cans, the heavy drop cloths draping bureaus and floor, the paint-encrusted ladder, my father's white cap that reads "Sherwin Williams" on his head as he reaches out a powerful arm to make to make perfect strokes of pale yellow on a freshly spackled ceiling. His overalls are covered with paint, the spidery mouldings gleam—the whole room changes before my eyes.

This was his inheritance from forty years, and twelve thousand rooms: permanently cracked and reddened hands, skin that never stopped itching from the poisonous lead, two hernias from the lifting and dragging of the extension ladders. My God, if you put together all the steps of all the ladders he climbed in his life you could reach the moon.

And this was his inheritance: pride in work well done, a total lack of bitterness, and a sweetness that can't be described.

My father had a great sense of humor, a humor that didn't come cheap. It was born of his having to leave his own mama and papa when he was sixteen to escape the czar's army. (Jewish soldiers didn't often survive in the Russian army, as their enemies were behind them as well as in front of them.) It was a humor that matured with years of work on the railroads in Hanover, Germany; a humor seasoned by crossing the ocean three times to get to America. The first time was from Germany to Cuba in 1923. He voyaged with his best friend, Abe Spiewak, who would later, in New York, introduce Leo to his beautiful sister, Reyzl Spiewak, who would marry Leo and give birth to Estelle and me. Abe and Leo came to Cuba because it was then the gateway to the new world. But with a change in the immigration quotas, that gate, like so many others before it, was closed in their hopeful faces. My father's humor grew in steerage, returning from Cuba to Germany, when he found ironically and luckily that the immigration list with his name on it had at last become active. He arrived here finally in 1927.

My father's sense of humor was one that flew in the face of things. It was a humor that held wisdom because he laughed only at himself, never at other people; and it was a humor that insisted life is not a joke. Three times across the ocean to get here, forty-eight days in a coma to die—and in between, fifty-three years of living in Brooklyn.

I come to my parents' door. My father opens it. He smiles shyly. I give him a cigar that cost me a dollar. "I bet it's only twenty cents," he teases, as he puts it in his shirt pocket for later.

"I can't lift my arms above my head," he says and smiles. Terrible new cracks in his hands he shows me, and smiles again.

Double hernia he has, but the noodles in the chicken soup make him giggle as they slide down his throat.

My sister calls. "Hello, my dear," he says.

My mother cooks, he does the dishes, claiming the water softens his hands.

When he sleeps he sometimes cries out, knowing that life is a nightmare. When my mother sings her Yiddish songs, he glows proudly, knowing that life is a dream. How lucky he is to have found such a beautiful bride, how lucky to have both a son and a daughter ("Don't be so nervous," he tells us). And lucky with grandchildren; lucky, even, to have some old photographs left of a family that perished in the Holocaust—luckier still to have three nieces who survived.

"I live the life of a prince," he said to my mother, just a few days before he fell into a coma. "I have everything—delicious food on the table, a warm apartment, a wonderful young wife who sings better than a bird, children who love me, three *sheyne* grandchildren, holidays in the country. Who has it better?"

My father lay dying for much of a winter. Even the doctors said he wouldn't last two days.

Three glasses of orange juice, three times across the ocean, two children, one loving wife, many countries, twelve thousand rooms painted over and over by now—harvest gold, avocado, new colors applied by new immigrants. But underneath these extra layers lived the handiwork of my father's powerful arms, his delicate humanity.

Guinea Golden

Jerome Badanes

The dime sticks to my palm and glitters
as I whirl to the sun of bay seven.

Small girls spiral tricky castles
along the great Atlantic ocean.
Their mothers,
backed by umbrellas, bellies
nudging the horizon,
or some, on World War II army blankets,
their backs unhooked to the sun,
watch the young men's
body building calesthenics in the sand.

My mother dishes spaghetti from a jar
and says, "eat your lunch,
before you lose that dime."
I sit in the sand and fill my mouth
with spaghetti and chew
through lumps and lumps of it.
Grits of sand chill my teeth
and the white sun bakes my nose.

I watch the seagulls
washing their white wobbly appetites
and long to flap my arms
and strut like a seagull, or a commando,
and dip my nose in the water

and rinse my mouth,
split the waves like a P.T. boat,
sub-machine-gun my gallop to the beach
and inspire the driftwood to follow.
"No swimming for a half hour, you just ate."

I bite down on the dime and scoop
a narrow hole in the beach until
I feel wet earth
between my fingers, and twitch
with the image of black beetles.
Then I bomb the dime in, bury it,
and memorize the place
by where the life-guard lounges,
and, for insurance,
I squeeze a bottle cap in,
on top, and leave to scout the sea.

I spout like a whale and think
I'm a submarine
sneaking through waves for a better look
at the fortified castles manned
by amazons who will, if they spot me,
cut my fingers off,
scalp me,
bury me to my neck in the sand,
and dance without clothes around me
until the tide comes in.

My cold thighs burn
and my shriveled groin
feels warm and silly against the cold sand.

Jerome the pirate-marine
from Gibralter and Guadalcanal
With a knife in my teeth and the gold earring jangling,
with boots and a purple heart,
with Iwo-Jima bursting in me,
with silence, dripping wet, I storm the beach,
sidestep beer bottles and bones,
dazzle the ladies, careful
for the yellow ju-jitsu jungle fighters
behind umbrellas and baskets.

"Mama, hurry, the treasure."

I guide her safely beyond
life-guard lookout. There's
the secret cap. I kick it off.
I scoop the sand.
Everyone is watching, the queens in their towers,
the young men through their muscles.
The hole is deep.
My fingernails are bloody with beetles.

From Day to Day

My own dwelling
is at night
in the space of your
breathing in the
borrowed time in
the crystals of
quartz in my hand
in a snapshot in
their nakedness in
the pellets of death
in the consultant
his ear to the wall
in soundless expiring
of oxygen in the
frozen plumbing in
the wrenched gold
fillings in the
sour taste of your
coins in your gray
thickness of cities
in my child asleep
in the napalm in her
fists in a village in
Viet Nam in my mouth
of ashes in their
spread eagled spines
in a prophecy of

insects afflicting
my window in the
lonely space of your
breathing in your
separate being in
your woman's body
in your warmth in
our bed in the
borrowed time in
the rainfall easing
this darkness in
my own dwelling
in my own dwelling.

Late Night Footsteps on the Staircase

Hey
you!
break down my door and say something
I won't be silent or huffy or heavy
I'll prance on the tips of my toes a happy ape
who's learned to speak
alphabets will stick in my beard
and shake free and scatter
we'll whistle tunes from our lips
and those tunes will slow down
to the wheat field whispers of our flesh

All night long
I have thought about you America
in darkness
your deeds

Long live a hunger to feed each other.

Talking to Strangers

Hadara Bar-Nadav

I LEARNED THEIR VOICES, THE SPACES BETWEEN THEIR WORDS. I learned to interpret breathing, the long sigh or short breath. The I-don't-have-time-for-this voice. The monotone I'm-watching-the-news-right-now voice. I put together the pieces. It passed the time and helped me forget the gray loneliness of my cubicle, the computer I sat in front of night after night, the fluorescent lights that made my skin look green. At McMaster's Research in Paramus, city of shopping malls and traffic, I recruited people to attend market-research groups and get paid for their opinions. Tampons, canned peaches, aftershave, Colorforms—you name it.

The phone at my cubicle rang. It was Matty, cubicle forty-four.

"So, Pam, what are you up to later on? Do you think you could give me a ride?"

"Still haven't gotten your wheels back, huh? You must owe a million dollars by now."

"Hey lady, what's with all the lip? Can you give me a ride or not?"

Matty had lost his license, owed thousands in DWI fines, and needed rides home to Lodi, where he lived with his parents. Born and raised in Lodi, Matty was a twenty-eight-year-old pushy Italian with tattoos of Snoopy and Woodstock on his forearms. His black hair always looked wet, slicked back with heavy layers of gel, and his face and body were puffed up from years of drinking beer. Like other short men, he was careful not to stand next to me; I was 5'9" while he was only about 5'5." Matty was the lone male among the fifteen or so night-shift workers at McMaster's, mostly college girls like me who needed to work after class and moms longing for a little adult conversation.

The first time Matty was in my car, I handed him half a joint. He took it and smiled, "So lady, you want a toot?"

We stopped at a traffic light, and he watched as I sniffed coke off his chubby hand. I was nervous at the traffic light, and sloppy. I didn't tell him it was my first time. Most of the powder stuck to the outside of my nose and upper lip. Matty laughed as I checked my face in the rearview mirror. It looked as if I had dipped my nose in a pile of dry snow. When he leaned in to brush the powder off my nose, I thought he was going to kiss me. I even closed my eyes and felt that nervous tickle run over my wrists, which meant I was with someone I liked. When I opened my eyes again, the traffic light was yellow. Even though no one was behind us, I stepped on the gas. Matty seemed like he was somewhere else, staring out the window at the night.

When I got home at around 1:30 or so, my mom was asleep on the couch after her eight-hour shift at Linens 'n Things. Since I was in school during the day and worked at night, we didn't see each other much, which was odd because we lived in a two-bedroom apartment. It was good to see her restfully sleep. Sometimes I heard her cry as she slept, a warbling cry that sounded more afraid than sad. She was sixty-one with no real hopes of retiring. No money to retire with. My dad had died three years before. Mesothelioma. When he was in his twenties, he worked in demolition and later opened up his own series of businesses with campy names (Randy-the-Roofer, Randy-the-Handyman, etc.). He liked to tell people that I got my writing genes from him, though to my knowledge he never actually wrote anything. He died just after he turned fifty-nine and within six months of being diagnosed. At some point during his decline it occurred to me that demolition had destroyed him. I mean, it was ironic that destruction could catch up to a person and eat him alive.

I shut the door to my bedroom and turned on the television. I needed the voices, the hum, the little light and movement. I dropped myself onto the bed. After episodes of *Mash* and *Cheers* came the commercial. I had seen it before, some group of lawyers who represented people exposed to asbestos. A 1-800 number flashed on the screen with bright green dollar signs around it. Then a model-lawyer with pale lips, orange-tinted makeup, and hair that looked like bear fur sat on the edge of his desk and said to me: "Have you or someone you loved . . . ." I finally was falling asleep. "It could be on your hair, your clothes . . . ."

I drove Matty home four or five times a week. Sometimes we tooted in the car. More often, we stopped for a few drinks at a bar, where he would hand me a ball of tinfoil with the powder inside. No words. He would tap my hand under the bar and my hand opened. I'd slip into the bathroom every half hour or so. Sometimes I'd save up a couple tinfoil balls so I could have my own party at home. With his unending supply of drugs, I figured Matty was a dealer. His part-time job at McMasters explained to his parents and the IRS where he got his money. I didn't ask. Matty felt good about being generous and I liked him for it, for his ability to simply give.

When I was high, my writing was chaotic. I would write two or three lines in my notebook, then stop. Then another few lines about something else entirely. (*Write about eels, slick eels, their strange lifecycles. I miss my father. Randy-the-Handyman. I miss my father. My mother cries like a horse on fire. A whinny-screech. God, I need a new car, a new job. What should I do about Stephen? He's probably screwing some girl in a bathroom right now. Or a boy. Think: eels.*) Wide-awake and manic, I copied these fragments at home onto 18 x 24 sheets of newsprint and tried to map them together. By morning, I'd have a collection of incoherent loops and lines, latitudes I could never follow.

Working at McMaster's gave me ideas for stories, though I had never actually finished writing any. I had a lot of ideas. Fits and starts, and more fits. I had access to ready-made characters from the database—names, addresses, birth dates, occupations, range of household income, how many pets they owned, the make and model of their cars. I knew if they had cancer or diabetes and what medications they took. I knew the names and birth dates of their children. Winnie Suez had four kids, ages two, three, six, and nine, whom she drove around in a 1988 blue and gray Dodge van. She was a social worker, single, household income twenty-five to thirty thousand, which meant she probably was just scraping by.

I was a spy. A peeping Pam. Though I was a fifth-year college student, first majoring in art and then psychology, I finally settled on English. I fell in love with stories, like that one by Sherwood Anderson where a sexually repressed woman gets naked and runs through the rain only to bump into an old man and run home shamefaced. Working at McMaster's was like reading literature; I could study people's lives from a safe distance.

On the other hand, I knew I was being watched. McMasters had made me sign all these forms when I started there three years before, stating that I wouldn't reveal any trade secrets at any time during or after my employment. I knew my calls could be screened for "appropriateness of dialogue and training purposes." McMasters tried to be a top-secret, spy kind of place, but mostly it was all smoke and mirrors to make the clients feel special about themselves.

Supposedly the big bosses—invisible men no one ever saw—tapped our phones and could fire us on the spot if we were making personal calls or asking potential participants to lie. It was voyeurism on high; everyone watched everyone. We knew the pervy marketing gurus got off on watching participants through the one-way mirrors that divided their adjacent rooms. Happy to escape boring, middle-aged lives, clients flew in from cities like San Francisco and Chicago, got drunk on Bass Ale and Michelob, and ate soggy, cold Italian food while making fun of participants who couldn't hear the laughter behind the glass.

My supervisor Alan busted me for calling my non-boyfriend Stephen, who lived in Queens and was a junior-level stockbroker. I wasn't in it for the long haul or anything. We had met through a mutual friend when we were high on X. I guess we had a good time getting high, hanging out, and having sex. In the end, it could have been anyone. I could have been anyone.

When I slept with Stephen there would be a moment, more than a moment, when he was on top and I was just an idea, generic underneath him, the warm body, and he'd be elsewhere. Deep inside his need. Or fucking someone else, a girl he saw the week before on a bus or someone on *The Tonight Show*, Cameron Diaz with her red, ruined mouth. It made me feel invisible. It's not like I even really knew the guy—his secrets or dreams or the name of his childhood dog. The relationship only lasted about two months, a one-night stand that dragged on too long.

"I'll pay for the phone call, Alan. Sorry. Look. It won't happen again. Stephen and I aren't even seeing each other anymore. Here." I took out my wallet. "I'll give you five bucks to cover the call." I had hoped that letting Alan in on a bit of my personal life would make him act like more of a human.

Alan held up his hand. "I know how much you make, Pamela. You should hold onto your money now."

Alan thought he was so generous. I hated him anyway, and he knew it. Fucking phone nazi. He in his chintzy, thin white dress shirts. You could see his nipples poking through, which really freaked me out. He wrote me up for calling Stephen. Big deal. I had seven or eight "demerits" already. Maybe ten. I had stopped counting. Supposedly, three would get you fired. I guess there was a shortage of people who would actually do my job, throwing away life hours in the windowless dungeon where I worked. The place had the oppressive feeling of a dentist's office—gray on gray carpet every damn place I looked. Who the hell carpets their walls anyway? Perhaps it was there to muffle the screams.

I never told Matty about Stephen. I guess I thought it might turn him off, and I looked forward to seeing him, to getting high, getting off. Anyway, you're never supposed to talk about ex-boyfriends with a guy, right? Matty never said much about the girls he dated either, though he seemed to have a lot of women "friends": Angela, Lori, Tanya, Beth, even one named Lacey. They all vaguely sounded like strippers, and I couldn't tell what was real anymore. Real didn't seem to matter.

During our shift on Tuesday night, Matty called me on the phone. He was at cubicle thirty-four, and I was at forty-one. Two different rows. Calling each other was better than trying to talk across the hum of recruiters or getting caught like a rabbit in the lights, chatting in the middle of an aisle.

"Hey sexy, we're going to need to make a stop first."

"OK. Like for smokes or something? There's that Hess on 46."

"We need to stop at my friend's place before we go out."

(Empty space on the phone.)

"A friend? You mean like to pick up one of your *lady friends*?"

"No. Listen. I need to pick something up. For us."

(Empty space.)

"Oh. So, where does this *friend* live?"

I hoped my voice sounded flat and calm. Taking drugs in the bathroom at bars was one thing, but I didn't want to know where they came from. I didn't want to go to any creepy crack house.

Matty told me to turn off my car and wait in the driveway. He walked around the back of a yellow house, a small, two-level in Little Ferry with a metal fence around it and kids toys scattered on the front lawn. The wheels on a red-and-blue plastic bike spun in the wind, disembodied like in some horror movie where all the children are missing. The toys, the yellow house, the entire block seemed unreal under the hard fluorescent streetlights. I imagined walking up to the yellow house and knocking it down with one swift kick, and the next house would fall and the next, houses collapsing like dominoes, until the whole block crumbled to the earth. Demolition and dust. I thought of my father with a hammer in his hand.

Then I heard them, the hollow shriek of sirens. I ducked down in my seat, felt suddenly cold, then hot, and imagined pitbulls charging over the fence and police officers swarming my car. I kept looking around, checking behind me, scanning the street. I lowered my window so I could hear if anyone approached on foot and caught the blur of two fire engines followed by an ambulance crossing through the intersection to my left. I dug my nails into my steering wheel. Matty had been gone for more than ten minutes.

Finally I saw him step from behind the house and walk toward my car. I was almost giddy with relief. He was with a tall guy, 6'2" or more, with curly hair. I couldn't see much, a bulb inside a kitchen window doused them in gasoline-orange light.

There was a tap on the passenger side window and when I turned, a woman smashed at the window with a bat.

"You fucking bitch. You bitch. You stupid fucking bitch." She kept swinging.

At first the window sank inward, but didn't shatter. As I shrank down in my seat and rolled out of the driver's side door, my thumbnail got caught in the door handle. It was a dumb thing to do but I froze, squatting against my car, my left thumb in my mouth, my other hand over my head while this girl screamed and smashed both windows on the passenger side.

I heard Matty and the other guy come running. "Trish, what the fuck are you doing! Trish!"

I peeked over the hood of my car as the tall guy twisted the bat out of Trish's hands and threw it on the lawn. He wrapped his arms around her and jammed his chin into the top of her head. She was a tiny girl with oily black hair, who looked about sixteen, maybe seventeen. I could see that she was bleeding from the mouth. I couldn't tell if it was from the glass.

Matty got into my car. "Pam, get in here. Pamela, get in to your car."

I watched the tall man and tiny girl disappear into the shadows on the side of the house and waited for the screen door to close behind them.

"Pam, listen. It's not so bad." He stopped. "What the hell happened to your hand?"

"I don't know. My thumb. I have a towel in the trunk. Wait, here are the keys." I started to cry. "Get the towel for me. Please, I can't get blood on my dad's car. Christ. This is my father's car, Matty. It's my father's car."

"I'm sorry, Pam. Listen. I'm sorry."

"You don't understand, Matty. This is my father's fucking car!"

"All right, so we'll get it fixed. Calm down. Listen, I'll split it with you. We'll get it fixed before he even notices."

"Matty. Matty." I reached over and held him and clamped my teeth shut so I wouldn't cry out loud. I held him and held him and he let me, and sometimes he was my father and sometimes Stephen or even Matty and sometimes anyone at all.

"Pamela. Oh, God. Oh, my God. Call the police! Someone broke into your car. Oh, God." My mother snapped off my TV, grabbed my arm, and sat me up in my bed. I glanced around the room to make sure no evidence was out in the open.

"Mom, I. It was. Oh, the windows. It happened at McMaster's. Some respondent got angry."

"A respondent? Angry? I don't understand. How would a respondent know what kind of car you have? My God, how would they even know who you are? You never give out your real name, do you? Do those people you call know your real name?"

"Mom. No. Look, I'll get it fixed. Calm down. Shh. Sit down." As she sat on my bed I draped my arm around her shoulders, my head nestled into her neck. "It's OK, mom. Look. I'll get it fixed." My hand started to throb; I slid it under my blanket.

"No, you won't. NO YOU WON'T! McMaster's will pay for it. They'll pay. They are going to pay for it!" My mother's voice shivered. "You know, that car belonged to your . . . ."

"I know, Mom. I know." My father's car, a black 1991 Honda Accord wagon, *Randy-the-Handyman* nearly peeled off the driver's side door so that only the white *R* and *H* remained. "I'll talk to Alan tonight, mom. Don't worry. I'm sure they'll pay for it. It'll probably just take a few days. OK?"

My mother frowned and looked at her watch. We both knew she had to leave for work.

"Pamela, I don't want you paying for this." She got up to leave.

"I know, Mom. I promise I'll talk to Alan tonight." I nodded in affirmation as she closed the door.

My hand ached through to my shoulder. Though I had two large Band-Aids wrapped around it, my thumb was a deep blue down to the joint, the thumbnail torn clear off. I reached under my bed and pulled out the bloody towel from the night before and stuffed it into my backpack to throw away at school. Underneath the Band-Aids, the skin was sticky and raw. It looked like a third-degree burn, pink in the center, yellow and wet around the edges.

Overall it was a big drag to be on the phone saying the same thing four-hundred times a night for days on end until we recruited enough forty to forty-five year olds who ate Campbell's soup three or more times a week. Once our quotas were met, we got a new script. Sometimes the new script was a relief, my mind numb from repetition. My job alternated between being mildly entertaining and depressing as hell. On any given night, people on the other end of the phone would yell: "How did you get this number? I'm calling the police," "Do you know you are interrupting my dinner for this bullshit?" or "Take me off your fucking list," people who had forgotten they had signed up to be in our database. Occasionally there was a "Thank god you called. I need to get my oil changed" or "I'm going to Bermuda next week and could really use the cash." People who understood the game.

I relished the idea of free money, the New Jersey Lottery, *The Price Is Right.* I dreamt about going to California and winning both showcases on the Showcase Showdown. I understood the game, the beautiful idea of getting money and cars and a new living room for free. I even kept a notebook of million-dollar ideas. A tattoo that would be absorbed into your skin and disappear in five years. A chain of bar/restaurant/laundromats located throughout New York and New Jersey like they have in San Francisco. A Christmas tree with branches that light up in different colors, making ornaments a thing of the past. An ice-cream cone with a cup large enough to hold a full pint of ice cream. My most recent masterpiece of an idea was clear toothpaste—no white foamy flecks on your clothes. I wanted my mom to retire. Shit, I wanted to retire and maybe finish writing some of those goddamn stories I was always starting.

There were lawyers from Georgia and North Carolina who promised us thousands, hundreds of thousands for my father. When he was still alive they asked us, they asked him, impossible questions like what he ate for breakfast in 1974 and what spray fixative he had used, what friend he had worked for (already dead), what shellac, what floorboard, work gloves, dust mask (there wasn't one). Then he died. At first they called and sent letters in triplicate for my mother to sign, and then they sent only two or three form letters a year in a hard, jumbled language that made her cry in her sleep.

And no money came.

Sure, I fantasized about money, but I still had a conscience. Unlike some of the other recruiters, I would only nudge respondents a little. If a man was one haircut away from the quota, one gin and tonic short, I'd say: "We're looking for men who use ____ three or more times a week and you said one to two." Then I'd wait to see if the person on the other end of the phone understood. If he didn't, I'd thank him for his time and hang up. But if he did understand and revised his answer, I would remind him before we hung up: "So, you use Lysol three or more times a week, right?" I wasn't stupid. If the people we recruited got disqualified, we wouldn't get credit. The person with the highest number of successful recruits per month got an extra $50 bonus. In three years, I hadn't won once.

Even though we genuinely were going to give people money for their time, they sometimes confused us with those other telemarketers, the ones who want to take up your time and give you nothing in return. I, on the other hand, was benevolent, a bodhisattva come down through telephone wires to give people money. All they had to do was believe.

And not hang up.

Matty and I never went to the same bar more than two or three times. Secret undercover. Lucky for us, there was no shortage of crappy bars in New Jersey. Most of the places we went to played eighties metal and pop—Whitney Houston, Pat Benatar, Metallica—and had fake palm trees or other Malibu-type themes going on. Bar owners must have thought themselves ingenious for their choice in plastic decor when all that really mattered was the booze and ass.

It was a Wednesday night at Knickerbockers in Hackensack, and Matty and I decided to play electronic Trivial Pursuit with drunks in other bars across the United States. I was getting a bachelor's degree in English but managed to blow every literature question that came up. (*The Voyages of Doctor Doolittle* was written in 1923 by what author? According to *1984* by George Orwell, who is watching you?) I vaguely knew the answers but just couldn't pin them down. My brain seemed fuzzy and slow, and choosing one answer over another didn't make any sense. High and drunk at a bar, flicking switches and knobs, watching lights jump across a monitor, what the hell did I care about the right answers anyway? I thought it was comical, but I knew Matty was getting pissed.

"Pam, are you even paying attention? Aren't you some freakin' English major or something? I thought you were supposed to know this shit."

I laughed. "Who is watching you? Who is watching *you*? I think that fucking monitor is watching us. That's the funniest goddamn question I've ever heard. Like that monitor is a one-way mirror or something, like at work. Spies everywhere!"

Matty raised his eyebrows and sighed. He was not amused. He glanced at my thumb, and I tucked it inside of a fist. I knew it was ugly, the nail a purple-black nub and the skin underneath waxy and pink.

"Do you want to see this?" I waved my thumb under his nose. "I call it my party favor. Look at my ugly monkey finger. And this is what makes me human. This says I'm an intelligent human being. And it's broken."

Matty shrugged. Even his mouth shrugged. "All right, Pammy. All right. Let's calm down here and focus, OK? Focus. How about another drink?"

"How about another drink? How about another fucking drink? How about hooking me up before I head to the bathroom?"

My voice came out hard and with more edge than I wanted. Matty looked surprised and then smiled, a sad kind of fatherly smile like he was putting on a good show for some kid while the whole world disintegrated around them. He locked onto my eyes like it was the first time he had ever really seen me—or the last. That totally burned me up. Wasn't he so goddamn generous, so wise, so fucking in control. He handed me an entire vial under the bar and held my hand even after I squeezed it into a fist.

I had been upgraded.

Matty stared at me with that serious, sorry smile on his face. I almost started to cry and bit my tongue to distract myself. I slid the vial into my pocket and stared down at my thumb, afraid to look Matty in the eyes. It was so quiet I could almost hear the heartbeat in my thumb. For the past couple of days, it had been beating hot and hard. I wasn't sure if that meant it was infected or healing.

Before I realized what I was doing I looked up and kissed Matty. He didn't pull away. Silence seemed to surround us like a vacuum, a kind of slow-motion blur. I tasted the sweat on his upper lip, salt mixed with a pinch of lime from his Corona, and wondered where the cheesy music had gone.

It wasn't really a romantic kiss—skin pressed against skin, a momentary flash of warmth. It just seemed like something we had to do, I had to do. And then it was over. I felt shy in front of Matty for the first time, gave him a quick smile, grabbed my purse, and walked quickly into the bathroom for a line. When I came back out feeling sexy and victorious, Matty was playing pool, standing around the pool table with three guys, one who wasn't wearing any shoes. I stared at Matty from the bar, but he wouldn't look at me. A glassy chill hovered in my chest and stayed there. I sat down and watched the ice in my drink try to melt.

****

There wasn't much to say as I drove Matty back to Lodi. Sure, it was a little tense in the car, but we also were beat tired and usually didn't talk much on the ride home. The high and the crash that follows.

The plastic patches I had made in place of the missing car windows rippled hard on the highway and threatened to tear away in the wind. I listened to the sound, a succession of fast, flat, slapping beats. God, if my father were alive to see this. Randy-the-Handyman's car with garbage bags and electrical tape pretending to be windows. What a great way to honor my dead father's memory. Yeah, a walking advertisement for disaster. *Let me be your handy man, and I'll smash your windows. Let me into your car, into your life, and I'll smash it to pieces.* If my father could see me now, he'd probably cry.

I turned off the lights and pulled into Matty's driveway. He stepped out of my car and stood there with the door open, reached into his jacket, ducked his head back inside, and handed me an envelope. His lips were dry and pale. He looked tired, with bluish rings under his eyes, and his face looked pasty in the yellow car light. I picked up the envelope. Inside was a stack of twenties, maybe a couple of hundred in total. I put the envelope down on the passenger seat, looked Matty in the eyes, and slapped him. My hand simply lifted and swung.

"What do you think, Matty, you can buy my fucking affections? Fuck you. I'm not some fucking coke whore." I knew I wasn't. I knew I was reading lines out of some script, taking the plot to its natural end. Matty had never once tried to touch me. Not once. Why hadn't he even tried? It was a question among questions I wouldn't let myself ask.

"You know Pam, you can be a real asshole sometimes," he said, nodding his head. "This is for your car. Your father's car. And tell your mother to stop worrying. Her little girl's got it all under control." Matty slammed the car door so hard I felt the vibration shake through my jaw.

After Matty didn't show up to work for three consecutive nights, I asked Big Annie about him. She was the one who told me he had quit McMaster's. Turns out he found a job painting cars and doing custom design work for an auto-body shop near his house in Lodi. For a moment I thought I might throw up. I only had a little coke left, enough for maybe one or two more nights. I sat down at my booth and called him.

On the phone, he said, "I like airbrush work. It's real creative. Makes me feel like an artist. You know, creative." He laughed. Turns out he had been working at McMaster's as a temporary fix until "the right opportunity came along."

Matty and I talked once more by phone after that. I heard him light a cigarette, his voice tight, his breath hard as he drew in and closed his teeth. He had paid his DWI fines, got his car back, and was thinking about asking one of his girlfriends to marry him.

"You know, Marie. The one who works for that day care in Clifton?" I didn't. "Yeah, well, she's a good girl. And my mother loves her. She's Italian. And Catholic."

I avoided dead space on the phone and made sure to congratulate Matty quickly. I wondered what she looked like—his mother, and Marie.

After we hung up, I didn't cry or anything. I had a database of 34,000 people to call, some of whom actually wanted to hear from me. As for Matty not being around, I figured I'd start cruising the bars. There were enough men around who seemed interested. And the next night and the night after that, I'd still show up for work and get paid to talk to strangers on the telephone.

Bricolage and Blood

Hadara Bar-Nadav

I'm stuck here in the abattoir,
a fancy word for *eat my fatted heart*.

I've been a cow before
two lives ago and a woman
who gave too much in between.

It's all tautology, a cyclic chewing
on the same bit.

Call it cud—in this life
my tongue mixed with grass
and in the previous, merlot with tears.

I've been patient.
I've been given something to do
and I've done it phatically.

So much noisier a life ago when I choked
and died in a strange man's bed.

> I had seen death in his face,
> the beautiful skull
> articulated beneath his skin.

OPEN CITY

I wish I were in my last life
or my first, but for now I'm dying again
(a redundancy in red)

and the familiar passage
smells like blood.

Hadara Bar-Nadav

I Used to Be Snow White

                    but I drifted
and the seven small men
who set up video cameras left.

My thirteen-inch face floats
inside the television like a cake
of soap behind glass.

You prop me on the edge
of your dresser, splay
my antennae to spear the stars.

I dance until your satellites
blow, the static buzz
exchanged for romance.

Thank you for the candle
and ashtray though I've no
matches, no cigarettes.

Also, I'm cut off below
the neck (O, the things
I'd do if I had hands).

Still, I feel so close to you.
Whistle to me across
this expanse.

To Halve and to Hole

At three A.M. when I'm glass again
and millions of little red chairs dangle
like minarets, twinkle

like teeth. So they don't flatten my head I wish
for a black hat. I wish for one black hat
and then more.

I am jealous of men with black hats.
How fine it must feel
to be cupped.

At dawn the glass is full of pleases,
orange mixed with pink and the sun
bleeds out.

I sit in a red chair festooned with light
and two kinds of kneeling, catch teeth
in my hat and bleed out.

Look, we're all in roses now.
Look, the eyes gone like a surprise
and a soft fur in the holes.

We used to be so spiny, red fretworks
of shadow and bone. How beauty suggests
beaugeste and the ribs part

themselves for breath. And then the great
unraveling, a spool of blood
and bread.

Remember the blue feather and
leather circlet, boiled wool shaped
to your form?

What's holding us up anymore
I don't know. Close my eyes,
try to recall.

The Life of a Stone

Jill Bialosky

SHE TORE OPEN THE ENVELOPE. WILLIAM SENT HER A FOSSIL OF A dragonfly inside one of the stones he'd uncovered building his wall, and wrapped around it was a note saying that he missed her and needed to see her. She was nearing the end of her first year of graduate school. She explained to Adam that she would continue to model for him but that she was going back to try again with William. Besides, he was married. She booked a ticket to Chicago for a weekend, happy that William was finally ready to see her.

"I knew you'd come." William was in the backyard letting the dogs run free. "Eleanor, your hair smells so pretty," he said, embracing her.

He saw his role once his father left, the last child at home, to take on the responsibilities of the house and keep his mother company. He divided his time between his mother's and his own apartment in one of the buildings his father owned in Chicago. He took Eleanor into the woods to see the progress of the stone wall and the minute he smelled the fresh air, his face brightened as if the world had not yet pressed against him. All the laying of stone and the time he spent riding his horse had given more heft to his body.

"Do you know there's life in a stone, Eleanor? It takes on the memory of a place." He reached down and handed her a piece of the stone that had broken off the larger rock. She looked at the pine leaves on the ground and branches that had fallen. In the air was the moisture before rain. It was cool and she wrapped herself in William's arms to keep warm.

"It's so nice to be with you like we used to," William said. "Words are never adequate. I loved you before words. When I looked at you that first day on the rink I knew. You see things in me I don't have to express. Our words are these stones. I'm glad you came back."

The next day he took her to his dim apartment that bordered a slum.

"I don't like it here, William," Eleanor said. "I don't feel safe. Do you have to live here?"

"I'm sorry. We don't have to stay." He considered for a moment. "It's why they call him a slumlord. He takes their money and lets the place go to shit. They have nowhere else to go. It's why I can't leave. What do you think I've been doing all year?"

She looked at him.

"I made out a system. I take what I can off the top of the rents each month without him knowing about it and I fix stuff for them. Mrs. C. doesn't have hot water. Mr. B. in 5C has busted windows. Sometimes I can't sleep trying to figure it all out."

"You look tired." She put back into place a lock of hair that had fallen over his eye.

"I'm just stressed. I have things to take care of, Eleanor. I can't let them down."

On the night before she was leaving William cooked her filet mignon and baked potatoes for dinner at his mother's house. She wanted to tell him about how intense and interesting modeling for Adam was, about the paper she was writing, but she refrained, thinking he'd be jealous of the life she had without him The meat was tough and she kept chewing it. "It's great that you are trying to help those people. But what about you, William?" she said, worried about leaving him to the woods and the apartment downtown.

"I have responsibilities here." He pulled out a piece of paper from his pocket. He shoved it across the table. It listed each apartment in the building, who needed what done, what repaired. "Sometimes when I brush my teeth I want to go next door and give my toothbrush to one of those kids with rotted teeth."

"You're good, William."

"Eleanor." He stopped and looked at his half-eaten steak. "I wish there was an alternative universe, where none of the rules apply."

"I know what you mean."

"The world creeps in little by little and sometimes I don't weather it well."

"Promise me you'll take care of yourself," she said, when they hugged goodbye in his driveway. "Don't try to do so much."

"Look, a falling star." She looked up and saw another fall. "That's one thing you can't see in that city. Think of me when you go to Central Park, Eleanor."

"When do I not think about you?" she said, holding on to the sleeve of his coat.

William said he had met a man on the streets of downtown Chicago who was trying to save his soul—a born-again Christian—when he came to visit her in New York a month later. The born-again convinced William that the end of the world was coming, that if he did not redeem himself he would go to hell. "It's strange," William said. "I mean to me hell is right here on earth." He said the man told him that if he embraced Jesus he would understand the puzzle of darkness and light. William had a curiosity for things and explanations not of the earth, and he knew how to listen.

They were lying on her twin captain's bed that also served as a couch in her one-room studio. "It made me think," he said. "I don't understand why we're here. I don't mean in this room. I mean cosmically. I mean why are we *here*? I don't like to think about it, but it's there, that question. Are we supposed to wake up every day and do the same thing? Eat, go to work, sleep? What's the point when there's cruelty? What's the point when people next door don't have enough to eat? It's always haunting me, that there's evil in the world. I don't understand the way the world operates. I don't want to spend my whole life making money doing something I don't like so that I have a bigger house, a bigger television."

"We're here to be good people, William. You have to find your passion."

"You're my passion, Eleanor." He took her hand and held it like you would a valuable present and then kissed it. "I have my dogs and the woods where no one bothers me and I have you, what else is there? I wish we could go far away. Live in the woods, sleep underneath the trees. Eleanor, do you think there are trees in heaven?"

It was dark in the room. Outside, in the hall, she heard a congregation around the pay phone, talking about keg parties and cramming for exams. She squeezed his hand. "Let me finish school. We'll figure it out then," she said, thinking maybe that William could never leave the woods. She suddenly felt ashamed of all the hours she spent in Adam's studio when it was William who needed her. Her eyes adjusted to the darkness, and in the dark she could see the shape of William's arm as he lifted it toward the ceiling and stared at his hand.

"Do you ever look at your hands and feel that they don't belong to you? Like they are not your own?"

"Yes." She lied to reassure him. "Of course."

"Hold me, Eleanor."

"What's wrong? Tell me."

"Sometimes I can't figure a way out of my own head. I can't stop thinking about how I'm going to get it all done. The electrical. The hot water when winter comes." Her eye wandered to the crack underneath the door and the stretch of light. She heard a sound of an animal in agony. She thought it was a dog or cat out her window. She had never heard William cry before.

"You're stressed. You have to calm down." She tried to breathe strength into William's neck. She held him and they fell asleep like brother and sister without making love. The eagerness to touch, to kiss, to be close to each other's bodies had distilled into something more urgent.

In the morning she took William to the synagogue on Eighty-eighth Street to consult the rabbi. "Something's wrong. You're not supposed to believe in Jesus. You're Jewish, for God's sake. " Even though she wasn't really religious, and barely went to synagogue, she woke up with the idea that William was in some kind of philosophical crisis and it was the only idea that made sense. "You can seek God, but he's a loving God."

But when they arrived at the door to the rabbi's chambers, William changed his mind. "I'm not going through with this. I'm okay, Eleanor," he said, when she was about to knock. "I don't feel so bad today."

There was a spark of light back in his eyes. He didn't seem so anxious. "I don't want to do this. Come on, I'm leaving tomorrow to go back home. You and I need to be together."

Before they left they took a peek into the synagogue. Eleanor's eye caught the everlasting light on the bema. "Look. God is watching us. He's taking care of you."

All the leaves had fallen off the tree on Broadway. It looked stark and naked. They walked back to her studio apartment. She looked at him in his wool sweater, and the bulk of him reassured her. William picked up a burnt-red leaf from the ground and pressed it into her palm. "It's the color of my heart."

She took it in her hand and put it in her pocket.

"You're okay now, aren't you?" Eleanor asked in the morning as William stuffed his work clothes into his duffel bag. "I wish you didn't have to leave."

They sat on the edge of her bed. William coaxed her down on the mattress and looked into her eyes. "It's okay," he said. "Do you hear the trees outside the window making love to the wind? Remember the sound. I'll be inside it."

They went to Broadway to hail a cab. Going to a fancy Ivy League University, studying literature—she spent days in her room smoking cigarettes, drinking instant coffee, and analyzing lines of poetry—and modeling for Adam seemed meaningless when she looked into William's searching, down-to-earth eyes the color of the forest. She had begun to believe that what mattered most was living through literature and art. She didn't live comfortably in the world the way that other, normal people did. But what if she was wrong? Watching William, she told herself that she might give up her ambition. That she'd drop out of graduate school and go back to the woods and simplify her life. As they said good-bye on Broadway, the wind biting their faces and sending up swirls of garbage and papers from the street, she held on to the lapels of his coat. She looked in his eyes. "I'll be home soon. Hang in there. It won't be long now."

William stopped and pulled her closer to him. "You have to know it isn't your fault. You have to promise me you know that."

She didn't know what he was talking about.

"Promise." A cab stopped and pulled over. The white light on top of the roof of the cab went off. She said nothing.

"Promise me, Eleanor. This isn't a joke."

"I promise," she whispered into his coat. She thought he was referring to the fact that she had left him to go to college. She stood by the side of the street, watching as he climbed in the cab, until it was long out of sight.

She collapsed on the bed in her room. She looked at the red leaf he had given her that she had placed on her dresser. It was curling up at the edges.

Mrs. Woods greeted Eleanor in the reception area of the hospital, and tears filled her eyes when she went to hug her. She had called to tell her that William was in the hospital, and Eleanor had taken the first flight in. Mr. Woods was watching the television in the waiting room. He looked like he'd been up all night. His clothes were slightly crumpled and the back of his hair matted where he had fallen asleep against the back of a chair. He stood up when Eleanor walked in. "He'll pull himself together," he said, his voice tremeling with emotion. He patted Eleanor a tad too forcefully on the back. "He's a little mixed up right now."

William looked pale and tired. He was wearing a hospital gown, robe, and a pair of white sports socks and pulled an IV pole that released his meds. when he came to the waiting room to find her. The last time she saw him she was putting him in a cab on the streets of New York City more than a month ago. "Please be okay," Eleanor said, pressing her face into his neck, hugging him with all her might. They walked slowly back to William's hospital room and lay down together on the hospital bed with its perfect corners. His hair had lost its shine. "What happened?" She finally asked.

"I kept thinking about what that man said about Jesus and Hell and not being saved and I started feeling funny. It was like being so far down in your head you don't know how to climb out. I forgot my name. Where I lived. I looked at my hands and my face in the mirror and they were not my own. I couldn't leave the apartment. I realized that a week had gone by, and I hadn't eaten or done anything that I could remember. I picked up the phone and called an ambulance."

"But what happened? I don't get it," Eleanor said again.

He looked at her blankly. "I'm worried about the dogs. Will you make sure they get fed?"

"Of course I will. Whatever you want, William."

Eleanor went to the hospital every day. She sat in the lobby when William went to group, and had his private sessions with the doctor, and then joined him in his room when they brought in his lunch and supper. She picked up the tin lids and said, "Today you're having turkey and mashed potatoes," and she moved the tray close to William and watched him try to eat. They watched television together. Eleanor held his hand. She looked at him for signs. The doctor called it depersonalization. What did it mean? That William was not a person anymore? That he had no self? She said nothing. She kept looking for William in his eyes, but the anger and spark had vanished. *Why are we here in the first place? I wish there was an alternative universe we could live in, Eleanor. When I'm building the wall I think about it. About where we could live where no one will harm us.* She thought about those words looking at the grayish hue to his skin.

He stayed in the hospital for a month. When he was released, he went to his mother's house to recuperate. Eleanor went with him, sleeping in one of his older brother's empty bedrooms. She called the chair of her department and explained the situation. She'd have to make up her work when she returned. During the day she sat next to him on the couch in the family room and held his hand. His loyal dogs were at William's feet. It was like they were in high school again, only they were in their twenties, living together in his mother's house. "Eleanor, you're holding my hand too tight," William said. "Can you let go for a second?" The days passed this way. It was so quiet they could hear the leaves shudder, the dogs whimper, the cats meow.

"You have to go back to New York," William said, after another three weeks had passed.

"I'm not going back."

"You can't stay here and watch me."

"I'm not leaving."

"Stop looking at me that way."

"Where are you?" She pulled him by the shirt. She was angry. "You're not in here anymore." She pointed her finger in his chest.

"I'm right here. This is me now."

She moved closer to him on the couch.

"I can't breathe, Eleanor. I have to do this on my own."

"What about the wall? Who's going to finish it?"

"I'm not strong enough." He looked at her, his eyes sad and lifeless. "You're crushing me."

"I'll go back." She touched his arm. "If you promise it will help you get better."

"The only thing that will make me feel better is if you go on with your life. You have to do this for me."

Was the pain in her body William's or her own?

"William took the dogs out today." "William went to work." "William ate beef stroganoff for supper," Mrs. Woods said, with forced cheeriness when Eleanor would call from New York to get a report on his state of mind.

Eleanor went back to the synagogue to see the rabbi. "My daughter," the rabbi said, "the mind is fragile. You have to have faith in God and what God has willed." She didn't mind being the rabbi's daughter. She left his chambers and sat in the synagogue, watching the light fight its way through the stained glass. She began to pray. It was what she understood one did when there was nothing else to be done.

She couldn't get the shape, touch, voice, image of him out of her system. They had that kind of telepathy with each other. She knew that the minute she looked into his eyes everything would be fine even though they'd been away from each other for more than a month. She surprised William and came in a day earlier than he expected. Usually she spent the first night she was home having supper with her mother, but that night she asked if she could borrow the car. She fixed herself up, putting on a skirt, the blue one with the white flowers, and a blue sweater that William liked her in. She fixed her hair the way William liked, taking the two front pieces and putting them in back with a clip, slipped in her favorite dangle earrings.

She drove downtown, parked her car in the apartment complex where William lived. Once she got out of the car, she pulled her long coat closer to her body out of fear, telling herself she had to get William out of that place. It was after six o'clock, pitch black. The wind was tough. In the lobby, Eleanor told the security officer that she was here to see William Woods. She asked if he would let her up without buzzing so she could surprise him, and he went ahead and let her. She remembered exactly what floor William lived on, what apartment number. The door was locked. She knocked on the thick steel. There was no answer. She pressed the buzzer and then pounded on the door again. *Why didn't you wait?* She wondered.

But she had seen William's pickup truck. It was parked next to where she had parked her mother's car. Maybe he was taking out the garbage or tending to a problem with one of the units in the building. She stood in the hallway for a few minutes and waited. Then she stepped back into the elevator, went downstairs, and asked the security guard if he had seen William. She looked in the mirror in the vestibule. She thought to herself, as soon as William sees me we are going to be okay. The security guard said he'd try to page him. When he didn't answer the page, the security guard accompanied Eleanor back up the elevator. She thought how strangely yellow his coloring looked under the florescent light in the elevator. She remembered that security guard's face as he proceeded to unlock William's door. He suggested she wait out in the hall after he flicked on the light and smelled its stench. Eleanor couldn't wait. She followed behind him. The room looked as if it hadn't been cleaned in weeks. Dirty clothes were in a heap on the floor. A filthy towel was on the back of the kitchen chair. There were empty Coke cans, pizza boxes, newspapers stacked on the kitchen counters and piled on the floor and on the coffee table. It smelled awful. It was the sight of that room, the fact that he hadn't cared enough about himself to clean up that made her angry. *William, why can't you take better care of yourself?* She thought. The security guard tried to usher her back out the door, but she wouldn't go. On the table was an empty vial of painkillers William's doctor had prescribed for a disk he fractured lifting stones for his wall.

William was slumped on the couch, his face pushed into the pillows, his back to her. She thought he was sleeping, even though the security guard tried to pull her away. "It's okay," she said to the guard. "I want to surprise him." *Nothing is wrong. William's sleeping.* She leaned over and kissed his cheek. It was cold. She put a blanket around him. He didn't move. "William, wake up. Get up," she screamed. The record player nearby was still on. *Everyone's leaving. And sunny skies has to stay behind.* The needle was at the end of the record, scratching it. On the coffee table was the last letter she had sent him, telling him when she was arriving. Next to it was a brush filled with strands of his hair.

****

Days later she went to the woods by herself and sat on the stone wall. There was still snow on the ground and she sat in the cold to be close to William. She heard his voice in her head. *A dry retaining wall is constructed without mortar or adhesion. It depends upon the weight and friction of one stone on another for its stability. Nothing exists alone, Eleanor. There is always balance. The first stones can be laid six inches below grade. There is no elaborate footing required for a dry wall since the stones are not bonded together and will raise and lower with the frost. In laying the first layer, larger stones should be used. A line should then be strung along the wall as a guide to keep the rest of the wall straight.* She had watched him drag the stones from one site to another in a piece of heavy canvas. *It's about endurance. I think of it as battling with what pulls me down, what takes the life out of me, and then building something beautiful from it. This wall is ours. Remember. One stone on another.* She pictured the way he had pushed her to the ground and started kissing her neck. *Let me look at those eyes,* he said. *The blue one is brighter today, Eleanor.*

She picked up one of the lighter stones and laid it on the wall. The wall was perpendicular to a creek, and she heard the sound of the water moving through the stones, reminding her of the living world. *What happened to all the love letters I sent you when we were apart? Where are the letters, William? Nothing is private between two people.* She lifted one stone, and then another, placing each one on the wall the way he had taught her. *One life spirals into others. I thought God would protect you. But I made a mistake. You needed to watch yourself. To make your own covenant with God. Didn't I mean anything? Why, William?* She held the blue stone, his favorite, close to her chest before she threw it into the wall, shattering it into little pieces. *How could you do this to me?*

The air was turning moist. Darker. Clouds closed in overheard. Small animals scurried for cover. She could see the gleaming edge of a piece of red cloth in between two slabs of stone. It was the bandanna he wore around the crown of his head. She used it to wipe her eyes.

It's my life to do what I want with, isn't it, Eleanor? If I want to stay here in the woods, behind this wall? She stood up straight and stretched her back. *No it's not okay, William.* Her muscles ached. Her hands were crusty with mud. *What about us—the people who loved you? We sat around the linoleum kitchen table in your mother's house trying to figure out what would possess you to take your life. We talked about the coffin you built out of wood for the sick runt of your cat's litter. Your dad was there. He was crying like a baby. We talked about the amazing care that went into the way you built the wall. What went wrong? We talked about how you liked to run in the woods with your dogs, the way you juggled for hours at a time.*

She propped herself on the wall and let her legs dangle over one side. William was part of God; she listened for his mysterious echo in the woods. Nothing. Only the wind sighed through the dense trees. The shadow of a slender deer. A hundred sparrows crowded in one tree. It began to rain—a drizzle so light she could barely feel it. In time the rain quickened.

She hopped off the wall and picked up a fistful of dirt. *I know you can see me, William.* The rain soaked her hair and jacket. Her wet pants stuck to her legs. She shivered. In her memory she saw the shape of him scoop up a handful of earth. He held it in his palm and sprinkled it into her hand. *Here, take this dirt in your hands. See all the minerals and crystals inside it. There could be souls in this dirt, fragments of bodies. We're all inside each other.*

Subterfuge

Jill Bialosky

I'll always say yes
to wanting to be in touch,
but there are rules.
What are the rules, she said, apprehensive,
longing not only for the rain to stop
(suddenly it built in force)
but to look out for the two yellow birds
that skirted through the field
the morning before, weaving their way
through the flurry of the yard,
excited by their own dare.
You know the rules, he said.
There are boundaries.
The field of wild brush
separated one house from the other.
Even when it was quiet you sometimes heard
the child screaming with laughter in the yard,
could intuit the mood of the house
and its inhabitants, share in their intimacy.
The rain turned to storm. It pushed
against the windows, threatened to seep
into the cracks underneath the windowsill.
It slashed against the shingles, as if the house
were a boat and subject to the tide of water.
In the wind's determination was a force
that wanted to carry you with it,

engulf you in its madness
and then throw you spent into the field,
sure of itself and its need to purge and punish.

A Sheep Is a Gift

Max Blagg

WE WERE TWO YOUNG GUYS SHARING A LOFT IN LOWER Manhattan, around the time Belushi died. We made a tenuous living by bartending and construction, or rather demolition, in the industrial buildings being restored in our neighborhood. We drank a lot, had sex with multiple female partners and took any drugs that were available. Juan was a very good artist, but his primary mission was to prove that all women were whores at heart, based on some unfinished business with his own mother, about which he released sporadic details, usually when drunk—she had once fondled or fucked him or refused to fuck him. Or she fucked his father, she wasn't his real mother, his real mom was a prostitute, and so on.

Some of his stories were so classically Freudian or fraudulent one suspected he had made them up or read them on the wall of a toilet. He preferred women who were already attached to a man, to confirm his theory of the holy whore, opening her legs for anyone, even when she was already spoken for. He put more effort into these seductions than into his art, though he was very good at both.

I wanted to be a writer but I spent most of my time in bars, drinking and making drinks. Safely ensconced behind three yards of booze-soaked mahogany, strutting and preening on my little stage, playing many parts; good cop, bad cop, confidant and father confessor, bullshit artist par excellence. Lord of the Cups, the Master Decanter, orchestrator of inebriation, foreman in charge of the general derangement of the senses. Ladies drank free all night whenever I worked. I put up with all manner of aggravation and abuse, twelve hours a shift, four nights a week. I detested the people I worked for and despised most of the clientele, these surly inhabitants of a mean dystopia who so eagerly swilled down my beakers of liquid lightning. But the money was good, all cash all the time. We lived by the motto of Jackie Gleason:

"I had it I spent it, it went."

Christmas was coming. The rent was due. A pile of chocolate colored powder lay on the table by the back window of the loft, a former machine shop with solid concrete floors and ceiling. Soundproof, bullet proof. A life-size mannequin with brightly painted lips and nails hung from a chain in the center of the space. Photographs, newspaper clippings, magazine and manuscript pages were randomly pinned and taped to the walls. A Selectric typewriter stood on a table fashioned from the graffitied marble wall of a toilet stall, lying flat on an iron frame. There was a crude bathroom in one corner and a dirty white stove, which looked incapable of boiling a kettle. Juan's easel and painting materials stood next to a huge rectangular canvas tent suspended by ropes from the ceiling.

Beside the easel was a large cage containing an Amazon parrot named Veronica, even though it was thought to be a male. Veronica had a limited vocabulary consisting mainly of Spanish swearwords, "*cabrone, chinga tu madre, pendejo!*" which it repeated loudly and harshly until a silk cloth was laid over the cage and the bird became instantly silent.

The powder on the table looked and tasted like chocolate, or cocoa. It was mescaline, allegedly, but nobody ever checked the provenance of these substances, we simply ingested them and hoped for the best. I was doubtful this stuff would get me high but in the absence of cocaine I sniffed a couple of lines anyway. Juan decided to pass on the chocolate. He would wait until we met Maya at the bar. She always had something. We walked out into a mild December evening. By the time we had reached Chambers Street I looked at Juan and realized that this chocolate wasn't Cadbury's. A vein was throbbing in his forehead like a snake under parchment. He looked as beautiful as a Caravaggio, still halfway innocent somewhere deep down in a storm cellar beneath this tornado of drugs and booze that continued to engulf us both and leave us waving and drowning on a daily basis.

A silvery glow like Saint Elmo's fire was running along the edges of the buildings that arched way up into a blue velvet sky, soft and luscious, a massive breathing canopy above our heads.

We reached Canal Street and stood there for some time as the traffic roared by. I studied the signs imprinted in the tarmac, trying to decode their hidden meanings. Their shapes changed with each passing truck. The walk sign glowed permanent red. Each time we were about to step out into the street a fresh wave of traffic came surging up from both directions, highbeams crisscrossing like searchlights at a border.

Then I saw the dog. Not the little black shadow dog that followed me around when I was depressed, but a fair-sized, cream-colored mutt. I studied its muzzle through the magnifying lens of mescaline. Probably a lab mix. Words sizzled and sparked in my head.

Was Labrador part of the dominion of Canada?

Dominion was a nice word. And death shall.

Were labs bred in laboratories? Laughter bubbled in the cauldron as I looked over at Juan, waiting with Aztec patience to cross the street, calmly observing the dog as it skittered through the traffic and by some miracle gained the north side of Canal.

Just as suddenly it swiveled around on big puppy paws and lurched back into the roadway. There was a screech of brakes and a bang. A panel truck had caught the dog square in the head and killed it instantly.

They killed my dog! My stomach bounced into my throat, then I remembered I didn't have a dog.

The driver got out and dragged the animal unceremoniously to the side of the road. We took advantage of this brief delay to cross the street, and walked on, unmoved by this small urban tragedy. Around the corner was La Cornue, the bar where Juan had arranged to meet Maya, his current girlfriend.

Maya was a long sensual streak of gogo dancer, Jersey stamped all over her, beautiful cornflower blue eyes already going blank from endlessly exposing her meat joy beauty to the salacious gaze of the neckless geeks who ogled her from the sidelines of the luck-free bars she worked in.

She didn't like what her beauty had brought her, and had begun to acquire scars, tattoos, any kind of imperfection to spoil and conceal whatever it was that made men stare and click their teeth and call out to her in the street.

The place was packed. Animal planet. Badgers and pigs and geese crowded the tables. Two hippotami were squeezed into a booth. A low mooing and the whinnying of horses occasionally penetrated the wall of music and noise. Maya was already there, lynx-eyed, serene among the quadrupeds. Two minutes after we had sat down next to her a man in a business suit approached our table. There was something asinine in his slender physiognomy.

"Why the long face?" I asked, but he ignored me and began jabbering to Maya. It was obvious they had some kind of history, he was probably one of her lovesick johns. His bland, expensive suit and red suspenders marked him as a toiler in the pits of Wall Street. One of the capitalist pigs we loved to hate, ordinary mortals who made vast amounts of money by some mysterious sleight of hand, standing around the stock exchange and shouting at each other all day.

The man briefly turned his attention to Juan.

"Oh, you're an artist," I heard him say, "well you must be starving, let me buy you a drink."

Juan's lack of fluency in English frequently enraged him, and I shared his frustration as the condescending donkey monopolized Maya with his tales of high finance. This arrogant interloper needed to be straightened out, and a punch in the face seemed too obvious. As I sat there, mellow yet judgmental, I suddenly remembered the dog. I saw a balance, with the dog in one scale and the donkey in the other, canceling each other out. Justice would be served. Just desserts.

"The desserts in here are not very good," I said to the donkey, "but I've got something for you, something special. Don't go anywhere." The ass was so entranced with Maya he didn't even hear.

I quickly left the bar and retraced my steps to Canal Street. There was the dog, still lying in the gutter, smiling, as if I'd come to rescue it from this undignified place. A medium size lab, maybe part Alsatian, obviously not fully grown—its paws were huge. I grabbed it by the scruff of the neck and carried it back toward the bar, a question flitting through my head. Why did it not seem unusual to be carrying a dead dog along West Broadway?

"Ah, don't worry about it," the drug answered as I reached the bar and pushed my way back inside, the dog swinging slightly as it hung from my fist. There was a scream from one table, a glass smashed on the floor. Stirrings of pandemonium. The bartender shouted, "You can't bring a dead dog in here!" That seemed to make sense, but was it really dead, or only sleeping? Why take a dead dog into a bar? I couldn't think of the answer to that question either, it was obscure as a zen koan, or the first line of a joke.

"Ah, grasshopper, you take the dead dog into the bar..."—now I remembered, I was giving it to the insolent donkey talking to Maya.

I approached the table and gently laid the dog across the broker's feet. The man looked human again, and stunned. Maya was smiling. She loved trouble. A trickle of blood from the dog's head leaked onto his shoes. The bartender, who knew me, had come out from behind the bar. "Alex, what the fuck are you doing? Why did you bring that fucking dog in here?"

"I don't know," I replied, and I truly didn't.

It had seemed the perfect response when I was listening to the man braying away, but now it seemed, not necessarily wrong, but somehow out of synch. Endorphins were scattering like roaches in my brain. Right, wrong, right, wrong, each time I tried to decide the focus shifted. I certainly hadn't meant to interfere with anyone's night out.

The bartender began to pick the dog up and bloody drool spilled from its mouth. He dropped it and gagged, then ran into the bathroom to puke. Obviously he had no heart for the abattoir.

The broker seemed too astonished to move, even though the dog had dropped back onto his feet. "It's okay Tom," I yelled through the toilet door, "I'll take the dog out. Where's his leash?"

Then I excused myself to the broker and hefted the dog again, feeling almost cheerful. I had something to do. For a moment I wished I were somewhere else and the dog was still alive, but that was the past, this was now, it was better and it was worse.

The crowd, already jittery, parted like the Red Sea as I walked back outside with the dripping corpse. Further down Grand Street a dumpster was stationed outside a building under renovation. I swung the dog back and forth to gain momentum and then tossed it underhand into the dumpster. Blood sprayed around as it flew through the air and tumbled out of sight with a dull thud. That last construction job had done wonders for my triceps.

But I couldn't shake a nagging sense of unease, the idea that something foolish had transpired without my knowledge. It caused little bursts of heated embarrassment that were quickly dispersed by the soothing action of the mescaline.

A small cluster of people from the bar had followed at a distance and were looking in my direction. They all had little purple colored haloes above their heads. What the hell were they staring at? They stood there like a flock of sheep. Was I acting drunk? I didn't feel drunk, what the fuck were they looking at? Juan suddenly appeared at my side. "What happened?" He seemed incredulous too.

"Where's Maya?"

"Oh she's inside. She's talking to the guy, he's really upset."

"She's inside? She's staying?" I said, astonished that she wasn't with us, outraged at her infidelity to the cause, whatever our cause was, after such a grand gesture on her behalf.

"Yeah, come on, we should get out of here before Rachid shows up. I heard the waitress on the phone to him." Rachid, the owner of La Cornue, was a notoriously moody Arab of Berber origin.

I didn't share Juan's sense of urgency. We walked up the street a few blocks to another bar where we knew the night manager.

Jimmy Furlong, known as 8 to the Mile, looked like Art Garfunkel might have if he had taken a lot of acid. He greeted us effusively and seemed unfazed by the fact that my hands were covered in blood.

"What's this, the Scottish play?" he asked, deadpan, and we laughed. Everything seemed alright again. Again. An echo. Again.

"You better clean up," said Furlong and directed me downstairs to the prep kitchen, out of sight of the customers ruminating at the tables.

I washed the dog's blood off my hands and walked back up the stairs. Maybe this wasn't such a good thing after all.

"What color am I now, Alex?" Furlong said, his massive afro throwing off sparks, as he handed us each a shot of Jack Daniel's.

I drank off half the shot, the raw heat of the whiskey burning my gullet.

"Do you want something to eat?" Jimmy said. We both shook our heads no. The burgers here were primeval.

To alleviate the constant irritation of greeting and seating people he didn't like, and serving them low grade meat and beer while struggling to maintain a veneer of respect and civility, Furlong spent long hours in his tiny music studio, making tapes that juxtaposed wildly disparate musical styles, tapes which often drove people screaming from the bar. The sound track now segued from "Dear Prudence" to a kind of militant Arab music, interspersed with what might have been the sound of camels mating. For me it had a terrible poignancy. Several diners raised their heads in alarm, trying to pinpoint the source of this cacophony. A surge of adrenaline almost lifted me off my barstool.

"I gotta go home."

I pushed the unfinished drink over to Juan, who poured it into his own glass. "Yeah, you should go home. I'm going to wait here for Maya."

Behind the plate glass window, Jimmy and Juan observed my progress as I stood outside, looked around and then began walking south on West Broadway. The deserted street stretched away for miles, a long tunnel framed by empty loft buildings. I walked carefully down the tubular, submarine alley until I noticed a crowd of people milling around the corner of Grand Street. As I approached somebody turned around and yelled,

"That's him, that's the guy who killed the dog!"

Another voice took up the cry, then somebody screamed up the street, "Rachid, he's over here!" The crowd opened up to reveal in the near distance the owner of La Cornue, Rachid, a tiny ball of malevolence in an oversize leather jacket, rapidly approaching, brandishing a chef's knife as long as his arm.

I felt oddly relaxed, like this was happening somewhere else, or that *I* was somewhere else, not on this street corner with violence about to ventilate the tranquil fabric of the night.

The crowd clustered around, hoping for bloodshed.

Yeah he killed a dog
He killed his girlfriend's dog
Took it in the bar
Threw a dead dog on the bar
Hit some guy with a dead dog . . .

I chose to ignore these random samplings of information. They belonged in another movie. Instead I focused my wavering attention on Rachid, who looked deranged, as if something really terrible had happened. I tried to cheer him up.

"Rachid, you appear like a mirage out of the desert.

"That jacket looks good on you."

"You, it was YOU who bring the dog?"

"What the fuck wrong with you, bring a fucking dead dog in my restaurant? You were my friend, my customer!"

Oh, not the dog again. Why was it hounding me?

I tried to change the subject.

"Hey, Rachid, do you have a license for that jacket?"

"Why the fuck you bring that dog in my bar. A dog is bad luck!"

"Why is a dog bad luck?"

"It is fucking bad luck, listen to me. A sheep is a gift. A dog is bad luck."

"A sheep? Well there weren't any sheep around, it was late . . . it was that fucking donkey, he killed my dog, one thing led to another."

"What donkey? That was your dog? How did that guy kill it? He's my good customer! You fucking liar! What the dog name?"

What was the name of the dog? I had no idea.

"I don't remember, but it had a mother and father . . . they killed my puppy!" I suddenly added, and burst into real tears, which lasted for seconds, followed by a gale of laughter.

The streetlights were pulsing in time with my breathing, ready to guffaw, the buildings were tittering, or sobbing, I couldn't tell, there was such a fine line between happiness and grief.

Rachid stepped forward.

Was he about to use me for bayonet practice? I didn't really care, the chocolate had completely euthanized my feelings. I tried to clear the cluttered deck of my medulla and launch a coherent sentence.

"It . . .was . . . nothing . . . personal . . . it was NOTHING!"

"You bring bad luck with you fucking dog! Stay the fuck out of my restaurant, next time I kill you."

"Oh okay, but," I paused, "the dog is the real victim here . . ."

Rachid, enraged by these non sequiturs, stepped forward as if to stab me. He feinted but didn't strike. However his swordplay deluded me into thinking I had been stabbed. I felt the blade pierce my thigh and my balls seemed to seek refuge inside my body, a strangely sexual feeling.

The shock of having my testicles go into hibernation almost sobered me up, and then the mescaline came coursing back in, lifting me up into the blue air of the evening. Ying yang my string sang. I looked down at my leg far below. There wasn't a mark on it.

I was suddenly furious that I had been tricked, not cut. It was just as bad somehow.

I considered decking this pint-size kamikaze, but Rachid had too many assistants, all more than ready to stomp me into the sidewalk.

I really wanted to explain, except that now I had forgotten why I had taken the dog in the bar, if indeed I had. English had become a distant language.

Everyone stood there for a couple of minutes, on the verge of mayhem, the night humming around us like a giant machine. Then Rachid turned and began to walk away, the backup team following him. A collective sigh of disappointment issued from the crowd. The show was over and there was no blood on the blade.

I was relieved to see him go, because he might easily flip out, like the natives occasionally did in Tangier, running amok in the souk and killing all the tourists. Maybe Rachid remembered that I had inadvertently saved his life a couple of weeks earlier, when I intervened in a confrontation between the Berber and his bartender late one night outside La Cornue. That time Rachid was wielding *two* butcher knives, facing off against a cold-blooded psychopath named Willy Gilman. Willy, a popular but temperamental bartender, had apparently and not too discreetly pissed in the ice instead of using the bathroom during the late rush. Willy was so cold he would have broken Rachid's neck and then claimed to have been hugging him, or stabbed him and said he was trying to give him back his knife. Even with two knives, Rachid was liable to get badly hurt. In a state of brotherly love generated by a combination of bourbon and quaaludes, I had foolishly tried to talk the two men out of a knife fight. Willy, after politely asking me to get out of the way, suddenly picked me up like a toy and hurled me about ten feet into the stacked bags of garbage that the busboy had just put out on the sidewalk. This sudden flight of the peacemaker through the night air was so astonishingly comical to the crowd of onlookers that it also precipitated a storm of laughter in both participants, and suddenly the duel seemed preposterous. Just like that, everyone was friends again. The crowd went back inside, where Willy served the free drinks that Rachid provided for what was left of the night. Rachid also insisted on buying the leather jacket I was wearing, even though it was far too large for the tiny Berber. Since I had just shoplifted it at Canal Jean, I was happy to accept the two hundred dollars Rachid offered, and that night I walked home rich and drunk in my shirtsleeves.

Now, two blocks and two weeks from where that friendly sale had taken place, Rachid stopped, removed the jacket and began to hack at it with the butcher knife, stabbing it repeatedly. After he had murdered the coat he threw it at me and stomped off with his little band of Thuggees in the direction of his bar. The crowd melted away.

"My tailor can fix that," I yelled after the retreating figures and burst into manic laughter once again, alone on the sidewalk, safe in the gelatinous clutches of mother night.

6/17/04

Max Blagg

The light was up at 5:45 A.M. and I rose to meet it
first hours of the day filled with rain
lightning over Montauk something
sticking in the craw, the seeds in the burst throat
of the songbird on the road, sunflower seeds.
Ken Kesey planted sunflowers by filling shotgun
cartridges with seed and firing into the muddy banks
that surrounded his house in La Honda
somewhere north of Big Sur where we once
wandered more like refugees than literary pilgrims
"Lord I am risen from that misery and I wait for you
like the sleepless man waits for the dawn."
I wait for you like the poor man waits for shekels
to rain from the sky instead of frogs and snakes,
familiar musculature, grazed anatomy
stirring pits and seeds
through the morning like sunlight
crossed the floorboards
close to the wonder and the wonder.
Read the psalms as the dog curled into
me and the night was cool again,
everything bearable everything
in the palm of my hand,
finger on the trigger
chakras loaded like shells
along my spine.

6/18/04

June spreads its beauty like a cloak like a
tarp on wet grass a trap for cats.
Young men reading *Briggflatts* gasp
at the streamlined God-built beauty of the thing itself.
Eat a peach, eat it down to the bone.

Welcome to the Year of the Monkey

Nick Flynn

(APRIL 2004) WE HEAR WORD OF THE PHOTOGRAPHS BEFORE WE see the photographs, we hear about them on the car radio. The man on the radio has seen them, he talks as if they are there in front of him, as if he is thumbing through them as he speaks—*The photographs are from our war*, he says, *and they are very, very disturbing*.

I'm driving north from Texas to New York with my pal Ben. Ben has been a human rights activist for a long time now, the focus of his work, at the moment, is Haiti; before Haiti it was East Timor. I've just finished a semester teaching poetry in Houston, the first significant amount of time I've spent in Texas, having been based most of my life no further south than Coney Island. Ben flew in from California a few days ago for this roadtrip. The car is a 1993 Ford Escort wagon—good, reliable, unsexy, cheap—a basic a-to-b device. I bought it in Texas with the idea of taking it north because, unlike the Northeast, a used car from Texas will be unlikely to have rust. You just have to make sure it was never in a flood—Houston, built on a swamp, is known for its floods. Houston, also, is seemingly endless—we hear about the photographs again and again even before we make it to the city limits. What connects the photos, the man on the radio says, is that each depicts what appears to be torture, and that the people doing the torturing are wearing uniforms, or parts of uniforms, and that the uniforms appear to be ours.

****

One thing should be said at the outset, in the spirit of full disclosure (*full* disclosure?)—these photographs appeared at a time in my life when I found myself wandering through my days with the first few lines of Dante's *Inferno* running over and over in my head—*In the middle of my life I found myself in a deep dark wood, having lost the way*. Much of this had to do with the fact that my long-term relationship, with a woman I loved deeply, had ended, and badly. That it had ended a couple years earlier only testifies to the fact that it takes awhile for things to sink into, or bubble up from, one's—my—unconscious. That I had been with another woman for part of those intervening years, and that that relationship was also ending (badly) should also be said, up front, if just to give you a sense of my state of mind. *Un*settled. *Un*centered. Maybe even *un*hinged. I was drowning, or if not exactly drowning then slowly sinking beneath the surface of whatever it was I was treading in, sinking into a profound, *un*speakable silence. I knew, somewhere inside me, that it was likely that this delusion (the delusion that I was drowning while standing on dry land) had nothing to do with the woman I was with, for I had felt it before with other women. I knew, somewhere inside me, that it was me. In the way these things sometimes go another woman appeared, and I convinced myself that she was a life raft, or piloting a life raft—all I had to do was take her hand, pull myself up, or let my body be pulled up. The thing was, this woman appeared before the other relationship ended, which was problematic—painful—and it soon became clear that I was the one sowing the pain. Would I really stand on another's head to keep myself from going under? Is that what I was doing?

To backtrack: about the long-term thing there is much to say—here I will say that our time together was the first sustained period in my life that I'd felt certain about anything. By the time we'd met I'd already become accustomed to hauling around this sack of gnawing uncertainty with every step I took. That it ended badly (I still cannot imagine a way it could have ended well, though I know this isn't true) drove me to my knees—no, that's not it—it drove me to a pond, I threw my body in and swam, hour after hour, I swam as long as it took until I had a good thought. Just one good thought. Some days, most days, it would take a long time, but finally I could see it coming toward me, across the surface of the water, and as it reached me I let it wash over me. If I didn't make it to the water, if I missed a day, then I knew I wouldn't have that one good thought and, I feared, maybe I'd never have another one again. By certain—most—reckoning I was to blame, though for a long time I held onto the desperate belief that I'd actually been the one most wronged.

Shortly after that relationship ended I got a grant, which had one stipulation: in order to get the money I had to leave North America for one year—*The Banishment Prize*, I called it. I ended up based for the next two years in Rome, hard to complain, except that I left a support system I'd spent the last ten years building up, a web of friends and routines that seemed to keep me, mostly, on an even keel. Without knowing it, and without seeking it, once I landed in Rome this support system began to slowly unravel, to break apart, like those photographs of Antarctica's ice cap falling into the sea. It should also be said that this personal crisis was nearly invisible to those around me, especially since the one who had been closest to me for the past eight years was no longer there, but this might be another delusion, the delusion that no one else could see how fucked up I was, when it is just as likely I came across as an utter mess.

> *note*: Thich Nhat Hahn has a meditation exercise I've been contemplating lately: *Knowing that my deeds are my true belongings, I breathe in. Knowing that I cannot escape the fruit of my deeds, I breathe out.* Thich Nhat Hahn also claims: *You can change the past by what you do today.* It would be nice to imagine this was true.

The man on the radio says the words "Abu Ghraib," words neither Ben nor I have ever heard before—at this point we don't know if *Abu Ghraib* is one word or two, if it is a building or a city, a place or an idea. The correct pronunciation has yet to be agreed upon. We're in my new-used car on an elevated highway over the desolate landscape of Houston—strip mall, strip mall, factory, fringe neighborhood, empty lot—textbook urban sprawl. Ben steers, I'm shotgun, navigator, though the only direction is *out*. A woman I will end up with one day will describe this landscape as *inhuman*, but at this moment I have yet to meet her. She is waiting at the end of this roadtrip, in New York, but I have no way of knowing this and she is not really waiting because she doesn't even know I exist. She will use the word "inhuman" months later, after I am back in Texas again and after her first visit, as I drive her to the George H. W. Bush International Airport, the one with the larger-than-life sized bronze statue of the former president, looking as if he is walking into a windstorm, clutching a book entitled "Winds of Change." Inhuman—I won't blame her for this judgement: before I ended up here Texas was, in my imagination, "the belly of the beast"—Enron, Halliburton, the death penalty—a preponderance of recent ills seem to emanate from the self-proclaimed Lone Star State. This was my vision before I arrived, but at this point, four months later, my vision has been complicated somewhat—Art Cars, The Innocence Project, Molly Ivins, Steve Earle, Daniel Johnson—and, unlike New York, the bad guys don't pretend to be good guys, they don't dress like hipsters, they actually wear black hats. I like Texas, and I like telling friends back in New York that I like Texas, and to watch their faces twitch.

The man on the radio describes the photographs—there are prisoners, there are guards, there are dogs. Hallways and cinderblocks and cages. Leashes and smiles. Many of the prisoners, he says, are not wearing clothes. The reason for this, he says, is that there appears to be a sexual element to what is happening, as we float past a church the size of a shopping mall.

Ben and I met in Amherst, as undergraduates at the University of Massachusetts. Aside from our studies, such as they were, we were both on the periphery of a group that called itself "The Radical Student Union." These "radicals" seemed to attract the most interesting, beautiful women, but at times the group itself felt strangely elitist, though, to be fair, in my early twenties I felt like an outsider nearly everywhere. Still today, sometimes—often—it takes a force of will not to inhabit that psychic periphery. After kicking around Amherst for three years something happened, something awful—my mother committed suicide. About this there is much to say, I've written about it before, but here I will only say that in her aftermath I dropped out, drifted for awhile, and eventually landed in Boston. A year later Ben graduated and also ended up in Boston, which meant our lives could keep intersecting.

In Boston we drank in the same bars, we did drugs together a few times, we met up at clubs called The Rat and The Channel and The Middle East. The radio station we listened to had a hardcore punk show on every morning called "Breakfast of Champions," which somehow calmed me. Boston is a college town, and we told ourselves there wasn't a whole lot to do, since we were out of college. I worked in a homeless shelter, Ben drove a cab. At the end of our time in Boston we both quit drinking, independently and unbeknownst to the other, though a few months into it we bumped into each other and sheepishly admitted that our numbers had come up. We then spent a year crossing paths in AA meetings, until Ben left for San Francisco, and I moved to Brooklyn. By the time of this roadtrip we hadn't hung out like this, with a handful of empty days ahead of us, in many years.

The man on the radio tells us that there is something else disturbing in the photographs—in many there are more people than just the soldier and the prisoner. There are others, others who are apparently not taking part in what is happening, other soldiers and others not in uniform—maybe CIA, maybe "private contractors," the man on the radio says. These others are not directly involved in the torture, at least they have not been photographed torturing, but at the same time they appear to be not at all alarmed by what is transpiring. Some are even looking away, as if they are bored.

That there are others in the photographs is disturbing, the man on the radio says, because it reveals a pattern, it reveals that this is not something out of the ordinary, but, rather, something banal, mundane, something very, very ordinary.

Are you listening? I ask Ben, and he nods. It's bad, right? Yeah, it's bad, Ben agrees, but it's nothing new. He begins to tell me about his last trip to Haiti. We've got to get a newspaper, I say, but the photographs won't be in the newspaper until the next day.

By the time we see the photos the others—other soldiers, private contractors—will have been cropped out, so we are presented only with the central tableau—the soldier and the prisoner. Or, often, just the prisoner, or prisoners, posed in such a way that it is impossible not to know that they are in pain—one can almost hear them, one can almost smell them. That the others are cropped out will make it easier for some, in the weeks and months to come, to imagine it all as the isolated acts of a few bad apples. In the weeks and months to come the term "a few bad apples" will be heard a lot. The issue of who did the cropping, who made that decision, the press or the military, will go unasked.

I ended up spending some time in Lisbon a year or so after my mother died. I took a train one day with a Portuguese friend to the town of Sintra, where she had to appear in court to clear up a minor traffic violation. While waiting for her in the hallway outside the courtroom, shafts of sunlight streamed through the dusty gothic windows, both illuminating and enshrouding the few people awaiting their turn before the judge. Knowing that light is always changing I took my camera out and snapped a picture. As I put the camera down from my eye I noticed that one of the people in the hallway was wearing a uniform, and that he was now walking toward me. I put my camera back in my bag. The soldier now stood directly before me, blocking my way, though I wasn't attempting to go anywhere. Half-a-foot shorter than I was, he whispered something menacing into my face that I didn't understand. Sorry, I said, I'm just a tourist, no problem, hoping my friend would appear and translate my way out of whatever was happening. But she didn't, and he took my arm and directed me toward a door. Once we passed through it we were in another hallway, and everyone in this hallway, six or seven men, had on the same uniform. The small soldier put his face close to mine and murmured *pelicula, pelicula, pelicula*, which I understood was the word for film. He gestured for me to hand it over. Just a snapshot, I said, just a tourist, no problem, and that was when he punched me in the stomach. It didn't really hurt, not as much as you might think—it was more of a shock. I looked around at the other soldiers—some looked at their shoes, some smoked their cigarettes, some smiled and looked away. I realized I was, at best, on my own. I held up my hand, no problem, I said, and reached into my bag and took the camera out. As I did he punched me again, in the same spot, the spot the doctor had pulled my spleen out of a few years before. This time the whole thing was more of a dance—he leaned into it more, I rounded my back, pushed my weight up on my toes, absorbed it. The words *I am far from home I am being beaten up by a soldier* ran through my mind. I had the camera in one hand, *pelicula*, he hissed, gesturing, and for some reason I started to rewind the film, for I didn't want to open the camera to the light and ruin the whole roll, though the little soldier kept murmuring and menacing and gesturing. When the roll was rewound I popped the camera opened and handed the roll to him, and as he held it in one hand he punched me one last time. Since he had the film I decided it was time to leave, so I pushed past him back out through the door. My friend was in the hallway, waiting, wondering where I'd been. Shaky, I explained quickly that I'd lost the film, and that we should leave immediately, before the door opened again. On the same roll were some photographs documenting work we'd been doing on her apartment, and she needed these photographs to get reimbursed by her landlord. So she knocked on the door, and the little soldier came out, and she explained the situation, and he refused, and so she asked to speak to his commanding officer, and soon we were outside, talking to a little general in a little jeep, and with lots of wrangling we got the roll of film back. Which is why I have a photograph of the soldier who punched me three times in the stomach. It is the other soldiers, though, the ones who merely smiled and looked away, that somehow trouble me more.

> *note*: Since Portugal had no standing military at that time I wondered who these soldiers worked for, until a couple years later, during the Iran-Contra hearings, Portugal was identified as "Country B," the conduit for arms to Iran—the soldier I encountered was, quite possibly, part of a paramilitary unit funded by the United States. Funded by me. I encountered the same type of non-regulation soldiers running around Costa Rica during the Contra War, and in fact nearly got punched again for taking a picture of one of them.

Ben and I finally break out of the vortex that is Houston, and now we're driving north on I-10, approaching the exit for New Orleans, where we'd planned to stop, but we decide to push on, to make it to Tuscaloosa before nightfall, where our friends Joel and Wendy have offered us shelter. Since it's likely I'll be based in Houston half the year for the foreseeable future I can drive to New Orleans anytime. We make a plan for Jazz Fest the following year, and push on into Alabama. We never get to see New Orleans again.

The man on the radio says he is holding thirty photographs in his hands. He says there are many more he hasn't seen, maybe hundreds more. At first he doesn't say how he ended up with the photos, except to say that they were leaked. "Whistleblower" is the word he uses.

We've heard the man on the radio before, his name is Seymour Hersh, the first time we heard his name was nearly thirty years ago, when he broke the story of a massacre in Vietnam—My Lai—the name of a hamlet that came to symbolize all that was wrong with that war—nearly four hundred unarmed men, women and children—civilians—rounded up, executed, many of them herded into ditches and shot. Photographs document that day as well, and the photographs made their way to his hands, and eventually to the front page of the New York Times. *Welcome to the Year of the Monkey*, banners over the streets of Saigon read that spring of 1968.

All these years later people still bring Hersh things that trouble them.

When the World Trade Center towers were still standing, masses of people streamed northward up Lafayette. I stood in a parking lot at Great Jones with the rest and watched smoke pouring from the one tower we could see. It was the day I was to pick up my plane ticket for Rome. What happened, I asked a stranger, but he didn't know. Smoke filled the sky—whatever had happened was still happening. In my mind the people streaming northward were all coming from the burning tower, I was relieved that everyone had made it out all right—that's how my mind translated that beautiful blue day punctured by smoke.

A few minutes later the guy I get my coffee from told me that airplanes had crashed into both towers. *Both towers?* A few minutes after that I stood with another crowd of strangers inside an appliance store on Broadway and watched the first tower fall on a bank of televisions. I could have stood on the sidewalk outside the store and seen it fall, but I thought there might be some words coming from the televisions that would make it all make sense.

As Ben and I listen to the car radio almost three years later I come to a conclusion—tomorrow all cameras will be confiscated from all military personnel—an order will come down and from now on it will be illegal to carry a camera into battle, or at least into a military prison. I announce my conclusion to Ben. Over the next several months I will make many similarly misguided pronouncements.

****

At Joel and Wendy's we sit outside in the languid Alabama night and laugh a lot because we haven't seen each other in a long time and the dinner is sweet and afterwards we pass around the *New York Times* and look at the few photos printed there: the now-iconic hooded man standing on a box, his arms outstretched, wires clipped to his fingers; an oddly small girl smoking a cigarette that looks too big for her head, a leash in her hand fastened around a naked man's neck, the man on his side, cowering. On her hands are green rubber gloves, which all the soldiers wear in the photos. The hands of the torturers are green, Ben says.

We are aware, eerily, that at the same moment an enormous number of people around the world are looking at these same photographs—this is the way the world works now.

One of the things that surprises me most is that some of the torturers are women. One of the things that disturbs me most are the smiles on the torturer's faces, men and women, smiling directly into the camera, and the ridiculous thumbs-up they are giving us. As if we are complicit.

Later it will be revealed that the photos were taken on digital cameras and burned onto cd's and passed around among the soldiers like trading cards. The photos acted as trophies, as mementos, some were even used as screen-savers. The photos thus exist as both documentation and souvenir. Later it will be revealed that the soldiers who took the photos threatened to distribute them to the prisoner's families, to their villages, to the world, as another level of humiliation. The photos thus function as part of the torture itself, the part of torture that concerns itself with humiliation, which, it will be revealed, is torture's primary purpose in our war, for any information gleaned is primarily bogus. And now that the photographs have entered the public realm, which happened earlier that day as we crossed into Alabama, it becomes even more complicated, because they then become about us, the viewers, as well. By looking at the photos we become, in some way, either witness or torturer. Or both. We become complicit, and then we either do something or we don't.

On some level, perhaps, as we look at the photographs, we become the tortured as well. I say this as we thumb through them, and my words are met with silence. At this point it might be grotesque to propose this. It is, at best, an *un*formed thought.

This first time I hold the photographs in my hands I don't remember that they are cropped—what is portrayed is enough to both fix my attention and make me look away. But even if the photographs hadn't been cropped it was never just about a soldier and a prisoner—there was always another, at least one other—there was always the photographer, who is either another soldier or perhaps one of these private contractors. The fact that someone is there documenting it all, documenting things that have gone on for centuries, but for the last hundred years or so always in the shadows, always with the screams muffled, also makes it a little harder to dismiss as an aberration.

It might be a weird godsend, I say, that they took the pictures, that the pictures exist. Like a curtain pulled back on a darkness that's been denied forever but now is there for everyone in the world to see and no one will be able to deny it happened. It happens. It is happening. No one will be able to say it doesn't happen.

On the radio the next day, on I-95 somewhere in South Carolina, we hear a veteran of the Korean War interviewed about the photos. He's in a coffee shop in Tennessee, and we get the sense that he is thumbing through the photographs as he speaks. By now the photographs are in every newspaper in the world. *You know,* he begins, slowly, searching for his words, *stuff like this happens in every war.* It's hard to tell if he's disgusted or merely baffled. He pauses, and his voice gets slightly more indignant—*but you don't take pictures.*

You don't take pictures. Ben, you hear that?—*you don't take pictures.* Alligator clips, mock fellatio, leashes, this is all mundane—*but you don't take pictures.* We spend that night with an ex-girlfriend and her family in a town called Snow Camp. She and her husband have two beautiful kids, live in a rambling farmhouse I've done some work on over the years. Ben and I help out cooking and cleaning up afterwards. After the kids leave the table we talk about the photographs. There is nothing else to talk about. My ex-girlfriend was part of the Radical Student Union when we met; she spent time in Nicaragua in the 1980s. Her husband works with small-scale farmers, helping them transition into growing other crops besides tobacco. She was with me when I took the photograph of the paramilitary units in Costa Rica, illegally funded by the United States, driving around in their little jeeps and their unmarked uniforms.

The next day, by the time we make it to Virginia, Rush Limbaugh has weighed in—*This is no different than what happens at the Skull and Bones initiation. And we're going to ruin people's lives over it and we're going to hamper our military effort, and then we're going to really hammer them because they had a good time. You know, these people are being fired at every day. I'm talking about people having a good time. These people, you ever heard of emotional release? You heard of the need to blow some steam off?* This is the moment before "a few bad apples," this is the moment when the soldiers are just like us.

Shortly thereafter, at a press conference on what has come to be called "the Abu Ghraib scandal," Donald Rumsfeld, the Secretary of Defense, will say, *I don't know if it is correct to say what you just said that torture has taken place, or that there's been a conviction for torture. And therefore I'm not going to address the torture word.*

The torture word. You don't take photos. Blow off some steam. We had planned to spend the night at our pal Kevin's place in Charlottesville, where he teaches at the University of Virginia—Sally Hemmings U, as Kevin calls it, in an homage to Thomas Jefferson's unacknowledged slave/mistress (note: as I write this I hear that Virginia has become the first state to formally apologize for slavery). After spending a few hours on the public green with him talking about the photographs we decide to push on, and limp into New York at three A.M, three days after we left Texas.

A few days later senator Trent Lott will echo Limbaugh's pronouncement that the photos show little more than what goes on at a fraternity hazing. Charles Krauthammer (I'm not really sure what Krauthammer, with his comic-book bad-guy name, actually does for a living) will be more explicit—*as Americans we must all be prepared to torture.*

When I land back in New York I will make my way to the woman who'd appeared to me as a life raft a year before. I will tell her that I am in no shape to see anyone, not fully, that I will likely see other people, though this will not stop me from going to her whenever I make my way to Brooklyn. And so we grow closer, over the weeks and months, but at some point I meet someone else, the one who will one day describe Houston as inhuman, and though I am still not ready to really be with anyone there will be less at stake, since we just met. For a while I will tell this new one about the other and for awhile I'll let it be assumed that I've stopped seeing the other, until I wake up one day, a year later, back in Texas, in love with two women, honest with neither, and in as dark a place as I've been in a long, long time—*In the middle of my life I found myself in a deep dark city, having lost my freakin mind.* I'd spent my sober years practicing being honest, and it stunned me how easily one lie folded into another, how I could be on my cell phone telling my lover (which lover?) I was about to go to bed when in fact at that moment I was driving to Austin. When I was with one I dreaded a call from the other, so my phone was always silenced; when I spoke I used the name *sweetie* or *honey* or *darling* so as not to make a mistake. Until I began to hear a voice, I can't pinpoint precisely when it started, quiet at first, comforting, murmuring that if I was dead then the mess I'd gotten myself into would be lifted, and the damage I was spreading would be made right.

A year after the photos appear I'm ready to leave Texas again, to make my way back north, and this voice is murmuring louder. I pull into New York a few days later and attend a ceremony to receive an award from PEN for a book I wrote that came out a few months after the Abu Ghraib photographs appeared, a memoir that deals with my relationship to my father and my time working with the homeless in Boston. The night of the PEN awards I will meet another writer who will receive the sister award for non-fiction, and we will be photographed together, smiling and shaking hands. Months later I will read his book, and find that it is, in part, a treatise advocating the use of torture. A book, in part, about the need to subjugate Muslims, whose religion, he claims, is bloodthirsty and demented. Confused, I will contact PEN and ask if a mistake had been made—PEN is an organization, one of the few, whose mandate it is to end political oppression and, specifically, torture. PEN will tell me that no mistake has been made, that the writer is entitled to his opinion. I will agree to this, but wonder why they saw fit to endorse his opinion with an award, which is prominently announced on the cover of his book, as it is on mine. In order to appear personally affronted, which I am, I will also say that I am concerned that there is a photograph of me somewhere in the world shaking hands and smiling with someone who advocates the use of torture, though really I think the affront is larger than just toward me. The torturers smile, I smile when I shake hands with a torturer, the President smiles when asked about Abu Ghraib—why is everyone smiling? Over the next several months I will contact the author and try to convince him to renounce his views on torture; I will contact the judges who chose his book and ask them what they were thinking; I will write letters to the *New Yorker* and the *New York Times*; I will threaten to give my award back; I will have the board of PEN vote on whether they made a mistake. I will become, in a word, a crank.

Crank. In one email to the writer I was photographed with (note: feel free to insert his name here: ____________; it's easy to find) I relate the old sheepfucker joke: *A man walks through his village, points to the school, says, I built that school with my own two hands, cut each stone myself, but do people call me Eric the School Builder? No. And you see that church, I raised the funds to have the steeple repaired, I worked on it for ten years, but do people call me Eric the Steeple Fixer? No. (pause) But you fuck one sheep. . . .* I point out to the writer I was photographed with that I found much of worth in his book, but when he advocates one little torture. . . .

I ask the judges, via email, if they agree that a little torture is necessary, given the world as it is today, or had they simply not read the book that closely. One judge tells me it is inappropriate of me to question their decision, one ignores me, and one tries to say that she doesn't believe the writer is pro-torture at all, that his position is more ambiguous. Hear No Evil, See No Evil, Speak No Evil. Welcome to the Year of the Monkey. I point out the article he has written, a tamer version of what he proposes in his book, which I had sent to them, entitled *In Defense of Torture*, and ask which part of it seems ambiguous. I don't hear from any of them again. Crank.

note: That the judges were three women somehow bewilders me, in much the same way that some of the torturers are women bewilders me. Is this what the pioneers of feminism envisioned?

> As Angela Davis points out, by now the term *equal opportunity* has been twisted to often simply mean *equal access to the instruments of oppression.*

At a party in Rome, shortly after I landed there, a few months after the towers fell, I met scholar who was researching the Inquisition. The files of the Vatican had just been opened, and so he had access to hundreds of years of accusations and forced confessions. The Vatican, it seems, keeps very scrupulous records, and this scholar was spending days reading transcripts of what amounted to a ridiculous question—*how long have you consorted with the devil?*—followed by a garbled plea for mercy, often just a string of vowels meant to replicate a scream. At this same moment John Yoo, Alberto Gonzales, David Addington and their minions were busy drafting memos and legal briefs which would set into motion and justify what the Abu Ghraib photographs will later document. At this same moment Colin Powell is slowly walking toward a world stage, to utter a lie extracted by torture from a man named Ibn Sheikh al-Libby in a cell in Egypt (not to be confused with Abu Faraj al-Libby, who is either bin Laden's number three man or little more than his chauffeur), a lie about chemical weapons and Saddam and Osama, a lie that will be used to justify a war. At this moment something quaintly called "yellowcake" is being folded into the same lie.

My book will be a bestseller for a minute; the book by the writer who advocates the use of torture will remain a bestseller for more than a year. The *Chicago Tribune* will write (with no mention of torture) that his book has "a pointed sense of humor." The *San Francisco Chronicle* (also with no mention of torture) will write that "despite its polemic edge, this is a happy book." And the *New York Sun* (my personal favorite) will write "this is a trip down Memory Lane." A book that advocates torture equals a trip down memory lane—perhaps an unintentionally accurate description of the secret history of America.

As far as I know, to this day, the writer remains resolute, certain about our need to torture. In his certainty he reminds me of our president, who declared, as the bombs began falling on Baghdad, *The outcome of the current crisis is already determined. . . .*

note: The South African artist William Kentridge writes something that speaks to this type of certainty: "To say one needs art, or politics, which incorporates ambiguities and contradictions is not to say that one then stops recognizing and condemning things as evil. However, it might stop one being so utterly convinced of the certainty of one's own solutions. There needs to be a strong understanding of fallibility and how the very act of certainty or authoritativeness can bring disaster."

Over coffee a few months later the head of PEN will tell me that the award isn't really that big a deal anyway, that he is considering doing away with all awards, that they are becoming more trouble than they are worth. I like and admire this man and all his good works, but why do I feel like a child whose father is threatening to take away his ball if he can't play without bothering him? Why can't I get the image out of my head that somewhere in the world there is a photograph of me smiling as I shake hands with a torturer?

But this isn't the whole story. In the months following the leak of the photographs I will somehow become, to use one of my lover's terms for me, a *pain devil.* Months later I will learn that she would wander alone at night by desolate traintracks, drunk, and lay her head upon the rails, muttering for me to just leave her in peace. Pain Devil—so named for the turmoil and heartache I sowed, so named for the pain she reaped, and I am truly sorry for all of this. Thich Nhat Hahn says we can change the past by what we do today, but I have yet to find a way to take away that pain. Early on, when I told her I wasn't in any shape to see anyone, that I would likely see others, she had intimated to me that she feared she might hurt herself, and this intimation did to me what it sometimes does, especially when it comes from the lips of someone I love—it flipped a switch in my lizard brain, the switch that starts the tape that murmurs over and over *you can save her*, that murmurs over and over *this time you won't fail.*

I am so pitifully naïve. Abu Ghraib turned out to be not much of a scandal at all, at least not in America. The rest of the world might now looks at us and our quaint Constitution with something like bewilderment, but what does the term "the rest of the world" even mean? Who are they, where are they? After September 11, 2001 there was a brief moment when it seemed the world might turn from black and white to Technicolor, when the world might come together to find a different path, but that moment quickly faded. Whatever scandal followed the release of the Abu Ghraib photos turned out to be more of a curtain pulled back on a shadow, like that scene in *The Wizard of Oz,* when it turns out that the one in charge is simply a scared, fat, lost, ungenerous man, except in this latest remake that man is us. The writer I was photographed with tells us that he began his book the day after September 11, which I take to mean he began it in the fog of fear. And as far as I can tell he is still wandering there, albeit quite a bit richer. I ask people sometimes if they've read him, and many have, and I ask what they think about his stance on torture, and they often go glassy-eyed—torture? It seems hard for them to keep it in their heads.

In the fall of 2006 the U.S. Congress passed the Military Detainee Treatment Act, which, among other provisions, essentially legalizes the use of torture. So this is what has blossomed from that day the photos appeared—I am so pitifully naïve. Hitler, Stalin, Mao—none ever publicly claimed the right to torture (though of course they did it), none went to their people and said, *we must do this.* Even Genghis Khan, that cartoon definition of barbarism, even Genghis Khan outlawed torture within his empire. I am so utterly confused, so utterly bewildered, so utterly sorry. What is America now, I wonder—the most honest country in the world, or the most lost?

Earth

Nick Flynn

last night, capt'n, I wandered the earth—a dream, I know & now
the dream's gone—the earth though, still spinning, outside these walls
& the sand, on fire, yes, still—the dream, the earth, poisoned, capt'n,
someone muttering *too late*—I marched, I staggered, a forced march,
yes, then I was digging, a grave, made to dig my own grave, a body
walked into this hole, I saw my own body, covering itself with earth,

~

a body becoming earth

~

I don't know, honcho, here we are—me & you & this room
again—& robert johnson, of course, with us always, mister
robert johnson & his badass guitar—*everytime I'm walkin, on down
the street*—& oh, yes, my question, my one simple question—
look at me: you think I want to be here any more than you?

—that's not the question

~

I had a girl, capt'n, who wanted me to whisper *whore* as we fucked, I
had a girl who tied me up—the walls, capt'n, two feet thick—packed
earth, baked earth, scorched earth—*they created a wasteland & called
it peace*—I don't know anymore what anyone wants

~

> *a note on robert johnson*—he sold his soul to play guitar, he sold his soul to *learn* to play guitar—adam & eve again, prometheus again: knowledge equals death equals betrayal equals endless & unusual torments—*they created a wasteland & called it peace*—listen, can you hear it? once upon a time, the devil begins, it took years before things got freaky—here we hit the ground, boots in the sand, freaky

~

a spigot, a hose, a floor-drain dead-center—it all drains into the earth, into the sand, somewhere outside these walls—you can smell it, your face pressed to the tiles, it tastes like your village, all tile you think all tile you think all tile you think all tile you think baked earth scorched earth hospital yellow yolk yellow dead yellow sulphur yellow

~

everytime I'm walking, on down the street, some pretty mamma start breaking down on me—robert johnson—dead in a swamp, dead at the crossroads, knife in his heart, ratpoisoned blood—fuck the wrong woman, fuck another man's woman, fuck the devil's woman, fuck the devil, fuck the usa, fuck me—*mamma please, stop breaking down*

~

> *a note on the my lai massacre, 1968*—Black soldiers, according to eyewitness accounts & court records, did not participate in the killings—they shot their weapons over the heads of the victims, they sat down & refused, some shot themselves in the foot. This has been a recurring problem for the military—how to overcome the innate revulsion programmed

into humans against killing another human being. This was first noted during the Civil War, when lines of soldiers would face off across a field & fire over each other's heads, for days sometimes, in a drawn-out pantomime of war. The barely trained soldiers acted like some primitive tribes— warriors, painted & menacing, shaking spears & yelling, but never spilling a drop of blood. Of course, in the Civil War, eventually, someone aimed lower—eventually someone always aims lower. The United States military has spent billions to crack the code of how to get soldiers to kill—the code of human consciousness, they call it. We shall overcome, they sing. At Abu Ghraib some black soldiers did participate in the torture of prisoners, but not to the same extent as the white soldiers. Look at the photographs—the majority of torturers are white, though testimonies of the victims describe abuses at the hands of black soldiers as well.

~

they point to the door, they say, tell us what we already know, we already know so tell us, tell us then you can walk—you tell them about your village, they could care less about your village—be a good boy, they say, stand, right here, stand on this tile, this yellow tile, don't even fucken breathe, stand until we say

sit—one hour, one day—buried treasure, dirtbomb, tse-tse fly—to bury a man you must first walk him into the desert, make him dig out an anthill—fire ants—then place him in the hole, pack the earth up to his neck, & cover his head with honey—as a child these things fascinated me—dirtbomb, dirty bomb, king kong, viet cong—now it's me, pointing to the earth, telling a man how deep to dig

~

she fondles you awake—*the red light was my mind*, she whispers, listen to what he sings—

~

> *week three: random thoughts re my duties*—If I understand the memo right, capt'n: we can use water, but we cannot use earth; that is, we can simulate drowning, but not burial—is that right? I love my country, capt'n, sir, I love my job, I want to do what's right—a question: if we cannot bury the prisoner, can we bury his son? I mean, can we *pretend* to bury his son? capt'n, does the memo say we cannot pretend to bury the prisoner's son, does it say we cannot make the prisoner dig his son's grave, does it say we cannot make the prisoner place his son in the hole, does it say we cannot make the prisoner toss a handful of dirt on him, does it say we cannot toss another, does it say we cannot, just to see what blooms? I'm trying, capt'n, to do the right thing
>
> & he has still not answered the question.

~

another dream—the one where the car I'm driving goes into a skid & I can't pull out of it—the one where I wipe my ass but the paper never comes clean. I dug a hole in the earth & sang a little song into it, I dug all the way to china. I made a fort, I ran a stick across the dirt & said, *this is my fort*, you cannot cross this line, *safety*, it's called, the other kids did what I said, they followed the rules

~

ain't no red light here, she whispers, *your village is gone*, *your village ain't no more*

~

yellow tile, metal chair, a liter of diet coke—tell us something, something we can use, tell us anything, tell us a lie. I am a barber, you say, I cut hair, only hair—oh, you cut hair, is that what a barber does?—well then, mr barber, mr haircut, put your hands behind you, wrists together, upsy-daisy, tippy-toes—

this is what we do

~

> *a note on alternative energy*—the center of the earth is on fire, the center of the earth is a planet spinning inside planet & one of the planets is on fire

~

we are tired, they say, we are done—they cut you
down, they hand you a shovel, they point to the earth,
dig, they say, you dig, a hole in the earth, you sing
a song into it, you squat down & shit, you fill it
with blood—the sun, the earth, the shit, the dirt, capt'n,
my mother, her ashes, I scattered her in the ocean,
my father, capt'n, I will scatter him in the ocean as well.
I thought death would be cold, I thought outer-space
would be dark—I never wanted my body
placed in a hole.

“I

didn’t

always

smoke.

Once

I

was

a

baby.”

(Sexton, page 199)

Giving Notice

Deborah Garrison

DEAR TOM,

You called and asked me at the eleventh hour to write some prose, since I don't write prose, and you wondered could I just say something about why. Actually I enjoy writing prose if it's not to be published under my byline as "creative" work. It is so functional and elegant for most of my needs; I could write jacket copy and what we in the publishing biz call "fact sheets" for hours on end, and often have to. (Fact sheets sound dull, but they can actually be lush, detailed descriptions, tinged by passionate advocacy—the first "selling" of a book, inside a publishing house.) Writing as work, daily work, brings its own kind of joy. Prose helps all of us stitch together the day, whether it's in a diplomatic email to a colleague or the brief message you know a spouse will receive on his blackberry while driving home. (How do people who don't enjoy writing prose even a little live in the email world?) In prose I can be respectful, knowledgeable, irritated, affectionate, helpful, or just downright informational. I used to love, before I was a book editor myself and had to cut it out, writing book reviews and bits of criticism, and discovering, as though for the first time when I tackled each new assignment, that clear writing is actually clear thinking. It was almost as though I couldn't think at all until the pencil was moving on the page.

But I've never turned to prose the way I do to poetry—when I really write, it's not what calls to me. When I give a poetry reading I almost always get the question, "What made you choose to be a poet? Did you ever try short stories or a novel?" That is, wouldn't it have been easier for you, and for your readers, if you'd chosen some other form for your visions? The answer is of course that I didn't choose poetry, poetry chose me. Poetry is the only form I have a genuine impulse toward, and even that impulse is very rare. I can't decide to write a poem because I think I want to or I happen to be sitting at my typewriter wishing. In some odd way the poem has to "come over" me. I don't mean to suggest some mystical reception, a divine power guiding my hand. Not exactly. But there's an element I can't control: I can't dial up or press into service the mysterious inner pen that wants to write poetry. It's for this reason that I'm doubly amazed at the gift of the novelists and short-story writers whom I work with, and the discipline—the slogging—that has to be joined to it; they surely need to be visited by inspiration (and it better be a more detailed sort than the fleeting detritus that can generate a poem, even a great one), but even beyond that they have to put their backside in a chair and keep it there. They have to actually live through time, hours on that damn chair, to produce the effect of real time passing in the lives they create. It's a remarkable thing, to make time pass on the page. It takes a lot of words.

I wouldn't know how to write a short story about seeing a girl in a short skirt on Broadway and why it makes me conjure a former self (but you would! since you were born to the story), or about a five-year-old's peculiar, instant grasp of the meaning of infinity. For me, these are moments too freighted all in one place to expand into dramatic possibilities over time. Even mentioning them here, in a prose sentence, makes them sound banal to me—examples dragged under the banner of some point I'm trying to make. I can't describe how I made them into poems without sounding idiotic and again, too purposeful. Maybe my problem (both blessing and curse) is that I only have one way of noticing—that is, what I know how to notice is not the unfolding, the development over time of character and situation, but situation itself, stripped down to its essence, flashing just once in a graspable configuration or image before it fades. If I miss it, too bad—there won't be a poem.

With affection,
Deb

A Short Skirt on Broadway

Deborah Garrison

See that girl?
See that quick
no-nonsense
joying in itself
walk?
Soft scissoring,
slight hitch where
the blades meet,
Then flash apart,
re-meet?

Just so I
Used to walk.
I used to have
"legs." The small
trill in the gait
like a half smile,
tossed free those who'd look.
Self-ish pleasure on my walk
downtown with nowhere
in mind to go

was the best kind
before I found another so
ordinary I wasn't going to
mention it. Have you
ever been in the shuttered room

where life is milk? Where you make
milk? And by a series of peppery
tugs, urgent frothings, symphonic arcing
spurts (how absurd, how bovine)
you leave yourself aside
for someone else?
I was milk.
She was milk.
Even *he* was milk.

Now when I hurry across
Times Square, pants-suited,
Bag crammed with papers,
no one sees me. And I'm not
walking in the city—that old simplicity
I've learned not to miss, not much—
but getting out
of it, westbound,
to feed her dinner.
I wish the milk had lasted longer,
but she got legs of her own.

Deborah Garrison

Add One

She's five.
Wants to know
What infinity is.

I try: you take the biggest
Number, you think the last
Number there is, and you add
One more.
See?
You can always add one.
So then the number's
Bigger still.
Infinity means—
The numbers go on
Forever.

She thinks. Index finger raised.
Swiveling innocently Elvis-style
Hips in her big-girl jeans
And shaking her pigtails
In a trance of musing. Then
Cocks her head, terrier-set:

"Is it like, God is still
Alive, making numbers?"

OPEN CITY

Now, who told her—it wasn't me!—
That God and infinity
Are spoken in one breath?
That what's infinite
Must be divine?

Who, I ask you?

Deborah Garrison

Both Square and Round

You moments I court—

Back of the head settled
in arm's crook,
rump in my palm,
the whole half a body
just the length of my forearm,
small face twitching toward
repose. From the window
lamplight or moonlight slides
on the creamy forehead,
the new-bulb smoothness
at the temples both squared
and rounding, the flickering play
of shapes suggesting, mysteriously,
intelligence within.
And the triangular
center peak, V-bottom
of a heart where pure skin
shades into the gold dusting
of first hair, nearly
fur, like halo's fuzz,
more light than matter—

What was it, just
then, I swore to myself
I'd keep?

As though I could hold
a magnifying glass
to time

and slow its shaping
us.

The Necklace

He lay idling along me,
one leg crossed at the other knee, jauntily,

tiny man at his dinner, when
with brio sucked me in and wah-wahed

his jaw in quasi parody of his quest—
drinking but playing at drinking,

rhyming his eye with mine
and his was full of laughter as his starfish hand

upstretched, twirling to conduct the air,
to turn a song from nothing, waved

high and snagged of a sudden
the slender chain, platinum whisper

at my neck (dangled from which,
a diamond his father gave when *she* was born).

He couldn't care!
Just tugging there—by accident,

or in a freshman stumble toward
intent?—was for him a joyous

purpose, a study of texture,
of that solid link that might resist

his pull,
Or not.

It took me a long minute
to unpeel that clutching paw,

and by the way it felt all wrong,
against nature.

See, if left to my own I'd let him
grasp without a thought

what was mine
and break it.

Arizona II

Jim Harrison

WHEN I WAS LOOKING FOR BERT'S PLACE I MOMENTARILY regretted drowning my cell phone when I could have used it for further instructions, but then I was inattentive at mid-morning feeling a certain warmth for Viv despite her slanderous letter most of which was true. I had also been distracted by the idea that I needed to get rid of all of these personal "issues" (as Marybelle would have it) in order to proceed with my sacred project of renaming the states and most of the birds. For instance, I had no intention of changing the name of the Godwit. In addition I was having trouble concentrating because of the alien desert flora that surrounded me. I had begun at dawn driving toward the fabled Flagstaff then slowly descending five thousand feet in altitude from the forests of the north to the hellhole of Phoenix, then turning east toward Tucson. When I found Sandarino Road running through the border of the Saguaro National Monument I was stunned as if I had suddenly been transplanted to Mars. Finally I located the smallish dirt road that led to Bert's place with its hand painted ominous sign, NO TRESPASSING. SNAKE FARM.

It was the strangest of days, already burning hot by late morning. Bert was out of sorts as usual and still wore a "Resist Much" T-shirt. Nothing should come as a surprise with Bert. There was a young woman named Sandra in her mid-twenties wandering around humming but it was hard to tell her age because her face was leathery, her teeth bad, though her body fairly nice. There were tell-tale signs of meth ingestion, a long time curse even in northern Michigan but only lately noticed by the authorities who still concentrate on the relatively harmless pot.

Bert showed me all the snake tracks in the sandy property and said vipers were hiding from the heat, adding that ground temperature reaches nearly two hundred degrees, enough to start melting the sneakers of the woebegone wetbacks trying to enter our country for work. He ignored Sandra when she took a pee in plain sight near a cactus called a cholla. She was evidently a free spirit or a nitwit.

We ate a nice lunch of garden tomato sandwiches which made my soul quiver because it was my first summer in over thirty-five years without a garden and my very own tomatoes. Bert had heard from his old Lutheran widow friend, now in her eighties, that Vivian had divorced me. While we were drinking quarts of ice tea Bert advised me to stay away from women under the age of fifty because they speak a different language. The words are similar but the meaning is different from what it used to be. Across the table Sandra was petting a tiny rabbit who nibbled a piece of tomato on her plate.

By midafternoon the sun had become reddish from a distant sandstorm and Bert cursed because the monsoons were overdue. Bert left pans of water spread around the yard for the snakes but said they usually traveled to his pond way out back. People in the area would call Bert in alarm and he would remove the rattlers from their yards. He said that the roadrunner bird would eat baby snakes but not the big ones. We were at the kitchen table and now Sandra was licking the rabbit's face as if grooming it. The house was quite bare except for the living room with its walls of books and a desk.

We went out back and Bert began yelling and cussing. A neighbor's cows, mixed-breed Brahmas, had gotten through his fence and were standing in his tiny pond. There were several of them and their feet must have torn up the pond liner because the water was draining away and the fish that Bert said were tilapia were flopping around. Bert beat the cows with his cane and they ran for the back fence breaking it down. Sandra fetched a bushel basket and she and I waded in to gather the fish but we got stuck to mid-thigh in the mud. Bert went for his garden tractor and a rope and pulled us out. "There goes my fish crop," he said.

We walked back to the house and Sandra said her first sentence, "The fish will stink." Bert hosed us off and within fifteen minutes the first Mexican ravens began to arrive. We sat under a tattered awning drinking a cold beer and within an hour I counted seventy-three ravens out at the pond gobbling fish and screeching at each other.

Bert showed me to a spare room that had an old air conditioner in the window buzzing away. I was relieved because the thermometer on the porch said it was a hundred ten degrees. It was siesta time but I had a hard time napping because of the strangeness of it all. I leafed through a picture book on cacti and watched the ravens out the window. They're a bit smaller than our northern ravens but behave the same. It occurred to me that Bert as an independent scientist rather than an academic one lived and acted more like an artist or poet. Such people came up to northern Michigan in the summer and the anthropologists and botanists were often as whacky as painters. While we were watching the ravens and drinking beer and I complained about the heat. Bert sent Sandra for a map and he showed me a mountainous area near the Mexican border about seventy miles away that would be ten degrees cooler and I decided to head that way in the morning. I asked him why he was using a cane and he said that last year after he came home from our class reunion he had gotten nailed by a diamondback out by his mailbox. He had his own anti-venom in the refrigerator but still lost a lot of flesh and the strength of his left calf.

I slept until early evening and when I came downstairs Bert heated up some coffee and set a bottle of tequila on the kitchen table. Bert was always handy at the stove and was stirring a pot of menudo which is tripe stew. We heard a pistol shot from upstairs and Bert yelled, "Sandra cut that shit out," adding to me Sandra was likely shooting at coyotes that were eating the rest of the fish outside the pond. He told me that Sandra was from Uvalde, Texas, and was a bit gun happy. He had rescued her during a drug seizure outside the Congress Hotel in Tucson a few months ago and she showed no signs of leaving.

At dark Bert set up a spotlight and we sat on the porch watching the snakes glide around chasing rodentia. Sandra walked among the snakes but they were bent on rodentia and ignored her.

"You can't keep a dog or cat alive around here but Sandra thrives," Bert said, pushing a snake away from the bottom step of the porch with his cane. The snake struck the cane with a thunk and broke off one of its fangs then crawled away with perhaps a toothache. I picked up the fang for a keepsake and when I turned I was alarmed to see Sandra take off all her clothes and flop into the hammock. She said, "Tequila," and Bert nodded so I went into the kitchen for the bottle, taking a gulp to calm my nerves. When I brought the bottle I looked away in modesty.

"A woman in a hammock is always faithful," said Bert. "It's a question of physics not morals."

The spot and porch light were catching Bert's face just so making him look older than he was, though I supposed this was partly due to nearly forty years of wandering in the desert. He had taught at the local university for a while but then had been "liberated" into being a private scholar by inheritance. It was then that I imagined that I probably also looked old to him. When you spend most of your lifetime outdoors you're not likely to look as smooth as a television newsman. A few years back Viv had bought me some skin care products but I told her I couldn't go to the diner for lunch smelling like a whorehouse. It was hard for me to admit that I had started my little fandango with Babe at the diner well before Vivian's downfall at the class reunion. One day after her lunch shift she asked me to fix her sink trap in her apartment upstairs. It took a full hour and I was there on the kitchen floor yelling out that she shouldn't pour bacon grease in her sink when I turned around and there was Babe in a silly purple nightgown. She put a furry slippered foot on my shoulder and said, "Let's go for it, big boy." All those years of fidelity went out the window. My friend Ad said that marital fidelity is part of the social contract and that the human mind is a cesspool of errant sexuality. Any Lutheran knows what Jimmy Carter meant when he talked about "lust in the heart." Of course civilization would be destroyed if everyone simply followed the smallest cues of lust but then it's also hard to imagine that the God of Abraham and Isaac is keeping a weather eye on our genitals.

It was getting late. I helped Bert set up a fine meshed framed screen along the bottom steps of the porch so when he got up at night he wouldn't be surprised if a snake crawled up the porch steps. Sandra had been singing nonsense syllables in the fashion of my brother Teddy then laughing, then drinking and crying. Finally she slept and Bert sent me into his den to get a sheet off the cot. I covered her and had thoughts about the wondrous physiology of women.

We tried to talk about Iraq but gave up with fatigue. Bert thought that nearly everyone in politics was a chiseler and I had had frequent bad thoughts about our boys being sent over there with bad equipment that doesn't do what it's designed to do. What good is armor if you end up in pieces? We were practically dozing in our seats, and then Bert lifted his pant leg to scratch his wizened calf. We agreed that most politicians were the rattlesnakes of the human race and then we said goodnight.

Another Old Mariachi

Jim Harrison

His voice cracks on tremolo notes.
He recalls the labia of women
as the undersides of dove wings
he retrieved as a boy for rich hunters.
Now in a cantina outside of Hermosillo
he thinks, I don't have much life left
but I have my songs. I'm still the child
with sand sticking to my dew wet feet
going to the fountain for morning water.

From *Nightlife*

Rodney Jack

Night of Friday, June 30, 1995

DREAMED I WAS SWIMMING WITH SOMEONE, SCUBA DIVING without diving equipment. We were holding hands, and our legs were like fins. We admired the beautiful sea life, the jellyfish. Maybe only I was, or we both were naked. I was enchanted by a Portuguese man-of-war overhead, the way its bladder-like cap went convex then concave. Suddenly it descended, all the stinging tentacles, although, in the dream, the jellyfish were the non-stinging kind.

Just before I woke up, I dreamt I went to Oxford Books to find a tarot deck. It was late and Oxford was the only bookstore open. I couldn't find the game section. Searched frantically. Went to Oxford wearing a scarf, bulky material I couldn't leave on my motorbike. Again, I think I came with someone who had gotten up out of sickbed. His presence was mostly sensed. I still can't picture the face.

Later in the dream, as the bookstore was closing, I made a last-minute dash for the tarot cards to no avail. Found myself in a labyrinth, a classroom or a building where, in a dark stairwell, I was trapped or lost, afraid of someone climbing the stairs, though that someone was also frightened.

Saturday, July 1

About 6 A.M. I got out of bed to start the black beans that had been soaking overnight. I was anxious to bake the bread. My hands are proof I have not been in the kitchen for some time. I have several fresh cuts: one made from a paring knife against the index finger while shaving the navel from a Vidalia onion; another cut was made by the "S" blade of the food processor as it slipped off the counter. When I fumbled to catch the appliance, the blade nicked off a bit of skin from the knuckle of my thumb. I also notice other injuries whose origins I have no idea about, except that I probably got them making the meal today, which turned out so delicious.

At about 4 P.M. Dude started getting ready for his weekend evening class. As is his custom, he asks me if his outfit is, or is not, flattering. No matter if I say yes or no, with or without conviction, he hardly takes my word for it. I've learned if I don't exactly prefer his outfit, but say that I do, chances are high he'll go back into the bedroom and change. We were club kids when we met. Nearly five years later, I suppose I fantasize him as club kid still. Maybe because of his amber eyes and olive skin, black is the color I prefer to see him wearing, although he says he's, "tired of being Goth." By the time he was ready to leave, having tried on several outfits, we were both exhausted, and it was terribly hot outside.

On the way to GSU, with what I intended to be an earnest attempt at comic relief, I asked Dude if he wanted to make a quick stop at the "Pakistani Burger King." Immediately he started into me with a solemn, didactic tone, asking why I insist on calling it the "Pakistani Burger King," since, "those people could be from India or some other Indus nation." I told him I don't think it makes much difference exactly what foreign country they're from, or rather they're immigrants or refugees for that matter. My point being—albeit inane and by that point decidedly needling—wherever they're from, they're not from here.

Then, as Dude can, he called me out for, "trying to get away with blatant indifference weakly disguised as the devil's advocate." He asked why I get so upset when I'm referred to as Latino (a frequent occurrence I mainly attribute to my being, as I was constantly called growing-up, "light-skinned"). "You raise your voice and say you're one-hundred percent (blank)!" I'm more than a little concerned by Dude's refusal to say, "Nigger." Apart from any negative associations the word may conjure, I fear, and fear he may eventually come to feel, that it's not only the word, but also the reticence to say it that looms like an imminent fatal blow to our relationship.

At the "Pakistani Burger King," as usual, I requested no mayonnaise on our chicken sandwiches, but, as usual, I got mayonnaise anyway. My subconscious assurance in the rote nature of the exchange, i.e., my request to hold the mayo being answered by receiving extra mayo, lies in my subconscious awareness of the adverse tone of my request. Nonetheless, when we sat on the molded plastic dining bench, and Dude pointed out the heaping servings of mayonnaise extruding from the edges of the sandwiches, I said I was going to take the order back. While swiping napkin after napkin over the drenched half of his sandwich, Dude tried to assure me it was alright.

His meek demeanor of gentle forbearance while swiping the bread fueled either my Libran sensibility, my confrontational attitude, or my overprotective tendencies toward him. At any rate, on occasions such as this (evident in the proceeding account), I attribute my actions to an inability to foresee a union such as ours enduring. Rather valid or invalid, informed by that uncertainty and doubt, I brace myself for inevitable separation. In which case, I imagine Dude may take away at least an understanding of the spirit behind my self-defensive mechanisms, while I attempt to adopt his aptitude for patience and tolerance.

The pretty Pakistani girl who took the order looked at me rolling her eyes when I exclaimed that I distinctly remembered requesting no mayonnaise. Then, using an approach used on me by a white Master Chief Petty Officer in the Navy, I inquired about her proficiency with the English language. I over-enunciated, "Do you know the difference between 'yes' and 'no'?" She turned away and started to shake the fry basket before sprinkling the potatoes generously from a tin of salt kept next to the bubbling grease. This reminded me that I had also asked for fries without salt, but got those crystal-encrusted, lukewarm and heat-lamp dried-out fries anyway. Again, I said, "Excuse me" to the pretty Pakistani girl, and when she got around to acknowledging me, I dropped the bag containing the faulty order on the floor next to her leg and demanded a refund. She summoned—I assumed—the manager, a short maroon-colored man in polyester knit slacks and a pinstriped dress shirt with the sleeves rolled up. He muttered something along the lines of a warning against, "throwing dings at my employees." I asked him, "What you gone do about it?"

While waiting in line to return the order, I had surmised my odds with him, and knew that more than likely the situation wouldn't come to blows (although I've been wrong before). He stood at least a foot shorter than me and was slightly smaller framed. Nevertheless, if I happened to have gotten him riled up enough such that he tried something rash, there might have been grounds for a civil suit, which might have served as consolation for both guilty and guilty feeling parties in the event I got my ass properly kicked. So, again I said to him, "What you gone do about it?"

Without blinking, the maroon-colored man leaned in, placed his elbows on the counter and composed his hands to give shape to whatever it was he meant to convey. In what can be possibly described (if there can even be such a thing) as a naive version of "playing the dozens," he proceeded, with sincerity, to relay his exact course of action. "Well-elle," he said, "Fahst, I take you nick, and rrrrrrring it! Den, I beat you ast rrrrrrreal goot!" By that time Dude had come up to the counter to say take him home. I was at the ready for a vocal joust, but I turned promptly around and left. Dude drove himself to class from the apartment. As I'm recounting this, I still can't help but smile at being bested in "the dozens" by the manager of the "Pakistani Burger King."

When Dude returned this evening, the bread had risen and the beans were well seasoned.

I'm somewhat surprised at the precision of wind. Last night it thundered and rained fiercely for over an hour. I went out this morning to see about the flower garden. The wind had shot pine straw like arrows through the heart-shaped leaves of the salvias. Our proudest, tallest, fullest celosia had dropped its outer petals into a rosette beneath its thick stem, and I fear for the other celosia, their survival.

Despite the garden's shortcomings, I have noted that where it lacks in depth, it more than makes up for with color. In the back of the garden, the purple impatiens have grown into a bushy impressive showing against the holly. The row of white periwinkle establishes a frontal border for the impatiens and a back border for the coleuses, which are doing quite well there in the sun I thought would overwhelm them. Within the red salvias I dispersed the few fire colored mini snapdragons that were left at the nursery. And, which I like to think of as a testament to summer, surrounding the entire garden are golden marigolds.

Sunday, July 2

Not much private time with Dude lately. Today I began cleanup of the spare bedroom-turned-office. Monumental task. If I apply and get accepted to American College, we'll need extra space where we both can study.

Postponed my scheduled run, because I was exhausted from the cleaning and the other day's weight training when I overdid it with dumbbells. Also entertained a case of hiccups. I cut a thick piece of yesterday's bread, buttered it lightly and tried to swallow down the spasms.

After my run, Dude's buddy from high school, Tyrone, stopped by. He and I were outside talking about being in the service. He reminisced about the Army and I talked about the Navy. Tyrone made an interesting observation, saying that America is so much more littered than overseas. I don't suppose I ever noticed, America being littered that is. I seem to pay more attention to nature, which is what I was doing at the time. The snapdragons and salvias (particularly the snapdragons) appeared to be withering. I've already had to uproot one plant; the rain has been steady, so I can't imagine why they're dying.

Today a nuthatch, wren, cardinal, titmouse, purple finch, and a grackle (which I recognized for the first time as distinguished from the common crow) landed on the feeder. The titmouse, I've noticed, is an aggressive bird that, while feeding, will attack any other bird attempting to feed at the same time. Then again, the titmouse will even threaten me when I'm nearby.

The three of us went to lunch at the Piccadilly. Two guys came in with a tranny who kept looking at me, or vice-versa. I have this fascination with drag queens. They're the quintessential thespians and muses; everyone should have a drag queen in his or her life. Salvador

Dali had his International Crisis, and Dude and I have our CeCe Boom. Interesting to me is that I can recognize a drag queen even out of drag. I'm not implying that the ability is such a big feat. It's easy to observe when the gesticulations and the body don't quite jive with the prescribed gender of the costume. I used to think it was just a matter of "acting" like females, when, through CeCe, I realized that there truly is such a person as an androgyne. I think CeCe is one of the bravest people I know.

Over lunch at the Piccadilly, Dude told me that Ms. Marie reported that she is again gainfully employed. Previously, Ms. Marie had quit her job as a collection agent to "get her shit together." She prepaid four months rent and was sitting back enjoying the cathartic rapture of Montel, Springer, and Oprah. She told me she realized that her life, and her drinking problem was not so bad, comparatively. That was in early May. By mid June an inebriated Marie came calling to announce that she was moving to Africa at the end of the month. I don't know what spurred that performance, but I had a feeling that Ms. Marie had neither the means nor the intent to leave for Africa, because, when asked, she did not know what part of Africa she intended to visit, nor whether she intended to remain in Africa or return to America. She simply knew or felt that she must "go to the motherland."

When we got back from the Piccadilly, Ms. Marie was sitting on her steps and serving us severe attitude, cutting her eyes, pretending to ignore us and acting appalled when she happened to glance in our direction. When she is perched on her steps, I usually stay clear unless summoned, since, when she assumes that particular position, she seems to prefer solitude while talking on the cordless, or gently shifting her shift while smoking a cigarette.

As yet I have not examined the American College catalog as closely as I've been intending. I must make note to get a grammar checker for the computer. Anyway, I'm looking forward to school, however not getting my adrenaline up, as it is questionable what condition my life will be in when October rolls around.

Monday, July 3

Last night Dude and Tyrone went out. I was having indigestion from the beans and rice we ate for dinner, so I didn't feel up to going. Probably wouldn't have gone anyway.

Purple tinged plants, what appears to be cockscomb seedlings, are sprouting throughout the frontal part of the garden. One side of the impatiens has been damaged. How? I don't know. This week I hope to transplant potted replacements.

Right now, as a result of my spring-cleaning, seven bags of junk—mostly collapsed boxes, newspapers, magazines and what-not— are in the apartment. Six bags are downstairs and one is currently being filled upstairs in the spare bedroom-turned-office. The management has informed us they will be cleaning the windows on Wednesday. Dude says I'm overreacting to think they'd go through the trouble of hiring a crew to clean all the windows in the complex just to spy on the interracial gay couple and find out what they already know, "They're sleeping together. Imagine that!" Of course, I realize the necessity of periodic maintenance. I also understand it's sensible for management to survey rental property. Suspicion and logical explanations aside, I still feel apprehensive.

When evening approached, I went out on my run. As always, I began by walking a block or so down Hermance Drive. The elderly couple that live in the house with the plastic flower adorned yard, were not standing out as usual, and I missed hearing their kind greetings as I passed by their home. They're both so beautiful—grey haired, and with smooth evenly colored brown skin.

Tuesday, July 4

I must remember to work on my vocabulary and review my humanities books. Broke my fast about 2 A.M. with Chinese food. Then I had cornflakes. The rest of the day I ate barley and carrot soup I had prepared in the slow cooker. I also had yogurt. I weighed myself this afternoon and I now weigh one hundred and seventy-one pounds. I started back cleaning the spare bedroom-turned-office. I believe I got five or so books organized on the shelves before I found something else to do. What had distracted me? I can't recall.

Rain sprayed the garden today, so I left the tending to nature. Soon I will plant replacements for the dying snapdragons and the damaged impatiens. I truly need a book on flower gardening. I found a book from Oxford called, *The Language of Flowers*, written in 1819 in response to ". . . Europe's enchantment with the ideogram language of the East and a budding interest in unusual and exotic plants." Interestingly, the book says that marigolds—which surround our garden—mean "Despair," and the impatiens in the back before the holly stand for, predictably, "Impatience." This means that the garden is contained in and inclusive of a desperate arc. Oddly enough, perhaps to counter or echo this sentiment, the red salvias within the borders mean, "Energy" and "Gusto," while the snapdragons symbolize, "Presumption," and the white periwinkle mean "Pleasurable Memories."

Since I arranged the garden prior to any conscious knowledge of the symbols, I've tried to consider what it all means. However, it seems I will have to wait until the revelation floats from the subconscious, in a dream perhaps. Meanwhile, I have yet to identify the earth-colored white-rumped bird I've seen twice now, both times in small flocks. The first time I saw them, they were in the front yard, flickering in the juvenile black cherry tree. The other time, while jogging, I saw the flock in a juniper brush on the vacant side of Peachtree Road.

Lenox Square put on their annual Independence Day fireworks display, and I went to see the show from (speaking of where I saw the birds) the vacant hill on the corner of Hermance and Peachtree. I sat about midway up and to the left of the plat. Before long a teenaged girl and a little boy sat nearby. With a solemnity beyond his years, the little boy spoke plainly and clearly. As he sat down he said, "It's a good night." Although a thunderstorm was approaching, cool winds drifted ahead of the showers, and, since I had encountered no mosquitoes, I was inclined to agree. Just before the finale, a mother arrived with her toddler. "Isn't that pretty, Tammy?" she asked the baby who shook her head gently, a finger hooked in her mouth.

The evening (following the fireworks) was spent tidying the apartment, making way for the "conscripted" window cleaners the complex promised would show up tomorrow. While cleaning, I again decided to leave the spiderweb hanging in the corner by the back door. One of its three gossamer eggs had already hatched, and dozens of translucent amber hatchlings dispersed in the web; that was days ago when I saw them. The next time I looked, they were gone. I imagined them lighting on the wind that came through the opened door, their silk threaded spinnerets carrying them outside and about the apartment. Indeed, I saw one of the babies crawling on my shirt.

Wednesday, July 5

In the potted coleus kept on the porch, a persistent oak seedling had established itself. I could but pinch it nearest to the bottom as I could, it being so firmly rooted for such a needle of a thing. Poor impatiens had taken a beating in the heat. By the time the window cleaners left, the plants lay wilting like torn balloons. However, after a drink of water and cooling down in the early evening, they fully recovered. Sincerely, I thought they were done for, judging from the condition they were in when I discovered them listless in the sweltering afternoon.

When the window cleaners finally made it down to our end of the building, Dude was leaving for his late afternoon class. The 'head' window cleaner attempted to analyze the situation. He asked if the office was my bedroom. When I said yes, that it is all mine so to speak, he went on to ask if I was subletting. "No," I said, "just visiting." To which, he responded with a smug, extended "hummmm…." Exactly the reason for my anxiety over their scheduled visit, though the windows (the ones that they cleaned rather) are sparkly clear. "It's been a good while," he said despondently, "bout seven years since these windows been washed."

While the windows were being cleaned, I began a workout, not knowing what else to do. The garbage collector came, to my surprise, a day early, so I took the opportunity to load his truck with the bags filled during my late spring-cleaning. I then ran my usual trek, and it was hot enough, but I like to tell myself that I'm of southern stock and perform best in the heat. I scarcely believe such a boast myself, in such intense heat as there was today. Still in shape or getting there. I'm holding steady at one seventy-one pounds, but plan to eat well tomorrow: great northern white beans slow cooked with ham. I also plan to bake wheat bread. I also hope to finish setting up the office, though last night I sprang my left trapezoid and shoulder when either moving furniture, or during today's workout. I can't remember ever being in such pain before. I've had to start taking Motrin.

At about midnight at the twenty-four-hour hour upscale Harris Teeter (grocer/deli), I found myself standing over the meat freezer, laboring over the steep cost of five dollars a pound for diced ham. I had just about decided to buy bacon instead, when at the back of the bin I spotted a single pack of smoked ham hocks—a steal at a buck fifty. Sinfully rich as the beans will be simmered with the hocks, having found them, I felt they were somehow essential to the meal. The black late shift cashier (notorious for her derisive commentary while either scanning or bagging purchases, i.e., "beans & rice, beans & rice, beans & rice...") seemed more appalled than amused when I triumphantly announced that I had secured the last package of ham hocks in Harris Teeter. Sister remarked, "I didn't even much know we sold these."

Thursday, July 6

I realize that there are two kinds of lifestyles—the healthy lifestyle and the unhealthy one, and that one has a choice. It's the part about having a choice, however, that I can't altogether grasp. Too much have I weighed circumstance against fate and tried to attach some sort of reasoning to the factors that constitute either. I feel helpless and doomed at times like this. I also feel afraid. My fear is deep, spurred by the horrors of my imagination, and by the real horror stories portrayed by the media, like that story I read in *Psychology Today.*

I know I must be optimistic, pursue the affirmative and leave fate to fate. I believe that one can make an effort to avoid situations that tell intuition something is awry. Two A.M., at CeCe Boom's, I played my part in the opera of urban nightlife, throwing leftover Independence Day firecrackers, smoke bombs and sparklers from the roof of CeCe's midtown apartment. The apartment building looks out onto the nightclub parking lot. Strobes of dance floor lights can be seen flashing like semaphore in the club's doorway. Even from a distance, the thump, thump, thump of techno-house music can be faintly heard, and, also faintly, yet deeply, felt registering in the soles of my shoes. The firecrackers we threw fizzled in the littered, dark and narrow alley where hustlers and clients—female, male and transsexual alike, retreated to snort bumps of coke or crank.

There we stood on the rooftop precipice, bearing witness to an elaborate choreography—various hasty and shrouded transactions in flesh and substance taking place in the alley accompanied by a percussion paced laser show. Simultaneously, on neighboring rooftops, other characters could be seen acting out dramas alarmingly similar to our own troupe's performance. All of us in our mid to late twenties, getting high, we play the fools, white flowers of purity and innocence metaphorically propped behind our ears. What direction has time mapped for me? I want desperately to deconstruct this surrealist, prophetic dream. What have I learned? Find peace. Reflect, not just on the negative such that light has no entry point into my life, but also reflect on what is perceived good. Practice the affirmative. Care for others, Dude, and myself.

Night of Thursday, July 6

I was living with Aunt Sylvie, and she was poor.

The President wanted me to do something for him, give a speech or something like that. Somebody told me he was looking for me, but when I went to see him, he didn't mention anything about giving a speech. He gave me a gift. We were in a room with a line of people formed beside him. He was handing each person a small, plainly wrapped box with one hand, while reaching out with his other hand to shake his or hers. Aunt Sylvie was also giving out gifts. Darren (my eldest brother) suggested she give away my piano. Aunt Sylvie refused, saying, "You know how I feel about Jack."

I was trapped in a house where the windows were nailed down. Escape was easy, though we (Darren, myself and others) didn't get around to it. I had proposed a plan to jump through the upstairs window wrapped in a blanket. Downstairs, some people were having a party.

Friday, July 7

Gale, Dude's mom clipped the split ends of his hair, and told us who had died recently, and who was ailing. She also mentioned menopause. Since Lawson, Dude's dad, doesn't talk too much, and as her generation begins to mature, maybe she feels helpless and somewhat alone. Then again, maybe I'm mirroring.

We talked about Gale's begonias, about how such vibrant and full plants grew from cuttings. The elegantly spun cup of a cardinal's nest lay partially hidden in the laurel hedge behind the tomatoes. Two little drum skins blotched with feathers heaved. A bird had taken shelter in the bird box. Lawson thinks it's a chickadee, but definitely some other small bird since he can't imagine what would lay such tiny eggs. pale beige and lightly peppered, folded in moss, pine straw and blonde—what he believes to be—dog fur. Gale picked two tomatoes from the vine. She advised that they'll need to sit in the kitchen window for at least a couple of sunny days to fully ripen. While she harvested the fruit, I imagine that the azalea seedlings Lawson recently planted, judging from their height and breadth already, will, come next spring, make a hearty pink and red blossoming hedge of their own.

Mosquitoes ate me alive while Gale and I stood around the tomatoes, talking about the vigor of the plants and eyeing the blushing fruit for the ones that were ripest. As I'm writing this, the whole account seems ethereal. The mosquito bites no longer sting.

That *Psychology Today* story still haunts me. The article chronicled the mind of a killer. In the story, a man in New York gets into a cab with a couple of strange women to go to their place "to have some fun." When he arrives at the apartment, he discovers that he's been set-up. The five hundred or so pound woman who lived there, and who was hired for the deed, binds him and locks him in the closet-turned-torture-chamber. For several days, she enacts these sadistic rituals, like pulling him out the closet and sitting on him while she eats supper and watches television. After the second week of such abuse, she impales him with a smoldering pipe. At the trial, the obese woman was unremorseful. She testified that the man must have been "queer" because when she "stuck the hot poker up his ass, he wiggled."

My dismay over the article has been so powerful that I have now begun to experience intense paranoia. What if our next-door neighbor Kenny's friend—that homophobe—becomes violent? He certainly knows where we live. Already, I've been thinking about buying a gun, about locking the bedroom and office doors, about moving. I suppose I'm tired, but I've always, or lately it seems, found the night threatening. I hate sleeping through the day and being so awake in the evening.

I must water the garden as I speak. I must discontinue my bad habits—smoking, masturbation; both fatigue me and cloud my thinking so that I am susceptible to the negative aspects of my environment.

Saturday, July 8

Today's roasted chicken dinner came out beautifully, but I vow to never cook a chicken again. It occurred to me while skinning the bird that by buying this meat, I've inadvertently contributed to its systematic death. I know that people can live off vegetables alone, and I have already started to do something about it. Dude and I have pretty much given up red meat and we're determined to give up meat altogether.

Realizing that the chicken is flesh—animal flesh, nearly made me sick as I tore the skin off in a great yellowish pimply sheet. I felt like a masochist. Certainly, if I value human life, I can value other animal life as well. To think about the living conditions of these factory churned-out chickens . . . I had to smoke a whole joint just to get through making dinner, though the foil wrapped bird emerged from the oven wonderfully aromatic, infused with a medley of bell pepper, garlic, onion and celery. Served on a side of white rice steamed in the stock, buttered and sprinkled with oregano, sage, and rosemary, the meal made for a Barmecide feast.

Tyrone came by this afternoon, knocked just as Dude and I had settled in for siesta. While the three of us were sitting on the porch, our neighbor, Reverend Foy who lives in the building across from us, came and stood on the slope appearing distressed and disheveled. He was there to announce, "I needed you reeeeeeeel bad the other day."

Reverend Foy explained how he'd come by the apartment, but his knocking went unanswered.

After giving it some thought, I vaguely remembered that Dude and I were upstairs and thought we might have heard an unusual yet distinctive clang. We recognized the sound, but couldn't readily discern its source. When we realized it was the brass knocker, I went to answer the door but no one was there. The sound of the brass knocker is so strange to us because, up until Reverend Foy rang it, we'd heard it rung only once or twice during the three years we've lived here. And, since on those other occasions the visitors turned out to be solicitors, we'd trained our ears to somewhat tune out the sound.

Reverend Foy explained that he had come calling because he was nauseous with hypoglycemia, and had just had an operation. He managed to have walked several feet (including taking a rather steep flight of concrete stairs) from (and back to) his apartment to ask for assistance opening a medicine bottle.

Although I can't say we're unaccustomed to unannounced visitors, a visit from Reverend Foy was nonetheless unexpected. We've exchanged pleasantries, but nothing beyond that. I might add that whether or not we're familiar with someone, does not in all cases ensure or prevent us from answering the door. By way of an excuse, weighed alongside the very real and sad dilemma of someone not having the strength to open and access a prescribed and proven source of relief, the matter of the brass knocker seemed trivial. All I could think to do was offer my apologies. To which Reverend Foy abruptly replied, "See you." He then walked across the parking lot, got in his car and drove away. Tyrone looked at Dude and said, "What's his problem?"

Tomorrow I fast, finish cleaning and arranging the office.

Seedbed

Rodney Jack

My cool November guest
has gone away from here.
Followed by a thwarted early spring.

Begins the objects the ill-wind swept:
the lounge chairs . . . Too bad
the series photographed in black & white

instead of the colors of summer,
Re: the wish I dared make,
which way did the wishbone break?

Solitude is the seedbed for the base
emotions. Until spring locks in, winter returns
with impunity, fancies itself humorous.

The field smells like wet fur
hidden in the tall dead grass stalks.
Bud by bud by tentative leaf, thus

the ivy-cased oak counts its gains and losses
following the sudden late cold front.
And, not in one fell swoop, the field made

fallow, like caution, in precise ironic increments,
in mockery of the swift hawk above it,
making moot the question, *Who did this?*

Black-Capped Chickadee Trapped in the Feeder

It was tempting, to let it struggle
in the bluish globe
it took such pains to enter.

Tiny, of course. The characteristic
white cheek patches, on closer inspection,
not altogether white.

Soiled, beating rapidly
with the sound perhaps only feathers make
against glass,

thin, translucent,
the fact that I took
the risk of injury; thus,

the striking similarity to my own charities
by no means escaped me, though
the feeder had long ago been emptied.

Rodney Jack

Perpetuation

Amid the squealing
swarm of starlings, voracious

for the grass seeds, I was
reminded of him.

The very morning he passed,
on the assumption of a pleasantry

I'd written in coincidence,
hapless, inferring to one

medication replacing another—
no longer effective.

Winter honeysuckle opened,
the mock-spring fragrance—

less and less from year to year.
Similarly, abruptly, the fall

surrendered to an onslaught of hail.
Still, for hours they fed,

a steady undulating
confluence of shadows

like a diagnosis: invasive,
aggressive and highly adaptable.

Now they outnumber all
our native cavity-dwelling songbirds.

The obituary reads:
"His battle was courageous...."

Lost in the mindless
deconstruction of "24 Hours,"

the song he admired, I wondered,
how many verses, phrases,

words, what patterns emerge
as ice from the ice storm melts?

Following the inevitable blackout,
strangers in a strange room

feeling, blinded and confused,
toward any door.

First Dossier Welcome Tour

Wayne Koestenbaum

HEIDEGGER HOTEL

In January 2002, broken, I read Heidegger's <u>Being and Time</u> and thought nonstop about hotels.

Heidegger was my hotel, an unfriendly, dominating domicile. I stayed for one cold, difficult month.

No philosopher, I entered <u>Being and Time</u> for aesthetic pleasure and for hotel gleanings.

My goal: to refurbish the meaning of hotel. As Heidegger says, "it is the business of philosophy to protect the power of the most elemental words..." (All my <u>Being and Time</u> quotations are from Joan Stambaugh's translation.)

Being-at-home, Heidegger says, is not the "primordial phenomenon." "Not-being-at-home" is more fundamental. To be not-at-home may mean to be <u>at hotel</u>. (Am I at home in this language?)

Hotel Women confused strangers, who expected women only, and were surprised to discover that men, too, resided there.

*

Liberace—or someone who answers to that name—admired himself in his private room's full-length mirror. To conquer vertigo from corridor conversations with other Hotel Women residents, he stared at his naked reflection. His groin, *primum mobile,* couldn't communicate. No one knew how to acknowledge it or house it appropriately.

I may deviate from Heidegger in this discussion.

Hotel presupposes home. To speak about a hotel is an oblique way to address home problems.

Do you check into a hotel? Or does the hotel condition check into you?

My friend referred to his lover's death, euphemistically, as "checking out": "Mark checked out." We "check out" when we cruise: "I checked him out."

Dwelling in the hotel state, my voice newly neutral and indifferent, I hope to override the "They" of home, of fixed domicile.

HEIDEGGER AND CUSTARD PIE

While reading Being and Time, suddenly I remembered a custard pie from the 1960s. I hadn't tasted it; I'd merely seen it, quivering, in its cafeteria vitrine. The relation between house and hotel is like the relation between restaurant and self-serve smorgasbord. The custard pie, trembling behind glass, is the hotel, offering itself.

Hotel existence uncannily suspends us above groundedness. To be in hotel is to float, or to tremble, like just-set custard.

Heidegger frequently uses the term "thrown." We are thrown into Being. And, I'd add, we are thrown into the hotel, thrown into its impersonal, public muddle.

*

Whitehead, Hotel Women's owner and de facto handyman, removed his shirt before repairing Liberace's shower, while Liberace lay topless in bed, perusing *Motor Sport.*

Whitehead thought, *Maybe Liberace appreciates my narrow waist, flat chest, shaved head, pierced nipples, butterfly tattoo, masochism, indiscriminateness.*

Whitehead worried about Hotel Women's emotional health but not its finances. His dead wife's stocks kept Hotel Women afloat.

Abstract thinker, Whitehead obeyed stern moral codes. No Hotel Women guest could rival his naïveté and sophistication—their rare, brimming combination.

*

Liberace was Hotel Women's most important resident, but his value was sinking. That trend excited him. His loneliness was well-known, as was his madness.

Slowness had recently overtaken his cognition—blissful

We turn away from work as a means of "taking care," says Heidegger. To check into a hotel: this, too, may be a mode of taking care, of refusal.

Hotel is a method of "not-staying." Curious, we stray; we enter the euphoric state of "never dwelling anywhere."

Hotel existence, because socially unattached, is silent, even amid noise.

We may take speed in a hotel room, and yet a hotel room more frequently finds us tranquillized and numb. Stranded, alienated, closed off from authenticity, in the hotel we commit what Heidegger calls "the plunge." We dive into "everydayness." We eddy. We "fall prey."

To be in hotel: is this an inauthentic practice? Checking into a hotel, are we freed from surveillance and ordinariness, or are we squashed and smothered by the "They"?

MORE "THEY"

Unfortunately, a hotel is the control station of the "They."

We have reason, therefore, in hotels, to feel intensely phobic.

Other than TV, and invisible enemies, there may be nothing, in a hotel room, to watch. (Mirror? Lover? Airshaft?)

What am I trying to discover in Heidegger? I want to clasp Being, apart from the particu-

turgidity. Unfortunately, he made too many social mistakes. His latest errors were stasis, confidence, alertness.

"I must accomplish great things!" shouted Liberace, alone in his hotel room. Career dependence unnerved him. He thought, *I don't want to care about fame, but I can't avoid striving for it. Quiet is what I need. Appreciate sunsets and tractors. Stay away from stars. They're querulous.*

Liberace looked at his nineteenth-century Bavarian glass dish, once his mother's property, now filled with salted peanuts. He loved that dish. Lonely and important, it had sat, long ago, on his mother's bureau; Liberace had read Shakespeare while that dish, gathering clout and braggadocio, waited.

Liberace thought, *If this hotel becomes too devoted to pornographic activities, I'm going to move across Dolores Street to Hotel Theory. I'll communicate to fellow Hotel Women residents my everlasting importance, and then I'll disappear. Relaxing at Hotel Theory, I'll brood on my separation from Hotel Women, that bordello.*

lars that locate and disguise it. "Hotel" uncovers a state of undressed Being, without presuppositions. In a hotel, Being is abstracted, naked. We suspend—or lift—the conventional identity tags.

HOTEL CHOPIN

Chopin is always "in a mood." (Heidegger writes that "Da-sein is always already in a mood.") Hotel mood is a running or bleeding of an emotion, as ink runs when water touches it. What kind of a mood is Chopin in? Can't pin it down. Labile, it spreads and liquefies before we can give it a name.

Fooling around with a Chopin mazurka, I perform non-activity, temporary location, rooms-to-let; I hang the sign (VACANCY) and respond to its open-ended call.

Dream: I rented a room in a dormitory-hotel. There, my friend S. gave me a blue perfume called Chopin. (The bottle was blue. So were its contents.) I marveled that Chopin was now an expensive French scent's name. (Then I remembered that Chopin was also a brand of cheap vodka in tiny bottles, sold as stocking stuffers and souvenirs.) Accidentally I'd left my friend's gift on her toilet lid. Didn't I value Chopin's blueness? Was it a depressed perfume?

*

After Lana Turner's studio workday ended, she drove her red Alfa Romeo down Dolores, which led circuitously from MGM to Hotel Women. Dolores confused her. It sprouted multiple, conflicting intersections, diverse streets bearing identical names. Sameness flummoxed stars, but plebeian residents had mastered misleading nomenclature, which created sullen, storm-cloud effects above taquerias and massage parlors. Hotel Women, large pink building with stained awnings, never to be cleaned, overshadowed its salmon rival, Hotel Theory, which might soon fold, intimidated by competition.

Lana parked her Alfa Romeo on Dolores.

"I could use morning and evening assistance," Lana said to Whitehead, who manned Hotel Women's front desk.

Whitehead agreed to mind Baby Helena when Lana was busy at MGM or socializing with other hotel guests.

She was grateful that Whitehead had volunteered to convert her life from maternal abomination into orderly vista.

She was not cold-hearted,

HÔTEL TRANSYLVANIE

The title of Frank O'Hara's poem "Hôtel Transylvanie" suggests that transfusions and transmigrations occur in hotels: Dracula, blood-mingling, identity-swap. In such hotels, guests share needles, bareback, and refuse all activities except for respiration and fornication.

HOTEL DREAM

Dreamt that I forgot the name and location of my hotel, either in Barcelona or Vienna. Feebly I told the cab driver, "I think it's near the Lido." The driver cruised the streets. Eventually we made it to a hotel that might have been mine. I'd inscribed in my appointment calendar the hotel's enigmatic initials: TH, or HT, connected to "The," or "Theory," or Heidegger's "They."

Underground tunnels linked the hotel to a major Jewish library, many-windowed, ultramodern. In its stacks I saw rabbis poring over texts. Then I walked into a mall, connected by subterranean passage to the hotel. I entered a men's clothing store—prices slashed. The clerks stared aggressively at me: I didn't speak the language, lacked currency... The suits on sale were illegit, sleazy.

I waited for my boyfriend in our elegant, ochre, unfash-

despite Dr. Ferrucio's claims: psychotherapist at MGM, he'd encouraged her to leave Ditmas Boulevard's spacious hacienda, temporarily, and relocate, experimentally, to Hotel Women.

Society unnerves me, thought Lana, while Baby Helena napped. Lana remembered her childhood home's grapefruit tree. She remembered her father's and grandfather's paralysis from horseback-riding accidents. She worried about Baby Helena's developing consciousness.

*

Lana Turner lay alone in her Hotel Women bed. United States, depressed, approached war with Germany. MGM did its best to cheer up phobic populations. Was it morally wrong to be gay during crisis? Lana wanted commensurability and parallelism. Bigotry, both local and foreign, dwarfed Lana's cognition. *If I could cancel my mentality, I would,* Lana thought; *but I cannot. I am Lana Turner, doomed to cogitate; doomed to reign; doomed to oscillate between my well-appointed hacienda on Ditmas Boulevard, from which I* ionable hotel—the color of faded brick, with seven hundred rooms, orange carpet, and coat-of-arms motifs in the wallpaper.

Did the stingy receptionist ever grant me a room key?

I walked onto a short dock and stepped into a rowboat. A windstorm resumed its assault.

HOTEL CORRESPONDENCE

A communication from a hotel comes from nowhere. The letterhead deceives, masks a lack of location.

"HOTEL"

Movies like Hotel, even in 1967, were passé. Its opulent hotel is a symbol of the film industry, in which Merle Oberon (the Duchess, her hair a complex, projectile, distracting stack) no longer belongs, though she is allowed, as a courtesy, to stay on—a dinosaur, like the segregated Hotel St. Gregory, owned by Melvyn Douglas.

Images:

Through the Hotel St. Gregory's lobby wanders a woman in a sari.

Downstairs in the oyster bar, Carmen McRae, in neon-pink mood light, sings.

Catherine Spaak, starlet dressed by Edith Head, doodles a self-portrait on hotel stationery.

Heavy hotel drapes block consciousness.

have inexcusably exiled myself, and this squalid, spacious Hotel Women room. She could not justify simultaneous residency in hotel and home; dining with studio bigwig Solly Freund last night downstairs at El Salvador, Lana had mentioned, self-critically, how morally dubious it was to maintain dual residences, but Solly had rationalized Hotel Women as Lana's "experiment in transiency" (as he put it), or her "venture into contingent dwelling." Lana irrationally feared being cut from Hotel Women's scene. She wanted to dominate every milieu, however marginal and degraded, and to widen her repertoire of locations.

Lana spent last Christmas helping Mildred, her mother, cope with vertigo in Boulevard Arms, condo complex in San Clemente. Mildred telephoned Lana this morning and said, "I forgive you for leaving home, miffed, on Christmas Eve." Mildred pardoned Lana for slapping her face.

*

Suddenly I remember the Monopoly game. Hotels were a high category of desire and attainment, superior to houses. A hotel was worth four houses.

A new efficiency-hotel empire is trying to buy the St. Gregory from Melvyn Douglas, but he doesn't want to sell. The potential buyer wants to run it as a "completely automated hotel"—like a car wash, without hands. Douglas, clinging to "old-time" standards, despises this new genre of "cheap-run joint," a hotel chain catering to "automatons" with "lubricants for blood."

Karl Malden, playing the hotel thief, escapes via a dumb waiter. The thief is the hotel's antibody—circulating, cunny, crazy.

The lift system short-circuits, sending the problematic elevator number three downward in a death dive.

A hotel is an arbitrary collection of human beings. Like other city-structures (stores, arcades), hotels throw strangers together in chance arrangements.

A hotel is a box, containing smaller boxes (rooms). The grid of cells gives formal-structure to the crowd's chaos.

A street, with its cars and pedestrians, is not a closed set. Its participants change every moment. A hotel's cast changes, but less frequently,

Balmy winter evening: Lana Turner drove her Impala from MGM to Cremona and Dolores, where Hotel Women sat, dilapidated and importunate, its bulk disfigured. She owned several cars. She couldn't survive without daily luxuries. Her attraction to Hotel Women was metaphysical: she never forgot lessons imparted by Professor Hal Hoffstrom, who'd impregnated and then jilted her, leaving her to raise Baby Helena alone.

*

Whitehead babysat Helena whenever duties or pleasures occupied Lana. Babysitting suited Whitehead's rigid, grid-ruled outlook. His taste for mental rudiments quelled hurricanes of recollection that assaulted him in grammar school and led hasty teachers to diagnose him "retarded." He could absorb information only piecemeal. With isolated facts he traveled far, but he could not leap between tidbits. *Disseminate my feeblemindedness,* thought Whitehead. *Arrest every guest's mind.*

and with greater ceremony. A hotel is a temporarily finite set—hence, a laboratory, a culture demanding dumbwaiters and thieves, bellhops and prostitutes, duchesses and switchboard operators, complaints and licentiousness, stairs and red leather armchairs, bathrobes and old-time hospitality, automatons and B-girl routines, a "colored couple" and a sari, drapes and credit cards, turbans and ashtrays, Presidential suites and oyster bars.

HOTEL DE CERTEAU

Michel de Certeau, in The Practice of Everyday Life, speaks of mutations that make a text "habitable, like a rented apartment." Or like a hotel room. I mutate The Practice of Everyday Life, turn it into a hotel text. Thus I make it habitable. I push the book away from its proper identity. I commit an act that Certeau calls la perruque (the wig): I steal time from the boss, divert it, use it for my own purposes. Certeau suggests that we might turn writing itself into a practice of la perruque; we might transform writing into an uncommon, useless thing. Consider this book, Hotel Theory, to be a diverted text, occupied for purposes other than its original intention.

We practice a hotel room, just as we practice space:

*

Lana Turner lived in Hotel Women so that she could taste its starry exclusivity and claustrophobia. *Ad nauseum* she drove down Dolores from MGM; she felt lightheaded from Thiothixene. She'd broken into sweats while shooting *Betrayed.* Clark Gable had called her "defective." Her fame would evaporate unless she quickly returned to Hotel Women. She depressed her yellow Fiat's accelerator and honked. She said, out loud, "I live in Hotel Women because it is possible to live in Hotel Women. I need no other justification."

In her room she contemplated upcoming disasters. At home on Ditmas Boulevard she lacked perspective. Here, in Hotel Women, she could leisurely think about confining hacienda and disobedient Cheryl. On vanity table she placed framed sweater-girl photos, out of date. *I'll tell Dr. Brice: I need empathy, not surgery.* She had switched psychiatrists. MGM had many. Dr. Brice. Dr. Rank. All were topnotch, able to dispense modern calmatives.

She continued to brood about her current locale and her

residing and walking are ways of turning space to account, defining and molding it.

Nothing gets accomplished in the hotel room. The hotel room is unthinkable, though I am trying to think it. I ponder the problem of the hotel room because I want to escape the "closed system."

A hotel room is what I say it is. It is a space I am choosing to practice, a space open to my definitional fever.

SPECULATIVE INTRODUCTION TO THE PROBLEM OF HOTELS

A woman lives in a hotel. She may be temporary, but as long as she resides there (two weeks, a month), time alters, and she becomes permanent—a hotel woman. She may never check out.

A deluxe hotel (five-hundred rooms) contains five-hundred destinies. Some rooms shift occupancy, night to night. Others contain permanent residents. Only the clerk can tabulate the indecisions. And the clerk is insufficiently philosophical.

At her room in the Hotel St. Claire, my grandmother kept a box of chocolates in the bureau's top drawer. She opened it to show me bonbons—proof of occupancy, supremacy, greed. It might not have been good candy.

My great-aunt stayed in the Hotel De Anza, less fancy than the Hotel St. Claire. From De

bad taste in men. *They call it Hotel Women, but its clientele is Hollywood homosexuals, starstruck pansies who consider it their ticket to Tinseltown, not their death sentence. When my last husband was alive, I never had problems with trash. My lover, Wallace, former tattoo artist, currently bookie, thinks he can hide with me in Hotel Women and regain virility, but he's wrong. Welcome to Hotel Women, world capital of impotence.*

*

Liberace admired his reflection. Early morning light entered Hotel Women and hit his naked, mirrored figure. He thought, *Perhaps my body's improved since yesterday. Harder chest?* He lifted dumbbells, then looked again and verified development. *Let Lana Turner ignore me.* He didn't mind being snubbed by fellow stars. Lana Turner was replaceable but Liberace was not. He contemplated his irreplaceability. Erect, it glistened. Fortunately, Whitehead didn't monitor what transpired in private rooms. He didn't want to be accused of molesting stars. Liberace dreaded losing personality and becoming

Anza to St. Claire was an appreciation, a hill.

Because, tonight, I am sleeping in the Hotel De Anza, I am happy to announce that this new slow tempo has become the norm.

generic; his identity, sealed, must never disintegrate. On Hotel Women's roofdeck, Observation Point, he sunbathed daily, nude no matter who else was present.

Time moved abnormally in Hotel Women. Several decades co-existed without quarrelling. Cautious residents considered it 1930. Dissenters dwelled in 1940 or 1950. Freethinkers attained 1960. Management didn't bother to correct chronological irregularities. In Hotel Women, time bent over backwards to make guests happy.

A Little Rock Memoir, Mostly About Other Things

Cynthia Kraman a.k.a. Cynthia Genser
a.k.a. Chinas Comidas

WHEN I FIRST CAME TO SEATTLE IT WAS A COWBOY TOWN. BY that I mean both a town with cowboys and a town going the way of the Old West, toward annihilation. Its fortunes, in the seventies, went boom and bust along with the fortunes of Boeing. When it was bust, as it was when I arrived thanks to the government's whimsical way of awarding contracts, it was full of the emptiness of withdrawing engineers and their families; that exodus made what Ross Perot later colorfully called the great suckin' sound of Americans losing their jobs. The city's older soldiers, those hollow-eyed sailors and out-of-work cowboys who resembled rural versions of Mitchum and Bogart in black-and-white clips, walked down wide vacant streets in staccato silhouette as imaginary dancehall music accompanied their iconic strides. The newest ghosts in town were Alaskan Indians who'd come in with the pipeline and couldn't get back. They drank, and I drank, along the edge of Elliott Bay in bars called IXL and Dew Drop Inn where you got four beers for a dollar and any change was in wooden quarter slugs that got you another beer. I was generally taken for an Indian, which meant that as a woman, I disappeared.

From this position it was easy to see things. One afternoon a white guy was flicked with a knife and blood ran down his forearm. It was exhilarating and repulsive. Just outside the door of the IXL, tumultuous clouds moved out over the bay. I could see where Frank Zappa went fishing from the balcony of the Edgewater hotel. Jimmy's purple haze clung to the horizon. The great drama of water and sky swept any remaining New York cosmopolitan civility out of me in a whipping iodine wave. I went back and used the last slug in my pocket, and settled in.

Seattle was one love, immediately, and Rich Riggins was the other. He was a lean guitar player from Eastern Washington in his mid-twenties when we met. I soon learned that his father had been a drunk, a failed salesman who became a drunk; on his deathbed he imparted a father's wisdom saying, "Richard, get your shit together."

Richard's childhood dreams were to be a car and to disappear, and there was something infinitely, tenderly vaporous in his edgy persona. Richard's brother-in-law came to visit us on Pike Street. His skin was tight and pink like a kid's, his eyes were untouched by strong emotion or any tinge of intellectuality. Over a drink at the Rainbow Tavern he told us he'd become a motivational speaker after running off with his Asian secretary and getting fleeced, then getting punished by his wife. They were now both Christians. He felt he was his own best advertisement for how to improve yourself by telling other people how to do it. He was American in a way I'd never experienced, the American of tentative, ahistorical gesture; he had his back to the Pacific like a scared kid huddled against a fence in an alleyway. For everyone, there was no place to go. The Indians at the IXL, Richard's money hungry evangelical salesman brother-in-law, the SILVA mind melders merchandising the will to power and their kin, the proto-Nazis upstate, and the chicken trade by the Market who were also the kids in the music scene, even Richard with his frayed smile, everyone was part of a desperation that felt strange and flowed into me like a drug. I was never more myself than in Seattle.

Richard had big blue eyes, a raw-boned body and milky freckles on his arms and legs. His red-blond hair stood away from his face and fell back. He had the teeth of a poor kid, which gave him a slow revelatory smile. He had a chronic rash on his left arm which made him shy. He played guitar, he painted. Sometimes he painted houses for a living. He had other jobs too. But whatever they were they all ended in a string of abuse from his boss, or from Richard, or both. He was never going to forgive his father in whatever form he took.

Richard wore an old tailored jacket over a worn white shirt and blue jeans, and when he leaned on a fence in the dusk I thought he was the most beautiful man, or thing, in the world. He took my breath away. I found out where he lived and crept into his window and made him kiss me. He had the longest eyelashes in creation. We invented a kiss that you did by closing your eyes against skin so the lashes were feathery lips.

You have to do something with someone to stay together. We had a band, Chinas Comidas. The band was made of everything from before the band, the days and nights Rich and I spent together in the summer and fall when rain in Seattle starts in earnest, refracting Pig Alley into a palace, bejeweling Harry the Preacher spitting threats at tourists, and casting a great grey cloak over islands we went to by comfortable ferries, drinking lots of coffee. And then at sunset the sky cleared in the pine-scented U District or up on Capitol Hill or Magnolia Beach where we could climb to a sort of treehouse and shimmy down a rope to the beach below. One night I couldn't get my foot disentangled and stoned, drunk, ecstatic, I just let go. I fell fifty feet. Somehow I caught the rope again and laughed a million years of doubt into the briny blackness. In the Northwest, transformation was the trope. The displaced were weird interlocutors of the soul about to reincarnate into a redeemer with multiple personalities. Lots of traffic on the astral plane.

Well, bands aren't like love or night walks, they're little bureaucracies and difficult families and in some ghastly way a team and a job. Debbie Harry once laughed at some critic who called her band "outlaws"—you can't be in a band for long without a lot of discipline and drive, and without riding wide of trouble on a pretty regular basis. Plus you need money. Plus you need to get along with people. It turned out I could make money as a copywriter at a place called Pacific Kitchens. They had to test every recipe multiple times so the band also ate off my job, and all our friends did too. We inhaled ham from "Pears Grace a Holiday Ham," which I wrote for Easter syndication to a few hundred papers, and of course pears through the kindness of the OWCPB (Oregon-Washington-California-Pear-Bureau) who was the client. And when Pacific Kitchens landed the Alaskan King Crab account we broke out the decent beer to ladle around a big pail of bouillabaisse. There tended to be a lot of noise when the band gathered which was hard on my writer's nerves—Dag cheek-popping a bass line, Brock tapping whatever, Rich grabbing the black-and-white Telly to play a riff for Mark—so I spent long productive hours on the fire escape, smoking Luckies and brooding on the driven existential lives of the mighty wharf rats running nimbly through the trash. Definitely good times. Definitely noise and a sordid whiff to everything. That was the point of the exercise and it was a mild dose of underbelly one got cheap and still steaming in my serene beloved Seattle.

On the olfactory and gustatory note, Chinas Comidas was named for places in New York that sprang up in the seventies serving Spanish and Chinese food. I liked the sound of it, I liked the mongrel culture it represented, and when a great local Tex-Mex singer Lily Benitez started calling me Chinas I was thrilled to be pseudonymous and eponymous and cool enough for a gorgeous girl like that to call to me from the stage. She was a honey-colored lesbian with a smoky voice who was not above the occasional drunk and disorderly for drinking the milk of paradise from one of her bandmates out in the parking lot of the Blue Moon, and she had an old pick up and a good dog. Like most people in Seattle she had a pretty little cottage with collected paraphernalia from her travels, a painted velvet map from Salt Lake, an inquisitive one-eyed plastic pink flamingo from Tampa, and a cup from North Platte that said "My Daddy Is the Biggest Trucker."

All the girls in Seattle weren't as lucky. There was an extremely active white slave-trade that had a retail outlet on Pike where girls in slightly dirty underwear did their desultory dances in a store window from noon until midnight. When the ringleader of one of these outfits finally got arrested his main girl told the papers "I don't believe he ever hurt anyone. He was always nice to me. He ran the water for my tub." My original keyboard player was a lap-dancer who came to me to ask if I thought this ruined the band's reputation—I reassured her that it probably improved it.

The roughest situation for us Northwest girls was the Ted Bundy rampage. I remember it well because I'd gone to the beach to read and fallen asleep up on the flat red rocks near the tracks with Henry Miller's *On Turning 80* under my head when holy smokes! Bang, whiz, the train came roaring by. What a rush. I was savoring the feeling of having my bones shaken out of my skin by a thousand tons of steel at a million miles per hour when a straight guy with a broken arm asked me to help him get his car trunk open, which it turned out was Mr. Bundy's opening gambit. Luckily I was just too buzzed and the guy looked like a real pain in the ass so I waved him away and said sorry. Which is how Henry Miller saved my life, scout's honor, the whole fucking Milleresque truth, which I pass on to women everywhere—stay away from squares and get enough sleep, even if it's in a dangerous spot.

Unfortunately the band wanted to sign so we all headed to L.A. We were unhappy there. In Seattle when I went to get a quart of milk I was greeted or insulted by a citizen critic. In L.A. I was accosted by boozy suits in cars because anyone walking was a hooker. Once I was stopped on the sidewalk and offered a job as a backup singer for a group who already had "a blonde, a black girl, and we're looking for a third." I said I didn't really sing by conventional standards. "So?" the guy recruiting me shrugged. "We fix all that later electronically." But even that remark was constitutive of a simulacrum that looked surprisingly like life when the contentless arrived full blast with full immersion into the L.A. punk scene.

In L.A. we played regularly with the Plugz, who were Mexican, and thought we really were Spanish-speaking, and did the band things; eating blintzes on Fairfax at dawn, running from the surfer-punk audience after a gig with Black Flag, touring with the brilliant Jello Biafra and the Dead Kennedys—but mostly we got held hostage for coke by soundmen at the Hong Kong or the Whiskey. Ditto the A&R guys. Richard and I had a little cabin in Silver Lake and I could walk to Griffith Observatory where I made watercolors of poppies that grew wild. Mostly the sun blazed and the nights were equally lit. There was no shadowy interior to constitute the personal, no question of the reality of anything nor anyone—the cartoon continued without captions as people pogoed to X while others held knives upright to hoist the dancers, whose inside autonomy, whose sensitive organs of feeling, whose life history as individuals, ha!, were quickly and completely remade for use, and then rolled, smoked or shot within the anesthetizing noise. There was action and reaction without pause, mostly the reaction of pain, which was the only experience in play; the pain, so sublime and nihilistic that it probably deserved some serious cultural or literary analysis (supplied *ad nauseum* by academic culture critics since the millennium), was, in L.A., not even registered in the usual places because the usual places—private conversation, newspaper editorials, thoughtful discussion after dinner, speculation between caresses in a quiet bed—were no longer located in this particular galaxy. L.A. has always been the mecca of the bookless mind. It was the natural home for an ethos that replaced purpose, even dreaming, with endless consciousness. It was a consciousness without reflection, a black pool that ceased to act as a mirror although the pool was chock full of dead primal truths like that gooey L.A. *memento mori*, the La Brea tar pits. The melancholy princes and princesses of punk, a sort of many-headed Hamlet, made memory into a straw man something like their father or mother, something originary and ghostly, which by pushing the plot development further they could then forget about revenging and in the end had to laugh about between mouthfuls of human flesh—sleep was out of the question as the pogoing continued past dawn, past day. Of course there was money to be made—this was L.A.—so it all went on and on rather longer than anyone had really expected.

An apotheosis of sorts arrived when we were invited by Los Lobos to be roadies for a show with Public Image Ltd. in East L.A.

Los Lobos did a great set for a largely satisfied audience and we all went to the edge of the backstage area to watch the reincarnated Sex Pistols. As Public Image came into view there was a change in the air temperature, the lights, the composition of basic elements. Altamont *redivivus.* A feral stench came from not only the pit but also the stage and even the black and bottomless ceiling. The crowd had changed, much as in England when the hike is over and tea is served the population transforms by noiselessly removing wellies and Barbours to become appropriate denizens of the best parlors replete with cashmere, bowties, pearls. Suddenly there were more skinheads and everyone was wearing faded black where the black definitely had its beginnings as categorically, fundamentally, dirt. The crowd swarmed and snaked. Johnny started a song and stopped. The guitar player spat on the crowd. Johnny threw nickels and pennies. Some mindless idiots dove after the change allowing others to knock them down and trample them. Those still standing drew chains from the shadows. Fights of all sorts were breaking out. The bass player broke his guitar on an amp and tossed it into the crowd. The drummer threw his sticks. The dancefloor, which had been a roller rink, thudded and bent. With one mind we began our retreat, helping Los Lobos to pack their equipment and get out. By the time we found our car the parking lot was filled with glass, fires, and the tire-marked naked bodies of drunk, beaten, and drugged boys and girls. The next day the *Los Angeles Times* critic called the concert a tour de force. But then he had the glassed-in VIP seats high up and out of sight of the slaves down in the Thunderdome.

We never went back to Pike Street. Of course I was the only one who thought we would. The band had dreams of glory. Anyway, for them L.A. was what Seattle had been for me, the great escape. So I never got back to the days spent listening to Hank Williams, Buddy Holly, Aretha Franklin, Lightnin Hopkins, Joan Jett. I would never again watch Rich make cowboy coffee, coaxing it with his hips, in our apartment above the fundamentalist Church of the New Light. We'd gotten the place by stepping up to remove the furniture and trash after our neighbor was found dead. Her little white dog cried for two days. Her sisters came, ripped open the mattress looking for cash, and left everything *in situ*. The body was buried in a Potter's Field. Our dear neighbor had been a drunk, too, and drunks, if they die drunk, apparently are trapped on the astral plane where they wander around often knocking things down in your apartment, if it was their apartment. So we built a little altar out of some of the debris for her wandering ghost to hang out, in the plastic flowers, ribbons, and a photo from the 40's of her sailor lover. Later he became the symbol for our record company, Exquisite Corpse. Later still we all left for different cities. But it was before that mattered. Before the band, before the million little compromises you make working with other imaginations and desires and neuroses. In the idea of a thing lie all its possibilities.

I had heard, as my foot first touched Pike Street in the colourless mist that day in the latter half of the twentieth century, so great a chord coming off the vacant neutral-colored streets, unfolding like well-used playing cards, off the acid iridescent sky, the bay suddenly closing its face like a shy child, that I listened more closely. There was a murmuring, a harmonic dissolve whispering "the end, the end, the end." Finally, finally, it was all post-apocalyptic. I could relax. The worst had happened. Any reflexive intuitions of wholeness became charmingly beside the point. Out of that promiscuous chord, out of the nothing, well, out of that came the music. The great American failure finally had a name and a place. I never felt afraid or alone onstage. Like everyone else in rock n roll, I'd come home.

Of course homes have their infestations. We had a bunch of Christers who had a band that hated us, the Enemy. They were invented by their former spiritual leader, some toad with a pencil mustache a good fifteen years older than his punk flock. These holy-roller crazy kids sabotaged our performances, tearing down posters, calling in wrong information to local radio stations, cutting the electricity. They finally invited us to their own private space, the Bird, and then hauled a huge garbage can up to the stage and rushed me. They got my duds dirty. This pissed me off. But in spite of the hecklers (who were legion; I could create a magisterial list of them rivaling Don Giovanni's conquests, but that would be a prose poem in itself) and evil twin bands, in spite of not being ever able to hear the monitors, in spite of every lying manager and lame local critic and stalker fan—if I could've pitched a tent and tuned in a TV set, I would never have left that sacred circle of light and noise that every stage became. Almost every stage, anyway, if you leave out the one at the Bird.

Seattle is a true *finis terre.* It had, in that era, all the negative energy of any good black hole. For our performances in bars and Masonic Halls we distributed handmade flyers with voodoo skulls announcing "*les mystères du rock 'n' roll*" would be on offer for less than the price of a drink. We spiraled down each day to end up in a practice or performance space that was airless, manic, brain-devouringly loud. That was great fun. And then, Seattle's ravishing natural beauty—Mt. Rainier rose out of our backyards. But when we went to L.A. we had to strike it rich. I couldn't stand L.A. or the idea of success in that bland sunny place. So I let the lunar ray beam me up and put me back down in the middle of nowhere.

For a long time there wasn't time or place except for bars, benches, short stays with friends. In St. Pete, Florida, which was also a bust town in those days, I looked out at a body of water scooped from the ocean into a paradisal gulf, and when my eyes were as full of blue as someone excluded from the transcendental azure can manage, I brushed off the sand and wandered with other ghosts. Jack Kerouac died screaming on those sunny streets. You are never more than five miles from water. If you're lucky you can still catch the psychedelic streak of a pink flamingo across the equatorial sky. It's a different ocean they've got there, and the night is higher. Now that I've returned to New York I find the nights keep me company, the close and foreign nights we have here in my hometown, so crowded with ghosts these days and nights that you never feel lonely. It's funny because when I listen to the band, our music, it isn't before but right now that surrounds me in an auditory nondirectional streaming, like the epiphenomenon of the new people walking their dogs by the eternal Hudson late at night, people with not only their own dogs, but their own dreams. Even though I came home a couple of ways and thought I got off the road when it happened, it never happened. Maybe that's the reason my little dachshund, Pushkin, looks pretty worried when I walk out the door. But he shouldn't worry. If life is provisional the music is forever and hell, I'm never going to leave my dog.

Little Gingko

Cynthia Kraman

There we were. You and me. You and me and
Eternity. Endless airless soundless space.
Pagoda of light. Pagoda like room.
Who loves life in an empty tomb? Who dark?
Who loves lack? Who loves kneeling in the snow?
Wherever we race, wherever we go
Nothing but the miles, the declining sun.

Pagoda of light. A tree in the street
Burnishes me like an effigy
Melts my ringed finger with its trumpetings
Ravishes the others into golden arms
Little gingko, little gingko, please kiss me!
Each one prays loudly to the little tree
But the little tree is kneeling fast to Time.

Here we are. You and me. You and me and
Eternity. Warming, ordered, coursing space.
Pagoda of light!—Pagoda like room!
How I loved you hard in that witless room
Signed for by the hour as if we bought time
And not endless longing, not ecstasy
The electric unfamiliar of eternity.

No Noon But Mine, No Heat But Yours

No noon but mine, no heat of noon but yours
As our equators slice the day in two.
No moony missing parts but we eclipse
Together—that's rule one!—no partial, small
Eclipsing either—listen—no nuptial
I'll go shopping, you do the cleaning up—
We both shop. Then it's both down on our knees.

My universe of pain your universe.
No north your south, no trading east and west.
When my storms gather, thunder on. And when
You feel a fine ice setting in I freeze.
Go south, I glare a solar eye at you
Go sleeping, dreams crash headlong in our bed
Go writing, get your language at our bank.

Get pissing drunk, I'll drink you down the drain
And nag for nag, and headpats, one for one.
Then I come crying—I drown in your tears
Until mice float like deadmen, ten toes up.
We make the earth one thing and many, then
A sudden saintliness occurs to you.
I'm peace itself. The cosmos breathes relief.

Cynthia Kraman

Summer Night Poem 1

Sometimes the contours of love are not human.
My dog's snout, his long, lovely scrotum.
Ah! So soft! you're laughing. But when our eyes meet
It isn't lust, but the turbulence
Of love that thrills through me. The light is brighter
Around his head. His breastbone lifting lifts me.
I dream his lowness, I dream him tenderly.

And so much higher than my hand is God.
Lips soft of softest soft should meet mine
If this were the unstoppable thing.
God is so high, I should wear wings, I would
Have eyes like cannonballs to take him in.
But if this love is love it has no name.
Not any figure or sex, no close thing.

My pajamas are the leafy air
And night hush. It is July and the sun
Reached just this year its furthest point from us.
Is absence of the Heat of Noon relief?
Or that he returns from now on? Which is it?
I can't wait for the answer. I'm awake.
The murmuring air under my tongue, loves.

Summer Night Poem 5

The night the night comes galloping
Awkwardly, it is a handsome giraffe
Who knows a famous writer we know
Who knows many people we would like to know
He arrives, a visitor we expected
A tall idea loping from the distance
And up the open avenues of late August

It's already August. The botanist
Is already planning future summers
We might have done some things with this summer
Cleaned books, written Shawangunks, dieted like crazy
But instead we did things with this summer
Pretty illicit, almost illegal
We slept in, we puttered around, we swam

We succumbed. We made love to this summer
Held it in our arms through its hundred nights
Smooched it up under its thousand stars
Then closed our eyes, became simpletons of sleep
In our dreams a tower grew like a weed
We climbed it into its thousands of stars
Up, up the giraffe's neck, into the day

Our Terrible Belief

Glyn Maxwell

YOU'RE BEAUTIFUL BUT CRYING.

Aren't you? Beautiful but crying.

Just sittin here of all places, beautiful but crying.

I'm sorry I don't understand what you're saying, I keep thinking you mean someone else.

No no one else sweetheart just you. Just sittin here with ya margarita. It's been a long day for you I reckon. Fancy another?

You know I am allowed to ask you that, cos you're looking at me like I'm what, I work here, right? Got a cash-till, got a towel, I can stand you a drink.

Beautiful. But crying.

Look at you, just sitting here of all places. I understand you, beautiful-but-crying. Quite a day, quite a day. You want to be alone and yet you don't want to be alone.

You know what you're half right.

I reckon. You come to where it's happening. Moth to a flame. Butterfly I should say.

Butterflies don't do that.

You're no moth, beautiful-but-crying. You know something?

I said you know something?

No.

You don't? What we learned today is that the world is a frightening place, but it can be beautiful too, and miracles can happen.

I'm sorry when did we learn that.

The whole world's beautiful but crying, the whole spinning planet is, for a little while longer. And you're beautiful but crying.

I'm not beautiful but crying. I'm not beautiful or crying.

Why does he keep saying you are? Where are you?

I'm in Arroyo's in Covent Garden.

Which one is it?

It's in the, you know, right by the, where the awful acts are and the crowds. I'm having a margarita.

Not which place is it, which guy is it who keeps saying.

I don't know, Minni, I don't come here. Maybe it's Arroyo himself.

Arroyo said? The owner of the place said you were crying? Does he want you to leave?

Beautiful but crying. One of the barmen. He said the world's a miracle or something. He said we know that now and I told him—

You're not crying, are you?

No.

I mean—

I'm beautiful though. Oh that was a bit loud. Joke everyone.

Did you really just say that? Suse!

It's filling up in here Min I can't keep this seat much longer. Hang on he's going right by again, he's quite tall; I could ask him he's gone now.

Is it Calum?

How do I know if it's Calum?

Ask him, he's the barman, is he Calum.

It doesn't matter who, I didn't think he meant me but he kept saying it, he kept throwing his stupid cocktail stuff in the air and round behind his back and I always wish it would go wrong but even with it spinning in mid-air he kept going "You're her, you know you are!" and I'd just shrug and he'd go "It's over now, it's okay . . ."

He was right about that.

What do you mean he was right about that? About what?

Right about how it's over. That thing we believed. Our terrible . . . belief.

What? Are you far away, Min, I can't sit here too much longer on my own you know I've had a terrible day. This is my second margarita I'm having. Also, plus, look there's something in it. (Excuse me there's look, what's that.)

(It didn't come with it last time, can I have one without it?)

(Thanks Calum.) Assuming he's Calum.

We all had a terrible day Suse.

Did we? I wasn't really monitoring anyone else. Where are you you sound weird.

I'm walking straight toward you and that's not Calum it's Liam. I mean hello? Nametag? Look at you with your drink! What's that, a margarita?

No a lucozade.

What's all that round the edges is it salt?

It is salt. Hi then.

I've never had one it's bad for you all that salt, are you supposed to, there's no TV in here, Liam could I have a margarita but without any salt? And why did you call my friend Suse beautiful but crying?

Look Min I suddenly sort of don't think it was him.

It wasn't him? You didn't say that, Liam? You don't think she's beautiful?

You do? He does!

It wasn't him *or* Calum, the one who said it was taller. We're sorry, it wasn't you, thank you, go away, get taller—

No I'm still ordering my drink! I'll have this one this Blue Russian in the picture. Thanks! That was easy! Number eleven. It's good having pictures.

Yay pictures.

It wasn't him, how embarrassing for you, Suse.

Well they all wear black, they all belong on a beach, they all do that trick stuff with the drinks, nothing ever smashes what's the difference.

Though that is *two different barmen both said you were beautiful. Good start to the night!*

Downhill from here.

I mean on a day of loss.

What?

Beautiful but crying!

The first one said I was crying. And now he's gone forever. Back into the outback.

You and your men.

What men.

What men, listen to her!

Yes, Listen to me. Listen to me. Because I may be, y'know, I may be dead soon.

Right!

Pardon?

Dead soon. Me. May be.

Yeah Suse.

Someone told me.

Right, I think that's too salty, how can you drink that?

Look what he's putting in yours.

Those are what goes in it, Suse, it has to be blue cos of the name so it needs something blue. It must be some kind of blueberry flavoring. It's what they use.

Not forgetting the vodka! Or you can't call it a Russian as vodka's a Russian look how he pours it in from way up high a Russian drink like a clear, clear stream of pure, blue—

Russian.

Russian—I wonder what that's for. He never spills a drop. Part of his act, that is, he takes our mind off things.

Actually he doesn't.

I can't believe today. Can you believe they did that?

Believe who did what?

You know! What they did! Where's there a why's there, there's no TV in here you'd think there'd be coverage.

Oh. The thing that happened. I had my own thing happen.

Twenty-four-hour coverage. People may have loved ones. God forbid but they may. They need to know even if we don't, and we do on a day of loss. I haven't seen any *coverage. Here comes my Blue . . . look at that. Thanks! I have seen the making of it, "Just how I like it!" I go and I've never had one! It's unbelievable those people.*

Charming sound you're making.

Mmm it's a cocktail actually Suse, you drink it through a straw? I'm drinking my usual at my local. Hardly! See that guy standing between the tables that's, you know who I mean from—

Yeah, Shane something from that—

TV I know who you mean and it's not.

It looks like him. No. From the side it did. Shane thing but it's not at all. God I can't believe today.

Min, can I just say—

They say it was ninety-nine minutes!

What was ninety-nine minutes? Who's they?

God did you even have *the same day the whole of the entire western world just had?*

No I had my own little day. Can I—

Ninety-nine minutes exactly, when the western world believed he was . . . passed away.

What are we talking about here.

You're giving me that look like you're going to ask me who *was!* Who *passed away!* Who *died and was reborn!*

Look at you!

I'm not.

You are though look at you!

I'm me, I can't see.

Who then. Who do I mean.

You mean him, the star, the star chap, Tom Bayne.

As if you didn't know, when it was breaking news all day and now it's it's now it's—

Broken.

And it's Thomas Bayne, never Tom, apparently he insists—

I'll try and remember that.

Yeah, we were broken too. For ninety-nine minutes.

Ninety-nine minutes.

No one doesn't know.

I heard someone say he wasn't dead. But I didn't know he was dead.

He was never at all*! That thing. It was never true! Except in the eyes of the world . . . It's like some people almost* wanted *him to be, you know, that thing. "Departed," he's said that in interviews, that you can rise too high, you can be shining too brightly, people turn against you, dazzled by your like, shining? There's dark forces out there, unknown terrors, that was in* Hello.

Some are dead, though.

Or okay. They are. Between eighty and a hundred are in that status. They were working on the set.

Set, what do you mean?

Suse this is embarrassing I'm having to be like you know the News myself, like what's her name Natasha Klabinski? "And today, in other news . . ." Or I'm like shuffling papers and agreeing with the man and waiting for the music to end.

What was I saying?

What set with a hundred people?

What set? Unbelievable. People in this bar have no idea you know nothing.

I had no idea they knew everything.

They only,

They bombed The Book of Revelation.

I'm sorry say that again.

They bombed The Book of Revelation. *They only went and bombed it.*

You mean, like an original copy?

Original copy of what?

The Book of Revelation. It's a book, Minni. Of revelation.

Well maybe in some museums it is, you're the reader, but not to the general public. No they bombed the set. They bombed the set of the film The Book of Revelation *starring Thomas Bayne which is due out in autumn 2008 though that may probably change and between eighty and a hundred people were you know, fatal casualties, and about a hundred and five more were you know not fatal but things like critical and stable, like they're on those lists, they're still counting but there's no TV in here weirdly of all things. There must be a way to give blood, or, sign a book of, you know. Imagine what they did. They bombed innocent people. Just innocent film people, going about their, their—*

Their film.

It's an act of total, you know, like pure evil.

Okay. I didn't know they did that.

It was in the deserts of Libya. It was just a location.

And Thomas Bayne isn't dead.

Some of the stars are. It wasn't just, you know, people you get in the credits, like, assistant this or third cameraman.

Thomas Bayne's okay.

He was completely apparently not, you know, scathed in any way. He had a day off filming, he was in a whole nother country.

But supporting actors are dead. Famous people are down.

You know this is probably bad taste Suse, but it was a thought I had, I need another sip of this…there's a blue flavor. It's just a question in the end. Some of those supporting actors, like, I don't know, those who were fatal victims of this atrocity, would they still do you think, I don't know, could they still be nominated?

What?

It's possibly not the time to think about it, but it may come up as a question. If they'd put in great supporting performances you know like selflessly, and the nominations are, if they'd put in great performances before, you know, the actual incident, with the, you know, the loss it's weird to be drinking a blue drink you only see that in films from the future.

(Can I have some crisps please really like now.)

Thomas will make a statement, he's bound to, about all this.

Then maybe we can kind of talk openly, say our feelings, he'd want that. It's hard to imagine it happened to him, or nearly did, but he's going to have to rise above it, for the sake of, just, us who survived.

(No I want ready salted, I hate these.)

But he's been among *the, among the. Departed I mean at least, in a way. For ninety-nine whole minutes, Thomas Bayne was among the, the departed even saying it's, just . . . For the sake of his fans . . . Can we have two menus Liam.*

I'm like I'm shivering.

Specials.

It's just so different from yesterday. That's what gets to me, Suse, it's just too different from yesterday, today, it's like today never even heard of yesterday if that's not too weird, you're the reader!

You used to say that at school.

Mm, you were the reader then. You're the reader now.

Actually you were a reader then too.

No but there was time then. Plus it was part of homework. Everything's different now. I mean even before now, I mean today everything's different. Now this, event, has come to pass. It's not a time to be reading in a way. You have to more keep your eyes open, like for packages? Not hide them in some book.

That's my whole like opinion on a day of loss.

Are you okay Suse? Are you crying? I can't tell. It's all right if you are but I'm not saying you are.

You never used to.

****

Good morning everyone. I'm your guide today. My name is Susan Mantle and I'm from Outer London. You're in Inner London. You're very welcome to Inner London and to this tour bus which, if you look closely, is red and two stories in height. The upper deck was added to accommodate the increasingly taller people coming to these shores in recent centuries. You might have noticed it doesn't have a roof and you'd be right there. See? Look! Don't be afraid. We're aware of that situation so don't be if at all possible. It's a nice October day if you notice. It's a Monday morning, so all these people you see down there to your right and left, these are working people of Inner London, that's right, get some snaps of them while they're there, whereas, whereas, you're all holidaymakers from, let me think, from the United States of America? Yes! Holidaymakers, makers of holiday! America! Beg your pardon? Kansas? The state of Kansas. The what? The Sunflower State. That's perfect. Tall big sunny flowers of America. Excellent. And tornadoes, right, yes, and witches and dwarves obviously, no? Monkeys with wings oh no I suppose not, that ain't Kansas is it, as she, well, specifically says. Ha ha ha, superb, ha. Ha can I not say what? I can't say dwarves. O-kay. I'll try hard not to.

But you two come from Nebraska, where, where they, well, where you two, are. From, good, you'll be able to, see the sights also. And then, remember them, there.

Here we go, we've started and the street we're on is called Oxford Street, that's right, Oxford, just like the university which shares its name. There's an interesting story (dwarves) about that. In the seventeenth or eighteenth century, you decide, a lot of people who wanted to attend Oxford University but couldn't really be bothered to make the journey would come to this street on a Sunday and all these buildings, which are now department stores, see, to the left, to the right, other way round, would transform themselves into Seats of Learning just for that single day. This one Marks and Spencers just coming up, this was called Christus Jesus College, and high learning went on in the seats and then, hey presto, the next day being Monday, it just looked like that again, with people walking past or going in and getting things they needed like trousers or soup. Strange but true. What's that? Yes, *Christus*, like *Christ* with *us*, or *U.S.* (that's good, Susan) then Jesus, like the gentleman who, you know. I'm sorry? Yes, died to save us all, ma'am, thank you. Died to save us from, obviously, further, further dying.

(Dwarves) this is Selfridges, or, Balliol. Are there any what? Ghost stories about that? I believe I, what's that? Ghost stories about anything? Well yes I was just coming to that, in regard to this very building. On every I think it's every alternate Friday in, in, June, Lord Selfridge of Balliol is said to, what is it, walk the floor. I mean on the floor, across it in a stately way. How did he die? No one knows. Just like that. One day he was there, being a Lord, lording it around, ringing the bell for service, muffins Jeeves, riding his high horse over the moors, the next day no one's ringing the bell, Jeeves sitting there, horse just saying now what, muffins in a foil pack and so on. That's how it happened. But he does this sort of, you know, moaning about it. It's . . . horrible, people have heard it. What's that, sir? And lived to tell the tale? No. No, sir, they didn't, sorry. This is Piccadilly Circus. It's not a real circus, but there's an interesting story about that because every last Tuesday in December . . .

It was a normal day Min, I was doing the morning shift and all the time I'm not talking my old rubbish I'm thinking about him.

The new guy! Him! Suse and her New Guy!

Right who I've met twice.

Yeah but who you were thinking about.

I didn't think I would be, I didn't think I felt anything. But the more I thought that, the more he just sort of came to mind, Nigel—

Nigel . . .

Nigel Pilman horrid name and I couldn't quite get his face right, you know, and for me that's a sign, when you can't get the face right.

He's the one I just know. *Then you can forget about that Josh.*

Hey thanks for that Min.

Put him behind you.

He's very far behind me. Who's there? No one.

I know, cos Nigel's the One!

Maybe he was. Maybe he is. I'm not sure he can be now. He's a tall dark stranger.

Yes and fanfare isn't that what we want?

Is it?

Hello! Yes!

Well it was.

What do you mean it was, that's like saying it isn't now.

It's what I wanted this morning. I thought the day would be all about him. Only now he's, he's like at the other end of some, forest.

Like in that film.

What film?

You know. With the forest. She was trying to reach him but he was like in flashback? It was to do with Time, and how you can never—or though I think they did in the end. They proved you can. I like these coasters. I'm going to ask them where they got them.

Well I was on the tube all the way he was on my mind, *it* was, that he was right, Nigel Pilman, "Nigel Pilman," can't be helped, he was just right, it had to be him I was even, I was even saying my name and this is deeply sick with his horrible surname attached—

God Suse!

Susan Pilman and I don't even intend to change my name ever but—

God.

I couldn't stop myself.

I can't believe you sometimes.

I sat there like a fool, like someone at the start of a joke: There was this girl sitting on a bus, right . . .

Who was that, Suse?

Never mind.

Here come our starters.

Sufficient Time

Glyn Maxwell

Sufficient time has passed, and now the girl
who was last seen has broken out of local
news and made the nationals.

Sufficient time has passed, and now she sheds
her surname and her given name and takes
a pet name for as long

as no one knows a thing. Sufficient time
has saddened the police, who bring that name
to conferences and briefings,

explaining why today and yesterday
look so alike. As if in sympathy
their own names shorten.

Sufficient time has passed and you can go,
everyone can go. The days that follow
will be given numbers.

Reality

Two cameras see
          eye to eye:
enough's enough.

Their lenses close,
          the focus goes.
They're fucking off.

They tug their leads
          from motherboards
and out of there

they're gone. The guys
          they blink their eyes;
the girls stare.

But who knows what
          they do or not?
No one can see.

Looks like we've got
          to do this shit
from memory.

Glyn Maxwell

Decision

He thinks it's time,
it was reported
by a minion.

He thinks he's "earned it"
it was snorted
in committee.

Believes he's ready,
echoed round
the gents' convenience.

His life is charmed!
Vice-chairmen nodded,
only noticed

once. *Charmed!*
the only chairman
sat and said so.

And he wants more . . .
he lifted pages
on to pages.

There is no justice,
he lamented
to the skyline.

Perfectly happy,
do you not think?
The meeting murmured.

Not fair at all.
And further murmuring
in agreement.

When one stopped murmuring
others did
but others started

murmuring more.
He was a statue
silhouetted.

Let him have it.
Silence fell.
Just give it to him.

Glyn Maxwell

Dust and Flowers

Everyone ever was shuddering past
In a rubbishy cyclone of them and the dust
And my eyes were attempting to follow each face
I would lose in a blur like a chariot race

So I'd try that again, and to anyone seeing
I seemed to be somebody stuck disagreeing
And shaking my head sort of slowly forever
Like somebody dreadfully stupid or clever,

Then you broke the surface between it and me,
And you were as still as nothing would be
If it thought for a moment, and I was the same
For no time at all till your face and your frame

Were nodding my head up and down on its stem
Like a flower in the rain at the height of a storm,
But afterward too, like a flower in a breeze,
And always, which doesn't have flower-similes.

The Arms of Half

Smoke at the horizon,
Something you remember, something
Up, something uttered,
          Darkens and detaches,
          Can slow the inhalation,
          Elongate a smile, set
          The cool head nodding.

Fire can keep it going,
Something in reserve, something
You have reserved the right to
          Set off across the desert,
          Illuminating uplands
          Bare and bright as foreheads
          Little hands are climbing.

Soot in the new morning,
Something disagreed on, something
Stooped toward and sifted
          By half a country. Half
          Will kick it up like fullbacks
          And stand in its dispersal
          A time until instructed.

Fall of Man [Continued]

The first man first notices
        actions have a past,
though there's only been one action yet:
the first man can extrapolate,
        hurtling this fast

under the jungle canopy...
        oh god he knew he knew
before he, during it, after he, he
knew, she knew, it knew! and me
        I'm telling you.

And where on earth till death
        will he wander when he's done
with running, where will he huddle when he's
done with wandering? under the trees,
        though searchlights shine

nightly for him. Meanwhile
        he staggers, utterly free,
too out of breath to breathe a word
about it, all of life a chalkboard
        knowledge-gray,

trackless; on he stumbles,
          who will do what he wants
now with what he's taken, now
he can't be found, for how
          can what he wants

be far? Only in time
          crisscrossing beams will meet
exactly when he's nowhere else
and stay with him until he kneels,
          as his green heat

betrays him to the dawn.
          And then he'll bow down low,
prostrate in light of what was done.
—Until you look and he's long gone
          and you should go.

Johnny Stinkbait Bears His Soul

Thorpe Moeckel

YOU KNOW THOSE GUYS THAT SLINK AS IF FROM THE CATALOGS, glossy with all the finest, talking vectors of cast and other crap, latest Gore-Tex jockstrap clamping their nuts like a vise—they are not me. No, I'm worse.

I'm a gearhead in reverse. I fish in found things. For wading, thrift shop sneaks are best. Reclaimed soccer cleats are crap—trust me. I fish with flies tied with beard hair and milkweed down. Once I tied a muddler with Her pubes thinking it would make me lucky. No luck.

For one thing it's boring shopping in stores stocked with all the latest, some know-it-all pretending he knows it all looking to hook you. And don't think those dinks fish barbless. Hardly ever release you.

Besides fishing, redemption is oatmeal each morning in a small china bowl with white blanch marks where I scraped the barnacles. Each morning this bowl and the oatmeal in it and the coffee, too, is a boat drifting me back to the day in Maine I stepped on it while casting a dog-hair (German Shepherd) Deceiver for stripers in the Presumpscot River on a drain tide.

I caught nothing that day. I casted. I waded. I was happy. I found a bowl. There are days like this. You go about them like you've come unglued from living and maybe you are living for once. I don't know. I don't know shit.

The day was hazy and I was wearing waders found at Goodwill for four dollars. They leaked a little, even though I'd duct-taped the slit along the seam. It was nice, really, feeling the water swash around my right foot, the wool sock doing its job. People are always giving people hell about fucking sheep like they never wore wool. Like we aren't all shepherds. What the hell.

I like recycling barns, dumps, second-hand stores, garage sales. There is no junk. There are things nearly new, things with potential. You and I, we have previous lives too. Our souls have inhabited many hosts and many are our compatriots. That fish I caught or that kid caught, I forget his name, in Scarborough Marsh a few weeks after I found the bowl, you see, we knew that fish.

That was a fish!

The kid was one of my clients, as once with a forged degree I counseled teenagers. Truth is, I let places counsel the kids. My office was where I liked it. That day it was an Old Town Tripper I got off an outfitter who used it as a clinic canoe on rivers more rock than water. It was nearly bulletproof with Kevlar where I'd patched it so it would float again. We were paddling around, shooting the breeze, him an orphan living with his sister, the lead-guitarist for a dyke-punkabilly band, Rugged Twat. Once I would have said to myself, poor guy, but not anymore.

I had my nine-weight between my legs with forty feet of line stripped out, trolling a shrimp pattern tied with snips of hyperpink Chia Pet fuzz. Wacky fly but a good one. We were floating awkwardly and rapping the general way. Him testing the waters, me trying to make him feel safe and maybe lift a laugh or two out of him. "What has two eyes and no mouth?" I asked him.

"What?" he said. A heron whispered over us then like some cargo glider loaded with tanks of mystery.

"Mississippi."

My nine-weight is a fiberglass antenna plucked from an Army surplus jeep, then threaded and glassed some eyes to and a grip. It works good, if you know how to work it.

"I thought Mississippi has four i's?" he said.

"It does," said me, clinically. I wrenched a stern pry. The kid paddled like there was no tide, like we were in a park pond, shitfull with swan and geese. "That's the point."

"Was that supposed to be therapeutic?" he asked after a minute. I wanted to flip the boat then, but kiddo was on so many meds it would have been fineable to dump him most likely by the EPA.

That rod I gave two years ago to my pop who bends it for drum now and sea trout in the Lowcountry. Or so he says. Two winters ago, pop's divorce came through with his second wife and then a day later his pop, who I knew as Big Ron, passed on. The Her formerly known as my wife had kicked me out a month prior. It was okay because me and pops were buzzing on a day, ripping the lips of sea trout and knew if nothing there was always sea trout.

I'm a fish, you see. More than a fisherman, I am a fish. I become the fish that I cast for. It so happens that last evening in a stream so anorexic with drought and wasted besides with acid rain from the crap spewing from the coal-fire plants, I stalked brookies. I became a brook trout. Don't ask me to explain it.

In exchange for the nine-weight, Dad gave me a one-weight that bends like a gymnast and is more sensitive than my pecker. I employ it in the quest for brookies near my place in Hurt, Virginia.

By now you've probably guessed that I worked with mixed up teens so long I am one, again, only now in a man's body, which is not good but kind of fun in a desperate and joyful way at least if you know how to work it.

For instance, I finagled some plastic barrels off a pickle company and made me a houseboat out of scrap lumber I drug from rivers in Virginia where I came after running from the detox. For a time I lay low with a guy who once was a friend but had become too big for his britches with the bucks he made as a full-time prescription med dealer. With fist, bat, and bottle, he gave me retro plastic surgery one night in a blackout, says him, and anointed me Johnny Stinkbait. I am grateful forever. Later I found a surplus library bookmobile, a six wheel, eight cylinder with a rivet-solid Grumman body, and drove it onto the barge I built on the lake here that is brighter this morning than a National Merit Scholar. Plugged in a potbelly and a few sundries, so here we are.

I score oatmeal from the nearby commune that makes and sells hammocks, tofu, and their own Don't Panic It's Organic-brand oats. It's good. My bowl is best. I hold it cupped like a breast. It is not true like a wheel is true. It must have been wave-altered in the tides as it was. I eat from it with my eyes and eat it with my eyes, from its blue paint in bold strokes, the trees and mountains, birds and rooflines. It is white with blue on the white and know that I stepped on it as much as it reached for me, this bowl tossed or swept from some deck and what has been eaten from it and who turned it and who it will be with next are questions that smooch me like any unanswerable.

From this life afloat, a moped when its running scoots me to the hills where I sneak around for brookies with no need to paint my face as years of staring life in its black and blue one has done it for permanent.

Her. Her was good. Sweet wife, Her gave and gave. Wore a mishmash of vintage elegance gleaned from the same wherever junkheaps that I love, Her, and filled those digs like nobody has or ever will, if you want to know. You don't want to know.

Then Her dumped me passed out at the detox. I guess it's like when men had women put away for menopause, menstruation, witchcraft, and such—comeuppance. "Scorned one make the beloved a patient," reads the headline. I blitzed and Her said, "Go on. Be ADD, an everythingaholic. Take your Intermittent Explosive and Language Processing Disorders, to name a few," Her said, "and go on." On I've been. I mean, why not a little mental hygiene via spiritus of grape, hop, and rye? I'm a sweet tooth, and like my sugar fermented.

I tell you they're wrong who say that matters only you and your woman. The only sanctity ever was fishing.

Knew it when I ripped a snagged treble that came back hungry for my eyelid, pops and pal paddling for my six-year-old screams thinking snakebit. Knew it then and that was Arkansas. Knew it pulling bluegill from golf course ponds with mushrooms and Styrofoam for bait. Knew it learning to swim across the Coolasagea, rod in mouth, catching underwater eddies, losing no ground even in flood. Knew it that year I only fished with corn because dad did with flies. Knew every cast was a metaphor for faith better than scripture. Knew it as a plebe sneaking nights from barracks on Parris Island to throw a mattress-foam crab pattern like pick-up lines for ladyfish in the tidal flats of the Broad. Knew it in blackwater swamp and clearwater glade. Knew it on the Kennebec, the Maury, the Potomac, and the James. Knew it in the Bitterroots, the Alleghenies, the Sangre de Cristos, and the Coast Range. Knew in Cape Breton, Cape Hatteras, and Cape Fear.

Jesus knew so, too. Consider him at the Sea of Tiberius, at Gennesaret—such bounty, henceforth, etc.

But I'm telling you Her, she was this plumpness of good French-Canadian, Lewiston, Maine breeding who stocked boots at the Salvation Army in Bath—mercy—Her'd hook me up with such fine scores and nice knockers like catfish head, each one of them puckered and few whiskers.

So this kid is quiet and me quiet and the reel starts screaming I grab it and feel that pull which could be the Almighty Himself. "Dag," kid says. Kind of whispers it. "What is it?"

"Fish," I say. The marsh is in my hands and the sky on it at once and I say, "Kid take this, take this and keep the tip up and let the fish run but keep the tip up the line tight."

"Dag," the kids says over and over, quieter each time.

I say, "No dag, this is the shit." And kid still won't take the rod like he knows it will hook him harder. "Take it," shouts me. "Keep the tip up."

"Doesn't it hurt the fish?" kid asks.

"Yes, but it hurts you worse. It hurts you best," I say as he takes it and the sun starts blinding me right out his eyeballs so full of the life through the line rod bend grip is kid. "Keep the tip up, kid," I'm panting. "Let it run." That was the best counseling I ever did.

Someday I will come rich and famous writing a book on Piscean Therapy. The kid turned fish. I saw it with my own two bloodshot ones. He evolved, by golly.

I dance now to think of it. There is room to do on the deck I put on the truck-houseboat's roof. And I sing a little jingle. Pluck a slide ukelele one potato two potato three potato four. Heart, I sing, you are a poodle-eating carp with tampon strings where your eyes used to be. You are dace and you are blowfish, heart. You are muskie and lamprey, madtom and sturgeon. You are bloatest grouper and sublimest bonefish.

Kid played it good with me screaming keep the tip up as love and fear breakdance in our chests and the boat follows the fish running for the rice thick along the tidal mud and some place gillinstinct know and no other. Kid got it next to the boat on that barbless shrimp pattern, and he is watching and breathing heavy. "What now?" he asks after a minute.

"Let it go," I say, reaching to release the hook.

"We're not eating it?" kid asks.

"No," I say. "We're setting it free. Watch it close." It is a lovely striper, mix of bayonet and starlight. "Watch it go."

Now I eat from the bowl. I take my oatmeal with peanuts and goat milk. Someday I'll be a striper. I'll be salt. I'm evolving. I know it. I was chub. I was out of season brown trout heavy with roe. Friends, you've got to be a fish, there is no other way to live.

Dream of My Father

Thorpe Moeckel

To get upstream, not to the source
   but somewhere close enough
to smell its gifts and risk
   being forgiven, my father
made a pole, whittled a length
   of cedar. The shavings,
they reeked of urine at first;
   with air, with time, they softened,
and he cupped them to his face
   as though they'd speak, as though
he'd hear them with his nose.
   Water, he heard, broken water
was all he could taste. One
   might say it was long, that
the work consumed him,
   but he took it slow enough
to be quick and he failed
   perfectly. The scrap was soil
soon and my father too,
   but near the end, when
he hauled the tired body
   of his canoe on the shore
for the last time and handed
   the pole to me, the wood
was smooth with use, and in
   a voice meant for roots,
worms, cooler, darker heavens,

  he said, "The tree when growing
had hardly been straight
  and once carved was even
more bent, but it brimmed
  with moon and grape and translated
the bottom of the river
  for my ignorant hands." I shook
his right one then, still know
  like the itch after a sting
that pulse of stone, grain—
  a gentle, sinuous gift and custody.

Thorpe Moeckel

Nature Poem, Inc.

Fir needles like the eyebrows of some eyeless face
that doesn't see
but wears a look; isles of moss
in rot-sunk pine, the wood

less a version of flesh
than a marrowing inward,
which is soil
in somebody's book, maybe the starfish
that freakdanced here

before the ocean retreated
or the land rose,
confident, magmatized, relieved
of some weight. Ice

is heavy, sure—what about frozen blood,
stuff they used
to fuse the kid's arm back on
in Florida last week
after they shot the shark to fetch it

back. *Jeez, stupid shark—*
pick on somebody your own size,
the taxidermist might etch
in brass

under the mounting for the museum
of the strange & miraculous, which could be
anywhere these days
or any other
one took the time to look. It takes

to look. See
the porcupine quill under the over-
hang of the boulder,
that Pleistocene Big Mac

sauced with spore bearers
and ferns like winged things about to
and always taking off, cliff divers
in mid-coast Maine's little Acapulco. You know
that caring means frolic

as much as attention
if frolic means being real. Who knows
what those raindrops mean
in the luminous

grocery bag of the spider web
staring—are they eyes?—
at the branchwork's atmospheres; maybe
they're listening to the thrush
who's listening to the squirrel, twitty red streak, scream

bug out, buddy,
even you sapsucker, meathead,
leaf—kiss me,
or bug out.

Thorpe Moeckel

Mussels

Plucked from ledge, from water below
lowest tide, and stowed in mesh
lashed to the stern;

we eat them now, steamed in brine—
succulent nubbins, tongues not our own—
as much for ritual as appetite,

the foraging: there's health in that.
Like eating the sea, a distillation—
we're licked towards breathing, toward

the tides that turn, yet you ask,
you ask: why do the ones
that never open nourish us most?

At the Co-op

What kind of listening is this, could it be good somehow
that even as Bill speaks,
carefully, fingering his goatee, I know that later I'll take
his dream, (the telling like

late-light on a wind-swept lake, bobber going under), home,
and sit on a bench that those
slow woodworkers, love & necessity, will make of it,
watching my daughter scoop

a bloodroot of flesh from the trout's cheek, the one I'm about
to buy, the one I'll overcook.
It's Tuesday, the signs tacked to the board—*humidifier for sale,*
local healers, folks

wanting rentals, *water view, rustic OK*—are feathers
of a closeness bird, and as we
brush them, snaking the aisles, my friend Bill, the sole employee,
roots his dream of bones,

parents, television & veils in the throat's rocky soil. What
becomes us—the things we want,
or the things we want to get rid of? It's loaded, his dream, as full
and real as the spinach, chicken,

and Rag Mountain Trout; and as I imagine Bill in bed that night,
Roberta & him, tangled
driftwood on the river of sleep, even their breathing holding hands,
we talk about life, the disasters,

the Scotch tape: his father's tumor: how I'm sick, he's sick & illness
is the cure that won't quit. I want
to stay, put an hour toward our discount in, stocking granola,
pistachios, flour, or sweep,

keep up this dance with Bill. But today what stays is the leaving
and what leaves is the coming back—
why else the Reiki master's free consultation, a juicer
for twenty-five bucks, *like new?*

Beautiful Jazz

There was an elephant last July in Bowdoinham, Maine,
in the shape of a man
go-going a trombone, rocking heel to toe in river sandals;
snake-charmer of the clarinetist coming in
like different magic from the same source. Children
digging a hole perhaps to resurrect joy
or its cousin, plenitude,
wagged their heads as though ants
boogied on their eardrums, as though they wanted them there.
Sometimes the clover
tapped its feet. We were outside, on a farm, the band
set up in the half-built barn, timbers up
like some monument to the music
in wood—breath,
design. I wasn't
sitting with my wife but could see her,
and was thinking about her nipples, how they've changed
since our child storied
their history; and now that she's weaned would they
do some new yoga or what, when this kid—a teenager really—
conjured so many breasts
with his keyboard. There was something
of the badminton player
in his wrist & arms. Or goodminton as my daughter
coined it. I mean
he was crawling up
the giraffe's neck of the bass

when the brass-snouted elephant spelled
thirteen synonyms for longing
on the day's naked back
just as my wife winked & blew me a kiss. Truly,
I embellish. Beautiful jazz
makes me horny.

That there are others in the photographs is disturbing, the man on the radio says, because it reveals a pattern, it reveals that this is not something out of the ordinary, but, rather, something banal, mundane, something very, very ordinary. (Flynn, page 57)

The Taking of the Government Center, 1996–2006

Greg Purcell

THE MAN AT THE PODIUM IS SAYING, WITH A STUDIED PHILOsophical flourish, the problem with the world is not that it's enormous—we can very easily imagine the enormity of the world, but we require great skill and resources to traverse—that is to say, ah, *encompass*—it, to work ourselves out from our epistemological center and past, above, ahem, its every minute workings. I call this cartography via the global market via the individual via the product. This what I call *gross* of being throws into harsh light the irony of our situation. For any account of massive physical space is sublime yet the sublime must be forwarded through an accessible act of ingenuity, I seem to have lost my place in these notes, excuse me . . . His flabby animated face turns on and off in the light of his slide projector, and beside it his index finger jogs in the air.

R. and, he assumes, the businessmen around him were willing to attend this conference—titled "Postmodern Marketing Strategies and the Construct of Globalisms"—only on the condition that they would be finishing up around 7:30, just in time to get back home and watch what could be the final game of the NBA playoffs. It's not that R. himself particularly cares about basketball, but for the past four nights of the playoffs there has been a great riotous celebration enacted by the neighborhood whenever the Bulls win, and the Bulls are up three games on Utah, and R., loving spectacle, doesn't want to miss a thing.

But it's already 8:15 and it's likely that the game is already half-finished. Even now there might be guns firing into the air above his street.

R. is listening not only to the great fat drone at the podium, but also to the sounds of businessmen shifting in their suits, redistributing their asses against the creaking aluminum chairs. He is listening to their muffled coughs and sighs. Everywhere, watches are brought discreetly into view and brought back down to dangle at a flank or to rest on a defeated lap. Collected, these repetitive movements and sounds begin to become oppressive, the sound of one great impatient thought finding voice in the tense timekeeping of a hundred individuals. In the back of the room, an ancient air conditioner hums in dips and waves.

R. is a graduate student in literature at the University of Chicago. He wants no part of this conference. If there was a reason for him to be here in the first place, he can't remember it now. R. remembers explaining to his advisor, a man in a tight fitting dark cotton suit named Doug, what his thesis was going to be titled. He explained that it was all very preliminary, that he was really only making sketches, attending seminars like this one. R. said he thought he might title his thesis "The Semiotics of Brokerage." The gaze of the man in the tight fitting suit bore down on R. then, and glinted skeptically.

A couple of red-suspendered types swayed in the seats in front of R. What exactly does this mean, "Comparative Forms of Global Cooperation?" said one of the men. He was looking at an item in tomorrow's program. He sounded a little drunk.

They think we're idiots, said his friend.

Ingenuity, the drone continues, does not of course come fully realized in a flash to the preordained "visionary" but rather it comes from the movements and buying habits of a society collectively and unconsciously defining itself . . . in purely binary terms they can give you the nod or they can give you the shrug . . .

R. is thinking at this point that the man at the podium must have just passed the two-hour mark, and that he was only now defining his subject in terms of binaries. Yet he leans forward, and his eyes are fixed on the man, not as if he were listening, exactly, but as if he were about to throw an icepick right into his fat slab of chest.

A shadowy figure up front asks how this sort of globally competitive thinking might affect his company's corporate restructuring commission. R. wants to shoot him an ice pick, too, but the man in front is too far away to really acknowledge it, so instead R. just lets out a puff of air and looks down into his lap.

Management must be brought to bear on these issues, the drone answers. That they are either unwilling or unable to cull these resources is not so much a *tragedy* as it is a *tragic paradigm* played out on a grand scale . . .

Finally, the convention is let out. The streets are mechanically silent. The game is still on. Every so often a collective roar rises from the open windows of houses, but even that sounds muted, expectant, as if a new noise were waiting to rise up over the city, negatively, like a cloud pulling back over Schaumburg. The businessmen in their dark suits, their ties already loosened, spill out of the convention center, shading their lazy eyes from the sun and scatter, hailing cabs and wending their way between cars in the parking lot. It is as if someone had dropped gray oil on a plate of shallow water.

R. waits for the bus. There are a few people at every stop, shifting uncomfortably on their hips, craning their necks and checking their watches.

But it is a brilliant day in terms of light. The weather is warm and the people are anxious. It is an experience that is felt collectively. R. rocks back and forth on his feet, and takes it all in, the fresh air, everything.

The bus arrives. R. is moving now over to his left, steps hard, steps again, and passes sideways through the packed aisle of the bus numbered 66, Chicago Avenue, westbound. The bus shudders against its own bulk as it rolls heavily, slowly forward.

R. has a small canvas bag and a book in his hand. He reels with the bus as it stops at the next corner, hisses, and then moves ahead. He is gripping the book hard in his fist so as not to drop it, and finds a place to sit near the back of the bus. These seats here form an angular U shape, and everyone who sits here without a book is forced to stare at his fellow man from across the aisle.

R is sitting just above the engine and brakes. Massive rotic squeals blow up from underneath the harried mothers, dressed in purplish pinks, always single, always surrounded by multitudes of wall-crawling children, the children squeezing under seats and into open bags.

And the sound blows up, too, from beneath the blue-uniformed transit workers slumping hard against their seats after having clocked out for the day.

R. sits across the aisle from the sliding back door. He reads his book from his lap, unconsciously disguising the cover from questioning eyes. The book is *Babbitt*, by Sinclair Lewis. Was this what he was reading before the conference?

R. entertains the idea that the conference has induced amnesia. He looks up frequently and with a blank expression surveys the scene around him. Mothers, hushing their children. City workers who always, at first glance, look like cops.

There is enough regular jerking of the bus that the stops go barely noticed. For instance, the bus stops, and a man with a thick pair of glasses frames too large for his head presses his way to the back door, hurrying as if from out of a daze to get off the bus. He pushes against the gray door handle just as the bus begins to pull forward. The door blasts an accusatory alarm.

Hey hey hey *hey*, he yells.

The driver hits the brakes with a conspicuous jerk, and just waits, looking straight ahead. The man with the thick glasses frames rattles the door handle and grimaces, repeating his partially literate complaint, and rolls his head around on his neck like a rubber toy. The alarm continues to bleat—R. thinks it makes a noise like a flycatcher electrocuting a struggling rat.

Everyone frowns and stares at the man with the thick glasses. A large woman in a pant suit furrows her brow as children with their mouths half-open buck lazily from her ankles. The driver, looking straight ahead, pushes an unseen button underneath the electronic change-counter. A green light flashes above the door and the door slides fluidly in and back. The man with the thick glasses frames bursts out with his fists clenched and the bus lurches forward again.

An off-duty Transit Authority worker, sitting to the left of the door, has opened his eyes, annoyed. His familiarity with the movement of buses seems ancient, unquestionable. He is an enormous black man and has himself firmly rooted into the nook between his armrest and the door-partition. His fat shakes with the movement of the bus, and his thick black moustache twitches.

Mm Mm Mm, he says. Three times, eyes closed, in a scolding tone.

The woman next to R. rolls around in her seat like a plush seal and R. wishes he could poke her with a pin.

The bus stops and jerks forward again. The rat-trap alarm system sounds.

Hey hey *hey hey HEY!* says a fat man in a big blue sweatshirt. He raises his arms in an exaggerated show of annoyance. Mrs. Pantsuit looks up again, eyes following the sound of the alarm.

With a sore twinge, R. realizes that he has been grinding his teeth the entire time he has been on the bus, and with some effort he relaxes his jaw.

The bus driver continues to stare straight ahead and again reaches, this time more slowly for the electronic release to the back door.

R. looks questioningly at the Transit Authority worker across from him. His eyes are open again. *Mm Mm Mm*, repeats the giant, flattening out his blue shirtfront. This one's not lettin' anyone off the bus on the firs' try.

Outside, very close by, there is a rapid burst of automatic gunfire.

In the dry cabinet there are mostly boxes. They form a deluge; beachball reds of ricotti, mostacciolli, a box of Raisin Bran, a book-blue package of chocolate cake mix. This, including the greens and yellows of cans billowing from the corners, a liquid brick-colored jar of turnips. The vividness of these objects throws the recess of the cabinet into a black pitch: from there one can make out the nondescript forms of forgotten objects, a package of saltines, twisted at the end, or a dry clove of garlic.

The refrigerator does not hum. It is unadorned. No magnets, phone numbers, or pictures from home—just a dimpled eggwhite surface, a couple of thin handles. Vegetables go undated, wrapped together in shopping bags. There are three or four half-gallons of milk forming a wall behind which random, unmarked pieces of tupperware are stacked. They look like bombs waiting to go off. In the door there are spicy mustards, plain mustards, more tupperware, a jar of too-dark olives, a jar of jalepenos, a plastic jar of chopped garlic swimming in olive oil, a bottle shaped like a perpetually fresh lime upon which a perpetually fresh lime with a human face is imploring himself to Stay Fresh. Formless lumps of tinfoil. Rags of wet spinach in a covered pot. Jars of red sauce, white sauce, brown sauce, pesto, teriaki. Cigars in the freezer.

Yet there is nothing to do with these random assemblages of things. No one is hungry. R. paticularly is not hungry, though he can imagine the exact placement of every one of his groceries before he ever walks through the kitchen door.

This food, he thinks—all of this forgotten food!—is the sign of some undescript good time. This is the economy of his household, probably of the world. Yet each item is blasted through with someone else's vague and terrible foresight. The food is saved but what is the food saved for?

Outside, a sort of riot has begun. The Bulls have won the championship. People are collecting on street corners, hands raised, hollering at passing cars which are in turn bristling with arms and legs and heads and hollering back. They all look overweight from a distance—fleshy silhouettes of girls, shirtless boys wth stout necks. Noise rises and descends in an arc from cars flashing by across Chicago Avenue. Probably no one cares that this is what they call the Doppler effect, the working of distance and movement on sonic vibrations, yet this rising and swelling of noise forms a quilt which, if not particularly warm, is at the very least distinctive. R. knows he has missed the game and finds the celebration less interesting now then when he had mentally pictured it.

The house that R. lives in looks from the outside like the sort of government building where people used to go to get some minor part of a larger project approved and stamped. It is long and gray and stands alone in front of the rubble of a vacant lot. The inside is gutted, open for renovation. For a government building it is small but for a house it is quite spacious. Yet the gray brick façade is alienating, and the part that R. and his roommate have rented—a space that must have been at one time a small cluster of offices grouped around a larger, central office—is windowless and dense and trapped.

R. is now deep in the heart of the former government building, moving from the renovated kitchen through a short hallway and past the bathroom which is really just a line of stalls with a stand-in shower attached. From either direction he can hear the sound of the other tenants banging away, making the dull ring of their hammers double and then triple through the congested system of rooms.

R. has no idea how many others there are. He runs into them now and again—pasty-faced, chalky with sawdust—nervously pacing from room to room. Every so often he will pass one of their rooms and the door will stand ajar. The windows of these rooms seem to have been knocked out and plated and barred in a hurry by unprofessional, burrowing hands. Brightly colored tarps have been erected over gray widths of drywall.

These are the sounds he's hearing now: sounds of work, hammers and saws reverberating through the white-cubicle guts of the old government building. The sound is never distracting.

R. thinks, shouldn't I get together with Brainard on building a few partitions for the common room?

The sounds fade as he takes a right, another right, steps over a mouldering pile of old jeans and tennis shoes, and works his way back into his own part of the government building.

He finds Brainard in the common room, hunching over a DAT recording machine. Brainard has propped open the emergency exit leading to the courtyard outdoors with a salvaged recliner—this is one of the only doors in the building, a door which can only be opened by a lengthwise metal bar from within—and he has crammed a microphone stand into the cushions of the recliner. The two bulbous heads of the mic are pointed outward, toward the courtyard in the back of the building, and a cord from the mic snakes in a thousand coiled repetitions back to Brainard's expensive machine. R. can hear the celebration outside, faint now, the sounds of passing cars now punctuated by the retort of firecrackers and gunshots.

I . . . says R.

Shhh, Brainard whispers, lightly turning a thick grey knob. *Doppler effect.*

They sit without speaking, faces pointed towards the invisible spirals of noise. R. soon finds that he is no longer interested in the noise. He skims a few pages of *Babbitt* and then places it back on his bookshelf. He wonders what he would have done with his time if he hadn't gone to see the pasty-faced man speak. He watches Brainard pensively hunch over his machine and begins to think about the paper he is going to write. He has a line running through his head, a fragment, dislocated from anything useful—something like *it is great to be a businessman in the bleakest weather.* It sounds great to him but would probably be deemed too poetic by his adviser. He writes it down on the back of a bank receipt, looks it over, decides that he'll keep it, and then wads up the receipt and throws it into the trash.

Shhh! Brainard turns to R. with a crumpled brow and puts his finger up sharply to his lips.

R. desperately wants to talk to Brainard about something, anything. He leans his chin against his hand and waits. Outside, there are squeals of tire-friction. Dogs are barking. Brainard channels his concentration out into the dark.

Much later in the night, Brainard and R. are listening to the recording. The DAT is replaying the lost squeals of friction, the dogs barking far off in the distance, the slight retort of firearms.

They talk about Brainard's project, the recording and looping of ambient sounds into *musique concrete*. R. says he prefers what they're listening to right now, the high register of the barking dogs playing against the low background whirr of muffled human voices. Brainard says wait till you hear the finished product.

They talk about nothing for a while. R. yawns and Brainard inspects some imperfection on the back of his upper arm.

Suddenly Brainard says, if you were four hundred feet tall then it goes without saying that you would be naked all of the time. Even if they let you walk around free it's not necessarily the case that they would be able to gather enough resources to get you into a pair of pants.

It is Brainard's self-appointed duty to destroy silence. R. doesn't mind. R. genuinely appreciates Brainard's super-lucid trains of thought.

And forget about going indoors, Brainard continues. Would you want to spend the rest of your life crouching inside of the Aragon Ballroom? No—you would sleep in Grant Park. In a sense, you would become Grant Park. Your gigantic naked presence would be undeniable. People would gossip about your privates. But forget about being a free man. The government would want you too much. Or a university. Within a few days of your discovery a semi truck with a cooling trailer would be speeding down to NASA with your heart in it. Same with your liver, your frontal lobe, your bones. All speeding to different places.

R. concedes some authority to Brainard in this matter, yet he feels small, feels himself getting smaller, as Brainard continues to speak.

So what if I were as large as the moon? R. says, interrupting.

As big as the moon? Uh. Well, then, you would be dead. Your head would be caught in outer space. Tides would change. You would have to stand in the ocean. The displaced water would engulf the world. These are the first things that come to mind. Other things would of course happen, worse things, maybe even the end of the world. The best thing for all of us would be for you to just die out there in outer space. Just float away.

R. stares at the miserable white wall, and imagines himself behind a podium, except instead of talking he is just moving his mouth, making the motions of talk, and the people are cheering, cheering and patting him on the back and just generally going nuts.

Unless! says Brainard. Unless, of course, by some supernatural means you were able to live self sufficiently, without oxygen!

Brainard is on a roll, his mouth moves and real words fall out.

Then you would become the world's best friend! You would become our other moon*! As friendly and as beneficial to us as the moon*, they would say! They would devise a way to send you out to Mars! Mars! You would have scientist friends who would send themselves up to greet you with—Gah!—with specially built space stations! Yours would be a fulfilling life, right? A fulfilling life, no doubt! They would pass on all of their knowledge to you and devise high-powered rocket boots as big around as Texas to be attached to your feet! For space exploration! There you would be, crawling around on the surface of Mars like a big white ocean, naked! Gah-ha! Wonder of nature! Man's best friend!

Brainard, excitedly runs out of material, and runs circles around the room with his eyes.

Oh, R. says.

He looks a little disappointed, as if he had had an entirely different scenario in mind. He stands up and takes a slow, deliberate look around the room. The recording has stopped and R. takes in the silence, languorously takes it in, and breathes through his nose like a weary vacuum cleaner. His gaze leads out from the hollows of his eyes.

Brainard, still sitting, looks up at R. apprehensively. He has forgotten about the moon, the size of the moon, the size of men in relation to the moon.

So, ah . . . how was the conference?

Which conference? asks R.

Global . . . says Brainard, and trails off, looking a little confused, almost frightened. Global *something*, he says, and looks down at his DAT recorder.

Global *something*, repeats R. thoughtfully. Well, let me know if you think of it.

R. rolls his shoulders around in their sockets and feels something good and grapelike pop within the system of bones.

I guess I'm off to bed, he sighs.

And that night R. dreams not of the Doppler effect or dogs or of the moon, but of the vast white spaces accessible only to the dreamless. The conference does not cross his mind at all.

Yet the conference has affected R. in deeper and more profound ways than he could have ever expected. He wakes up the next morning and calls in to say he's quit his job. He stops going to class. How exactly do forms of literature compare? he asks himself. If R. had ever cared before, he doesn't care now. Not that his emphasis was Comparative.

Outside, the dumb morning light wheels over the flat body of R.'s government building. Birds chirp and twitter and roll in their places like feathered things.

I'm sick of your incessant talking! he says to Brainard, and kicks him out of his apartment. Then he kicks the other tenants out. They file out wearily, Brainard lost among them; fat tenants, thin ones, tenants with one good eye taking a last sad and apprehensive look back at their persecutor. There is a buzzing in the back of R.'s head. He sees the 66 bus roll by as it does every twenty minutes and, incensed by its maddening regularity, the maddening regularity of the world, R. chases it for a block, shaking his fist.

You motherfuckers have no idea where you're going! yells R.

He thinks he sees a conscious, slant-eyed glare shot back by the driver. His first ever.

R. becomes purposeful then, and scours the government building from back to front. He throws out all of the belongings of his former tenants—backpacks, beds, bookcases, folders crammed with student papers, bills, unopened envelopes. He tears down the bedroom tarps, resurfaces the windows. He throws out the hackey-sacks, hats emblazoned with the insignias of sports franchises, tape-measurers. He throws out all of his own things; CDs, waterglasses, an old Goodyear tire.

Weeks later, the place where R. lives is a government building again. These weeks go by in seconds; the years, in half-hour spurts, and the government building does a brisk business. R. stamps figures, checks forms, and gets things done.

Then R. doubles. A year later he doubles again. His growth is exponential. The riots begin to die down, gradually, like the trickle of a dammed stream. Then they stop altogether.

Soon all news about the Bulls stops.

By the time my many selves have died, R. figures, smiling—yes, an old man now, dressed in the clothing of any old man, but stricter, in a way, more tweedy, more careful—by that time I will indeed be a figure to be dealt with on a global scale! Incomprehensible (let me check my notes, here), conceived, right, and reconceived in floridly expanding gross-flesh-estimates!

Soon he thinks he will have brought himself to the world.

I Have About a Billion Friends

Greg Purcell

I have about a billion friends
and each one sees the whole surround
which is why I never lie

one is full of light that bends
one weighs several billion pounds
one soundlessly flies

towards whom it soundlessly offends
and they'd seek me out just like a hound
with penetrating eye

and across the whole would I extend
and weeping, see the world around
and skeletons pass by

I have about a billion friends
like oceans breathing in the sound
of a single sutured sky

and to every beast they will attend
and man included in the loud
and choral lullaby

A System of Belts and Wheels and Mirrors

For Joel Craig

1.
The system was a good time while it lasted;
streamers of satin lint, and high on the air
we hung up angels where officiates smiled,
locked to officiates.
                              Everyone was at a desk,
and the desks were placarded with foreign names—
and right there we thought that if the desks
had somehow folded and become *Pierre's,*
then they could just as likely become
a sort of water fountain, whose numerous checkbooks 'plashed,
and they would be a bank that way.

Then, we explained, the system would work perfectly,
because who else would see himself as a pair of identical twins,
each with a snake in his hand, only one of the snakes was dead?
And though in the end we wound up playing hopscotch,
we did not worry about the singular war or the plural
parts of the war.
                              The blacktop was enormous,
and if the players on that terrible field,
their arms, police-like, spinning through the air,
sometimes seemed to be a bit foreshortened,
or sad when they should have been happy,

well, that's no one's fault, really. Just the clock
on the wall and the wish-list of weeping saints
catalogued separately in photographs
re-staging in detail the exact manner and time of their deaths,
constituting the most private high school yearbook
to have ever been made public. Now,
if we were half-blind as our saviors, we were yet saved.
That is to say we were happy. Then the system broke down.

The wars became religious and the drums beat
and those children I became were beating the drums.
The clocks ached from working and the worker ached
from squinting just so hard into desks which after all
were only desks—panelboard, nap carpeting,
little nails enveloping the floor,
and a secretary who began spiraling out like a game of dice.
So the system of objects moves! *I'm frightened!* They said.

The exterminator has called and said he would not come.
They are late all of the time, he said. This
is just one example. *Come on,* he said, *the others are waiting.*

2.

So if the light old business of buying a house
and thumbing through the *Index of Home Equity*
seems to have become a chore; and if you, K.A., or you,
my miniature Brilliantine, all tired after a hard day at work,
and in need of a little how-do-you-say-it-a-pick-me-up,
saw only *psychological* amounts of whisky in your glass,
that is not, of course, because getting drunk became a chore—
like the proof of the whisky, or the dumb act of swallowing—
but rather because the name
of a city like this,

(where the twins are left at home all day
to play with matches
with which they burn the pictures
of me, in my awkward house, and of my maps)
is a rattle, all modest,
and an upright bone in place.

My First Fairy Tale

Vijay Seshadri

1.

MY FIRST EXPOSURE, OR THE FIRST EXPOSURE I CAN REMEMBER, to the pleasures of narrative happened when I was a little over two years old, in Bangalore, in the second half of the nineteen-fifties. My father was in America, studying. My mother and I were living with my grandfather and his family in a house in the neighborhood known as Malleswaram. My grandmother had just died; the second- or third-earliest memory I have (the sequence of events is lost to me) is of making my way through a forest of adult legs to look into the room where she had been laid out on the floor, according to Indian custom, and was surrounded by her children, who sat in a semicircle and wailed and wept. My mother insists that I can't remember this, that I was too young, but I do, and remember many other things, too; the trauma of those weeks must have induced the birth of my consciousness. I remember the house was large, with mango and pomegranate trees and coconut palms in the garden and flowering bushes—hibiscus, I would guess—dotting the borders; with verandas, broad teak doors (I didn't, of course, know then that they were teak), broad windows open to the subtropical breezes, and cool marble floors, which left a smooth sensation of stone on the soles of my bare feet. It had a long driveway leading from the imposing iron gates in the wall that separated us from the street to the port cochere at the main entrance. Sometimes a car, probably a Citroën but maybe an

Indian-made Ambassador, would be parked there, its driver idling near it.

My grandfather was entitled to the car and driver because of his position in the administration of the state of Mysore, of which Bangalore was the largest and most important city. He was the chief engineer of the state, and had reached a position eminent enough that it made the subsequent and rapid decline of his fortunes in the next decade even more unaccountable and shocking. His narrative is the one that dominates my mother's side of the family, and it has a tragic arc, given shape by the elements that often define tragedy—hubris (he was caste-proud, proud of his intellect, and indifferent, or seemed indifferent, to the vulnerabilities of others); fate (which took form in my grandmother's untimely death, in his diabetes, which he was too self-indulgent to control properly, and in the terrible, self-destructive rebellion of some of his children); and a series of incalculable, unforeseeable, and disastrous coincidences. It was anything but a fairy tale, and not just because it didn't have a happy ending. Unlike a fairy tale, it had no conclusion. Its morals were forever withheld; its meaning could never be resolved; nothing came full circle but, instead, trailed off into the enigmatic and incomprehensible. I sometimes think nothing is more important to my mother than finding a way of telling her father's story that will force it to resolve. She tells it over and over again, to herself, to us, to whomever will listen, re-creating in helpless, frustrated, Balzacian detail, in order to find an escape hatch of narrative conclusiveness and thereby free herself, the early triumphs, the pride they engendered, the recklessness of this self-love, and the horrifying fall, which she avoided witnessing by moving to North America with my father after he received his degree and won a post-doctoral fellowship in Canada. About that fall, for no reason I can see—since she was blameless and couldn't have imagined what would come—she feels unassuagable guilt.

Indians have a talent for grief. I remember a lot of crying going on in that house after my grandmother's death, weeks and weeks of it. Her many children would get together in little groups and talk and weep and weep again, or go off singly to weep in corners, on staircases, near the well in the garden. My babysitters were my teenage aunts, but because of their grief they were lax in watching over me. The house had a large interior courtyard, along one side of which, near the entryway to the kitchen, there was a brazier of coals, over which, among other things, coffee beans were roasted in a round-bottomed pan. I must have been left to myself one day, and I decided it would be fun to run and jump back and forth over the brazier, which had been left burning and unattended. On one jump, I tripped and the coals scattered over my bare legs, giving me extensive third-degree burns. (I had the scars for a long time and I assumed that the discoloration of the skin on my legs was permanent, but looking just now, while writing this, at my legs, I find that, finally, no trace of the scars remains and the discoloration is entirely gone.)

I don't remember pain—the human body supposedly suppresses the memory of pain—but I do remember that I suddenly became the center of attention. I was carried up by the ubiquitous grief, as both an object on which it could focus and a distraction from it, and put in the bed my grandmother and grandfather once occupied (my grandfather wouldn't sleep in it anymore), a big four-poster in the biggest bedroom of the house. The doctor came, dressed my burns, and confined me to the bed for weeks. It was there, in a blistering South Indian April, while recuperating under the mosquito netting, that I first heard the story of the birth of Rama, incarnation of the divine principle, embodiment of kingly and husbandly virtue, slayer of the demon Ravana. The three wives of Darsaratha, King of Ayodhya, are barren. The king performs a sacrifice to petition the gods for an heir to his throne. Out of the sacrificial fire a divine messenger appears with a silver chalice full of *paisa*, an ambrosial liquid pudding, which Indians consume to this day, and which is made, in our household, of milk, sugar, cardamom, saffron, and either vermicelli, poppy seed, or tapioca. The king gives half the *paisa* to his first wife, Kausalya. She will be the mother of Rama, avatar of Vishnu. To his second wife, Sumitra, he gives half of what is left of the *paisa*. To his third wife, Kaikeyi, who will give birth to Rama's brother Bharata, he gives half of what remains (notice here the delicate hierarchical arithmetic at the heart of the domestic order of Indian kings). He bestows what little is left over on Sumitra, who because of this extra portion will give birth to twins—Lakshmana, Rama's shadow, and Shatrunga, bane of Rama's enemies.

2.

Do children like fairy tales? And, if children do like fairy tales, why do they like them? The answer to the first question has been deemed obvious by modern and contemporary culture (even though it doesn't follow that because fairy tales often have children as main characters they were told and subsequently written down for children). Yes, children like fairy tales (though I have known at least one child who couldn't stand fairy tales; his favorite bedtime story was about Hans and Peter, two boys in socialist Denmark who build a clubhouse out of odds and ends and invite their parents over for tea). And, moreover, as Bruno Bettelheim has told us, fairy tales have an important cultural function. They're therapeutic; they allow children to process the dark materials of experience. Fairy tales are useful, for both children and society, a notion which contains the answer to the second question. Children like fairy tales because they are an aid to cognition; they help them order the world around them. But is this actually the case? These assertions and explanations aren't self-evident, and seen a certain way they look suspiciously reductive. Could we possibly know what a child likes and why, or what the intensity of his or her approval is? How, for example, would I have responded at the age of two to a Nathalie Sarraute novel? Or what sort of stories was I telling myself? It's hard to say.

But I know that I liked the story of Rama's birth not because of its fairy-tale qualities—the magical potion, the number three, etc.—or because it was an illumination of, or an antidote to, the grief floating around me but because of the *paisa*. I've been told that the entire Ramayana was recited to me while I was recuperating under the mosquito netting in the house in Malleswaram, but the *paisa* episode is the only one I can remember from that time, and it is still the only one in that vast and various epic which has resonance for me, and that was because of the *paisa* itself. *Paisa* was a dessert I loved throughout my childhood, and food is something a two-year-old understands. I can make a case, in fact, at least to myself, that all the fairy tales I liked—the ones I encountered in the English-language school run by Anglican nuns, where I was enrolled at three; in the elementary school in Ottawa, to which I was translated at the age of five; in the grade school I went to in Ohio—had something to do with eating. The wolf eats or gets eaten; the idiot girl (hasn't she figured it out yet?) eats the apple poisoned on one side; the birds eat the breadcrumb trail; the abandoned boy and girl eat the gingerbread house and will soon, if they don't watch out, be nicely cooked themselves; Goldilocks eats the porridge (a delicious word that made my mouth water when I was a kid). I dislike Hans Christian Andersen's stories almost as much for the fact that his characters rarely eat in them, and certainly never with gusto, as I do for the punitive and hideous Calvinism that secretly infects each sentence.

I was a good eater as a child, and had a capacity for taking things as they came. I didn't have a trace of sentimentality about my grandmother's death (older and more vulnerable to human beings, I did grieve for my grandfather twelve years later, though I had hardly known him). I was puzzled at my mother's behavior, but not overly. Big things were happening around me in those weeks of death, grief, and burns, and I had snapped to attention. It would be years before events made as vivid impressions on me as the events of those weeks did. Also, and this has stayed with me, I developed, out of the different elements of which I was suddenly aware, an excessively precocious maturity about narrative, about stories and storytelling. I've read my share of fantasy fiction, but I have always taken greater pleasure in realism. I read Balzac all the time, and it would be nice to think that such a taste was vouchsafed to me in Bangalore when I was two. I enjoyed the story of Rama's birth. But I like to think that even then I knew it was just a story, while all the other things happening around and to me were anything but.

Fractured Fairy Tale

Vijay Seshadri

"You're coming up daisies, moose and squirrel,"
that same red-eyed, locked-and-loaded figure
intones in ten-second intervals—
blood grinning in his beard,
his finger squeezing the trigger. . .

But, gosh, Bullwinkle, isn't that guy the eternal recurrence of the same
reductive nemesis in whose name
the generalized life pulverizes
our beautiful particularities,
the horn of the moose and the tooth of the squirrel.
What's it all about, anyway?

"I don't know, Rock.
I don't even know that I don't know.
But if I had my druthers,
I'd just curl up by the fire with my books
—my books!—
cause they burn so nice and slow."

Wolf Soup

In the version of the Three Little Pigs
that I've been given to read my child,
the first two pigs, after the wolf has blown
their houses down
("Little piggy, little piggy, let me come in"),
find refuge with their perspicacious brother.
The wolf, for his part, displays no motivation,
only an impulse arrested
from his body's churning electrolytes
to demolish architectural follies.
He doesn't chase and corner the pigs.
He doesn't have a grudge against the race of pigs,
nor is he in the mood
for pig's knuckles or a nice pig's-ear taco
or even a simple ham sandwich.
And when he comes down the chimney
of the third pig's house—the one he can't
blow down, the one made of brick,
with its dormer windows
tricked out in blue, their trim
decorated with orange daisies—
he suffers for his motiveless malignancy,
in the soup pot waiting for him,
the lid of which has been removed with a
timely flourish, nothing worse than a scalding,
and runs back to his lair
somewhere over the hill.

Vijay Seshadri

Everyone has survived their lessons.
Everyone, as in the Last Judgment of the Zoroastrians,
is saved, even the wolf,
today exterminated
across much of the world, and almost so
in the forty-eight contiguous states.
The real story, which is locked in my desk
while I write this encryption, goes,
as you all remember, differently.
In it, the wolf eats the first two pigs,
but the third pig, the smart pig,
the shrewd, shrewd little pig, eats him in a soup
flavored with the turnips gathered
in a memorable prior episode.
Long did that pig rest a pensive trotter on the windowsill,
as he looked down the dusty road
travelled by the wolf.
His brothers were dead, his mother
unapproachable in her grief, and for weeks
the taste of wolf, at once unguent, farinaceous, brittle, and serene,
touched his mind with a golden fire.
In a pig's eye, he thought,
as his molecules began to recombine . . .
My son might be ready for this version of the story.
Like most four-year-olds,
he's precocious and realistic and bloody-minded.
He already knows, for example, that Jack
was nothing better than a common thief,
and has at some point observed
that giants let their fingernails grow,
sometimes to hideous lengths.

It was voyeurism on high; everyone watched everyone. We knew the pervy marketing gurus got off on watching participants through the one-way mirrors that divided their adjacent rooms. Happy to escape boring, middle-aged lives, clients flew in from cities like San Francisco and Chicago, got drunk on Bass Ale and Michelob, and ate soggy, cold Italian food while making fun of participants who couldn't hear the laughter behind the glass. (Bar-Nadav, page 11)

All God's Children Need Radios

Anne Sexton

Roses

Nov. 6, 1971

THANK YOU FOR THE RED ROSES. THEY WERE LOVELY. LISTEN, Skeezix, I know you didn't give them to me, but I like to pretend you did because as you know, when you give me something my heart faints on the pillow. Well, someone gave them to me, some official, some bureaucrat, it seems, gave me these one dozen. They lived a day and a half, little cups of blood, twelve baby fists. Dead today in their vase. They are a cold people. I don't throw them out, I keep them as momento of my first abortion. They smell like Woolworth's, half between the candy counter and the ninety-nine-cent perfume. Sorry they're dead, but thanks anyhow. I wanted daisies. I never said, but I wanted daisies. I would have taken care of the daisies, giving them aspirin every hour and cutting their stems properly, but with roses I'm reckless. When they arrive in their long white box, they're already in the death house.

Trout

Same day

The trout (brook) are sitting in the green plastic garbage pail full of pond water. They are Dr. M's trout, from his stocked pond. They are doomed. If I don't hurry and get this down, we will have broken their necks (backs?) and fried them in the black skillet and eaten them with our silver forks and forgotten all about them. Doomed. There they are nose to nose, wiggling in their cell, awaiting their execution. I like trout, as you know, but that pail is too close and I keep peering into it. We want them fresh, don't we? So be it. From the pond to the pail to the pan to the belly to the toilet. We'll have broccoli with hollandaise. Does broccoli have a soul? The trout soil themselves. Fishing is not humane or good for business.

Some Things Around My Desk

Same day

If you put your ear close to a book, you can hear it talking. A tin voice, very small, somewhat like a puppet, asexual. Yet all at once? Over my head JOHN BROWN'S BODY is dictating to EROTIC POETRY. And so forth. The postage scale sits like a pregnant secretary. I bought it thirteen years ago. It thinks a letter goes for four cents. So much for inflation, so much for secretaries. The calendar, upper left, is covered with psychiatrists. They are having a meeting on my November. Then there are some anonymous quotations Scotch-taped up. *Poets and pigs are not appreciated until they are dead.* And: *The more I write, the more the silence seems to be eating away at me.* And here is Pushkin, not quite anonymous: *And reading my own life with loathing, I tremble and curse.* And: *Unhappiness is more beautiful when seen through a window than from within.* And so forth. Sweeney's telegram is also up there. *You are lucky,* he cables. Are you jealous? No, you are reading the Town Report, frequently you read something aloud and it almost mixes up my meditations. Now you're looking at the trout. Doomed. My mother's picture is on the right up above the desk. When that picture was taken, she too was doomed. You read aloud: *Forty-five dog bites in town.* Not us. Our dog bites frogs only. You read aloud: *Five runaways and five stubborn children.* Not us. Children stubborn but not reported. The phone, at my back and a little to the right, sits like a general (German) (SS). It holds the voices that I love as well as strangers, a platoon of beggars asking me to dress their wounds. The trout are getting peppier. My mother seems to be looking at them. Speaking of the phone, yesterday Sweeney called from Australia to wish me a happy birthday. (Wrong day. I'm November ninth.) I put my books on the line and they said, "Move along, Buster." And why not? All things made lovely are doomed. *Two cases of chancres*, you read.

Eat and Sleep

Nov. 7, 1971

Today I threw the roses out, and before they died the trout spawned. We ate them anyhow with a wine bottled the year I was born (1928). The meal was good, but I preferred them alive. So much for gourmet cooking. Today the funeral meats, out to Webster (you call it Ethan Frome country) for a wake. *Eat* and *Sleep* signs. World War II steel helmets for sale. There was a church with a statue of a mother in front of it. You know, one of those mothers. The corpse clutched his rosary and his cheek bumped into the Stars and Stripes. A big man, he was somebody's father. But what in hell was that red book? Was it a prayer book or a passport at his side? Passports are blue, but mine has a red case. I like to think it's his passport, a union card for the final crossing. On the drive back, fields of burst milkweed and the sun setting against the hog-black winter clouds. It was a nice drive. We saw many *Eat* and *Sleep* signs. Last night the eater, today the sleeper.

Mother's Radio

Nov. 8, 1971

FM please and as few ads as possible. One beside my place in the kitchen where I sit in a doze in the winter sun, letting the warmth and music ooze through me. One at my bed too. I call them both: *Mother's Radio*. As she lay dying her radio played, it played her to sleep, it played for my vigil, and then one day the nurse said, "Here, take it." Mother was in her coma, never, never to say again, "This is the baby," referring to me at any age. Coma that kept her underwater, her gills pumping, her brain numb. I took the radio, my vigil keeper, and I played it for my waking, sleeping ever since. In memoriam. It goes everywhere with me like a dog on a leash. Took it to a love affair, peopling the bare rented room. We drank wine and ate cheese and let it play. No ads please. FM only. When I go to a mental hospital I have it in my hand. I sign myself in (voluntary commitment papers), accompanied by cigarettes and mother's radio. The hospital is suspicious of these things because they do not understand that I bring my mother with me, her cigarettes, her radio. Thus I am not alone. Generally speaking, mental hospitals are lonely places, they are full of TVs and medications. I have found a station that plays the hit tunes of the 1940s, and I dance about the kitchen, snapping my fingers. My daughters laugh and talk about bobbysocks. I will die with this radio playing—last sounds. My children will hold up my books and I will say goodbye to them. I wish I hadn't taken it when she was in a coma. Maybe she regained consciousness for a moment and looked for that familiar black box. Maybe the nurse left the room for a moment and there was my mama looking for her familiars. Maybe she could hear the nurse tell me to take it. I didn't know what I was doing. I'd never seen anyone die before. I wish I hadn't. Oh, Mama, forgive. I keep it going; it never stops. They will say of me, "Describe her, please." And you will answer, "She played the radio a lot." When I go out it plays—to keep the puppy company. It is fetal. It is her heartbeat—oh my black sound box, I love you! Mama, mama, play on!

Little Girl, Big Doll

Nov. 10, 1971

Out my window, a little girl walking down the street in a fat and fuzzy coat, carrying a big doll. Hugging it. The doll is almost as large as a basset hound. The doll with a pink dress and bare feet. Yesterday was my birthday and I excised it with bourbon. No one gave me a big doll. Yesterday I received one yellow wastebasket, two umbrellas, one navy pocketbook, two Pyrex dishes, one pill pot, one ornate and grotesque brown hamper. No doll. The man in the casket is gone. The birthday is gone, but the little girl skipped by under the wrinkled oak leaves and held fast to a replica of herself. I had a Dye-dee doll myself, a Cinderella doll with a crown made of diamonds and a Raggedy-Ann with orange hair and once on my sixth birthday a big doll, almost my size. Her eyes were brown and her name was Amanda and she did not welcome death. Death forgot her. (For the time being.)

Daddy Sugar

Nov. 15, 1971

O. called the night before my birthday, sticking his senile red tongue into the phone. Yet sentimental too, saying how it was forty-three years ago, that night when he paced the floor of my birth. I never heard of my father pacing the floor—a third child, he was bored. Isn't pacing limited to fathers? That's the point, isn't it! Maybe O. is my biological father, my daddy sugar and sperm. It ruined my birthday, to be claimed at forty-three by O. Just last Christmas, around the twentieth of December, he arrived out here with a secret package—my photo at sixteen (I never gave it to him. Mother must have given it to him!) and a lock of my baby hair. Why would Mother give a lock of baby hair to bachelor-family-friend-O.? He said, "I don't want to die with the evidence!" And then he drove off. Later, on the phone we promised to meet for lunch and have a confession hour. But I shy away. I am like Jocasta who begs Oedipus not to look further. I am a dog refusing poisoned meat. It would be poison he pumped into my mother. She who made me. But who with? I'm afraid of that lunch—would throw up the vichyssoise if he said: "Happy birthday, Anne, I am your father."

Brown Leaves

Nov. 16, 1971

Out my window: some wonderful blue sky. Also I see brown leaves, wrinkled things, the color of my father's suitcases. All winter long these leaves will hang there—the light glinting off them as off a cow.

At this moment I am drinking. At this moment I am very broke. I called my agent but she wasn't there, only the brown leaves are there. They whisper, "We are wiser than money; don't spend us." . . . And the two trees, my two telephone poles, simply wait. Wait for what? More words, dummy! Joy, who is as straight as a tree, is bent today like a spatula. I will take her to the orthopedic man. Speaking of suitcases, I think of my childhood and MUTNICK FOREVER. Christmases, every single year, my father tearing off the red wrapping and finding a Mark Cross two-suiter, calf, calf the color of the oak trees—and thinking of the wool supplier, Mr. Mutnick, who gave him this yearly goodie—he'd cry, "MUTNICK FOREVER." That sound, those two words meant suitcases, light tan, the color of dog shit but as soft as a baby's cheek and smelling of leather and horse.

Breathing Toys

Nov. 18, 1971

The gentle wind, the kind gentle wind, goes in and out of me. But not too well. Walking a block—just say from Beacon to Commonwealth—or over at B.U., I lean against the building for wind, gasping like a snorkel, the crazy seizure of the heart, the error of the lungs. Dr. M. wants me to go into his hospital for tests, come January. He's a strange one, aside from his stocked trout pool he keeps saying, "I want to save a life!" The life being mine. Last time we met he said, "You'll be an old hag in three years!" What does he mean? A yellow woman with wax teeth and charcoal ringlets at her neck? Or does he only mean the breathing—the air is hiding, the air will not do! An old hag, her breasts shrunken to the size of pearls? My lungs, those little animals, contracting, drowning in their shell. . . . Joy is still down. Meals float up to her. (I am the cork.) She lies on her mattress with a board under it and asks, "Why me?" Her little toes wriggling on the roof, her head lolling over the TV, her back washing like sand at low tide. As I've said elsewhere: the body is meat. Joy, will you and I outlive our doctors or will we oblige, sinking downward as they turn off the flame? As for me, it's the cigarettes, of course. I can't give them up anymore than I can give up Mother's radio. I didn't always smoke.

Once I was a baby. Back then only Mother smoked. It hurts, Mama, it hurts to suck on the moon through the bars. Mama, smoke curls out of your lips and you sing me a lullaby. Mama, mama, you hurt too much, you make no sense, you give me a breathing toy for World War II and now you take it away. Which war is this, Mama, with the guns smoking and you making no sense with cigarettes?

Dog

Nov. 19, 1971

"O Lord," they said last night on TV, "the sea is so mighty and my dog is so small." I *heard* dog. You say, they said *boat* not *dog* and that further *dog* would have no meaning. But it does mean. The sea is mother-death and she is a mighty female, the one who wins, the one who sucks us all up. *Dog* stands for me and the new puppy, Daisy. I wouldn't have kept her if we hadn't named her Daisy. (You brought me daisies yesterday, not roses, daisies. A proper flower. It outlives any other in its little vessel of water. You must have given them to me! If you didn't give them to me, who did?) Me and my dog, my Dalmation dog, against the world. "My dog is so small" means that even the two of us will be stamped under. Further, dog is what's in the sky on winter mornings. Sun-dogs springing back and forth against the sky. But we dogs are small and the sun will burn us down and the sea has our number. Oh Lord, the sea is so mighty and my dog is so small, my dog whom I sail with into the west. The sea is mother, larger than Asia, both lowering their large breasts onto the coastline. Thus we ride on her praying for good moods and a smile in the heavens. She is mighty, oh Lord, but I with my little puppy, Daisy, remain a child.

Too complicated, eh?

Just a thought in passing, just something about a lady and her dog, setting forth as they do, on a new life.

Thanksgiving in Fat City

Nov. 25, 1971

The turkey glows. It has been electrified. The legs huddle, they are bears. The breasts sit, dying out, and the gizzard waits like a wart. Everyone eats, hook and sinker, they eat. They eat like a lady and a bear. They eat like a drowning dog. The house sits like the turkey. The chimney gasps for breath and the large, large rock on the front lawn is waiting for us to move into it. It is a large mouth. Autograph seekers attend it. They mail it letters, postage due. They raise their skirts and tease it . . . It is a camera, it records the mailman, it records the gasman, it records the needy students, it records the lovers, serious as grandmothers, it records the sun and the poisonous gases, it records the eaters, the turkey, the drowned dog, the autograph seekers, the whole Hollywood trip. Meanwhile I sit inside like a crab at my desk, typing pebbles into a boat.

A Life of Things

Dec. 2, 1971

They live a life of things, Williams said. This house is stuffed like a pepper with things: the painted eyes of my mother crack in the attic, the blue dress I went mad in is carved on the cameo. Time is passing, say the shoes. Afrika boots saying their numbers, wedding slippers raining on the attic floor. The radiator swallows, digesting its gall stones. The sink opens its mouth like a watermelon. Hadn't I better move out, dragging behind me the bare essentials: a few pills, a few books and a blanket for sleeping? When I die, who will put it all away? Who will index the letters, the books, the names, the expendable jewels of a life? Things sweat in my palm as I put them each carefully into my mouth and swallow. Each one a baby. Let me give the jar of honey, the pickles, the salt box to my birthday. Let me give the desk and its elephant to the postman. Let me give the giant bed to the willow so that she may haunt it. Let me give the hat, the Italian-made Safari hat, to my dog so that she may chew off her puppyhood. Finally let me give the house itself to Mary-who-comes. Mary-who-comes has scoured the floors of my childhood and the floors of my motherhood. She of the dogs, the army of dogs, old English Sheep dogs (best of show), fifteen altogether, their eyes shy and hidden by hair, their bodies curled up wool. Mary-who-comes may have my house: the Lenox for her dogs to lap, the kitchen for breeding, the writing room for combing and currying. Mary will have a temple, a dog temple, and I will have divorced my things and gone on to other strangers.

Found Topaz

Dec. 10, 1971

The sherry in its glass on the kitchen table, reflecting the winter sun, is a liquid topaz. It makes a Tinkerbelle light on the wall. Sea light, terror light, laugh light. . . . There is less and less sherry, a cocktail sherry, very light, very good. It keeps me company. I am swallowing jewels, light by light. To celebrate this moment (it is like being in love) I am having a cigarette. Fire in the mouth. Topaz in the stomach.

Oatmeal Spoons

Same day

I am still in the kitchen, feeling the heat of the sun through the storm window, letting Mother's radio play its little tunes. Dr. Brundig is away, a week now, and I'm okay. I'm sanforized, above ground, full of anonymous language, a sherry destiny, grinning, proud as a kid with a new drawing. I'm flying invisible balloons from my mailbox and I'd like to give a party and ask my past in. And you—I tell you how great I feel and you look doubtful, a sour look as if you were sucking the ocean out of an olive. You figure, she's spent fifteen years attending classes with Dr. Brundig and her cohorts, majoring in dependence. Dr. M. (trout man, lung man) asked me, "What is your major problem? Surely you know after fifteen years?"

"Dunno"

"Well," he said, "Did you fall in love with your oatmeal spoon?"
"There was no oatmeal spoon?"
He caught on.

Angels Wooly Angels

Jan. 1, 1972, 12:30 A.M.

I feel mild. Mild and kind. I am quite alone this New Year's Eve for you are sick: having fallen in love with the toilet, you went on an opium voyage and fell asleep before the New Year. I heard it all down here in the kitchen on Mother's radio—Times Square and all that folly. I am drinking champagne and burping up my childhood: champagne on Christmas Day with my father planting corks in the ceiling and the aunts and uncles clapping, Mother's diamonds making mirrors of the candle-light, the grandmothers laughing like stuffed pillows and the love that was endless for one day. We held hands and danced around the tree singing our own tribal song. (Written in the eighteen hundreds by a great, great uncle.) We were happy, happy, happy. Daddy crying his MUTNICK FOREVER and the big doll, Amanda, that I got. . . . All dead now. The doll lies in her grave, a horse fetus, her china blue eyes as white as eggs. Now I am the wife. I am the mother. You are the uncles and grandmothers. We are the Christmas. Something gets passed on—a certain zest for the tribe, along with the champagne, the cold lobster hors d'oeuvres, the song. Mother, I love you and it doesn't matter about O. It doesn't matter who my father was; it matters who I *remember* he was. There was a queen. There was a king. There were three princesses. That's the whole story. I swear it on my wallet. I swear it on my radio. See, Mother, there are angels flying over my house tonight. They wear American Legion hats, but the rest of them is wool, wool, that white fluffy stuff Daddy used to manufacture into goods, wool, fat fleecy wool. They zing over the telephone wires, their furry wings going *Hush, hush.* Like a mother comforting a child.

Where God Is Glad

Joe Wenderoth

I HATE STRIP CLUBS. MY NEW BOOK HAS A PICTURE OF ME ON THE cover in front of a strip club, and when I show it to people and say *this is me in front of my favorite strip club in Baltimore*, I feel like I need to make all kinds of explanations. It isn't that I'm ashamed to be seen in front of a strip club, nor is it that I cherish the idea of being seen in front of a strip club. I guess when I step back and consider it, it seems childish to have one's picture taken there. What saves me, I hope, is the actual sign in the picture, which clearly distinguishes this particular strip club from most others. And then, too, the picture is good because the flash didn't work and you can just see my silhouette in the weird green-yellow light of the sign. That is, you can't see *me* so much as you can see *some guy*. The bar is called Tony's, and it's in Baltimore on Monument Avenue under an overpass on the outskirts of Highlandtown, not far from route 40, which is an industrial-trucking-prostitution-and-strip-clubs area. I lived with my wife nearby (though she was not yet my wife at the time, and has, since becoming my wife, declared that she never wants to go to Tony's again), and we could walk to and from the place. Indeed, we *did* walk to and from the place. Those were the days. So in the picture I'm standing in front of a filthy, dimly lit window with a painted sign in it. The sign reads:

ALL GIRL REVEIW
GO GO

****

Between the GO and the other GO there is a faceless buxom woman—she sort of reminds me of the cover of one of The Cars' albums—you may know the one I mean. Sort of like a fifties pin-up girl—very retro, very "stag." I guess what drew me to the sign at first was the misspelling of "review." The idea that, in the whole process of the making of the sign, there was no one capable of catching the mistake, or more likely no one who cared to make that kind of effort. This lack of concern for superficial matters quite faithfully conveys the essence of the place.

The first time I went to Tony's must have been in 1993 or 1994. As I said, it was a sort of neighborhood strip-bar, and I recall we decided—my not-yet-wife and I—that we would walk over and check it out one evening. Inside, there was a U-shaped bar to the right; to the left there was an open room with two extremely beat-up pool tables. Directly to the left, essentially behind the sign window, was one booth, the only seating in the place, save the bar stools and a handful of tables set up on both ends of the pool tables. The restrooms were in the back, behind the pool table area and behind a variety of broken machines and chairs and such. It was your basic dive bar, but dirtier, and more possessed of an under-construction look. Well, that's not exactly right—it looked more like it *had been* under construction, but construction had been abandoned for some time. What was really unusual, though—what stood out, let's say—was the bevy of dancers.

It was a bevy of three or four that first evening, if I recall correctly, and my subsequent visits have verified that this is generally the rule: three or four dancers in constant rotation. When we first walked in, the young woman who gripped the pole was overweight; I had never seen an overweight stripper, and so I found her dance quite compelling. She weighed two-seventy if she weighed a pound. The men at the bar did not seem amused, did not seem to feel that anything unusual or ironic was taking place. The dancer herself did not seem to feel that she, as a stripper, was unusual; she moved in the usual stripper way, swaying and thrusting and all of that, but with an added trick: she was able to manipulate the folds in her flesh, allowing patrons a view into a great variety of cleavages. I recall that she was particularly adept with her ass cheeks; she achieved a kind of quivering and then a kind of optical illusion as she endeavored to allow viewers to believe in the possibility of seeing in to the core, the secret binding as it were. The next dancer to take the stage was not as big as the first—she was middle of the road, as far as weight goes, and did not have a pretty face. What distinguished her was her left arm, which was misshapen, and also considerably shorter than her right arm. Her choice in attire stood out, too; she wore a one-piece Minnie Mouse bathing suit. She, like her predecessor, was conspicuously comfortable with her vocation.

We sat at the bar and drank, my not-yet-wife and I. We marveled and we talked of whatever was on our minds—that is, aside from what we were seeing unfold in front of us. The other two dancers that evening were—let me think—one was probably a thin, middle-aged blonde woman (thin save for a beer belly, that is) and one was probably an overweight black woman who shook her breasts violently. Tony's patrons that evening were white men and black men and us. Everyone was quite laid back. The bartender was Tony himself, and this has been the case almost every time I have been in; indeed, on the couple of occasions wherein Tony was not tending bar, he was seated at the bar. Tony is a small no-nonsense Greek man who, I later learned, went AWOL from the Greek navy in the seventies—somewhere in Central America—then drifted up to Baltimore and opened up his bar soon after. It is a bar, he claims, that has from day one welcomed all races; in Baltimore, this is not insignificant. But on this first visit I did not know about Tony's personal history yet. I knew what I have so far described. But then *knew* might be presumptuous; it's probably better to say that I *witnessed* what I have so far described—I did not *know* it.

The ladies—and they were clearly ladies—danced, and then they descended from the pole island and walked around the bar to ask for tips—a dollar, to be specific. Most strip clubs are constructed so that the strippers are able to approach, during their performance, the patrons seated at the bar, and to accumulate, thereby, their tips. This capacity to approach, mid-performance, in states of undress, is important, as it turns the front-row seating into a kind of challenge: to sit there is to confess, explicitly, your desire for that sort of intimacy. The capacity to approach also impacts, or challenges, the stripper; not only does it weave the achievement of intimacies into the dance—it at the same time marries the shedding of clothes with the accumulation of money. At Tony's, the dancer is not provided with the capacity to approach, during her performance, those who gaze upon her; there's just enough of a gap between the pole island and the bar to ensure that this is not possible. At Tony's, patrons seated at the bar are in some sense in the ideal spot; they're close enough to gawk, and yet not so close that they are made to pay for it. The main difference is really the way in which Tony's extracts the expected intimacy from public view and places it altogether outside of the performance, where, should intimacy continue to exist at all, it must exist as something less heard of. When finally the lovely tip-seeking lady arrives at your seat and asks you for a dollar—and by now she will usually have put her clothes back on—you feel more like you're tipping a pizza-delivery guy than a stripper. A dancer at Tony's makes her money when she's not dancing, and she makes her real money after she's combed the bar for tips. At that time, she will approach men in the bar, trying to find someone who would like to buy her a drink; the man who buys her a drink—and a drink for a dancer is steep—is entitled to sit close with her and talk as she drinks it. And then of course she might suggest taking him out into the parking lot. But what am I talking about here!—I am drifting away from the meaty crux, and I apologize for that. Let me get back to it: the living moment that is Tony's.

It seemed like every time I went back, something even more indescribable would occur. Soon after I introduced my brother and some friends to the place, we were over there on a Saturday night and there was a dwarf guy playing pool. This in itself would not be worth mentioning, but I managed to have a sort of run-in with the guy. He was playing pool, and he wasn't terribly good. I'm pretty good. But somehow he wins. My brother is, quite naturally, making fun of me, and so I say: "it's a fluke; I beat this guy eight times out of ten, easy." My rematch comes up and I miscue and scratch on an easy shot that would have gotten me to the eight ball. I am bitter, at this point, because the guy has been giving me advice all along—as if, because he beat me one time, he is some sort of pool shark. So he has this very easy shot that I have provided for him, and I am bitter, and so—well, you all know the rule about having to have one foot on the ground when you take a shot—of course, everyone knows this rule—well, the fact is, this rule would fairly disqualify my dwarf friend, so he ignores it. So as he leaps his torso up on to the table and arranges himself to take the easy shot to win the game, I say to him, from behind, and with just enough volume for him to hear: "one foot on the ground, pal." He ignores me and makes the shot. And the story has subsequently been etched into the weird crumbling tablet that is *our life at Tony's.*

The ladies have changed, over the years, and continually, but the essence of the ladies has not. I recall one night I was in there with a friend, and mostly it was Eastern European young women dancing, but there was one straight-up Baltimore woman. So she dances and then descends and makes her way down to us to get her dollars. Wanting to make conversation, my friend says: "Hey, what's up with the patch on your arm—quitting smoking?"

"Oh no," she says, "it's pain-killer."

"Oh man, what do you need that for?"

"Bone cancer," she says, and moves along to the next guy down the bar. Just when you think that the pathos cannot be amped up, just when you think you have truly met with the bottom of the barrel, there comes a deeper blow, a deeper affirmation of mortality. That is Tony's.

I've actually been meaning to write about Tony's for a long time and have not been able to do it. I love *going* there—actually approaching the physical social space that Tony's is—but approaching it *in writing* has always seemed wrong to me—has always seemed fundamentally disrespectful, fundamentally destructive of the sublime foundation. Now that I have stopped to describe the place in more depth, it seems clear to me that Tony's is not really a strip club at all. I hate strip clubs, as I said, and people who like strip clubs hate Tony's. Folks who like strip clubs seek something that Tony's *decisively* does not offer. Tony's is not "nice," does not feel like a risque Applebee's. It doesn't attempt to dignify the goings-ons it shelters. Your typical "nice" strip club maintains itself as a safety zone; its atmosphere tells you that you are dignified. It says: poverty is far away from here, and so you are safe. That the atmosphere is this way is not a small point; safety is absolutely required in a strip club, and this because of the delicacy of the intended spectacle.

If we stop to break down that spectacle, we can begin to understand why it need occur in a safe space. In the typical "nice" strip club, a chasm is constructed and then placed between the subjects and the objects. People—men, mostly—come in to gaze upon the objects of their desire, and these objects learn how to move about so as to maintain and intensify this gaze. The gaze pays. The gaze takes and then the gaze pays. The space wherein this transaction takes place must be safe—and conspicuously so—because that transaction is so delicate. The gaze itself is delicate. Why? Well, the gazer must convince himself that the gaze, in these environs, is worth pursuing. This is tricky because he must accept at the very outset that he will not be allowed to take any kind of next step; he cannot touch the object, and he cannot touch himself—he is required to inhabit the gaze without hope for the transformation it is ceaselessly making thinkable. This inhabitation is not static, however; it's full of drawing-nears. The challenge, for a strip club, is to create a consistently titillating drawing-near . . . without evoking frustration at the decided lack of arrival. This is, as I said, not an easy thing to achieve and not an easy thing to maintain once it has been achieved. Clear rules—and numerous experienced bouncers—are needed. At Tony's, there are rules, but—and this is really the amazing thing if you have ever been there—there are no bouncers.

Tony's is more like a hospital, really, than a strip club. Or maybe it's better to say a hospice. The sort of place wherein no one thinks about the prospect of discharge. At Tony's, one thinks: *life will never be other than this; I am sick, and this is a sickness that I will not outlive; this is the sickness that will take me all the way to where I have to go.* But there is something that's still missing in the analogy. *Think of Tony's as a hospice in which there is a celebration going on!* That's the great and mysterious leap. I've noticed a common reaction to Tony's—at least among the folks who are capable of loving the experience—and it goes something like: *how could this place exist?* Every time I go back to Baltimore, I fear that I will find that Tony's has ceased, and every time—knock on wood—my fears prove unfounded. Usually the existence of a public place is immediately understandable; one enters the place and feels how the place works, what the place is for, even how good it is at fulfilling that purpose. The longer one sits in Tony's, the more one wonders what it's for, how it works—even what its work could be. One wonders: *whose idea was this, and how did that idea not get vetoed?* That is the nature of the celebratory leap at Tony's; its very existence seems inexplicable from so many angles. In this, I think of it as akin to life itself. Or rather, it is akin to what we, from our decidedly limited perspective, call life itself—that throng of specific species that has somehow, flukishly, gotten through into this moment.

The typical strip bar is not likely to produce this sense of the inexplicable; its designers never intended it to produce this sense. They designed it to produce a chasm and to be capable of making use of that chasm. At Tony's, the chasm does not exist—it has never been installed. The woman on the stage, the woman who walks over to you and asks you for a dollar when she is done with her dance—that woman is no different from the woman you pass in the supermarket. She is no different, no more an object, than you are. She is a patient and you are a patient; she is as much a patient as you are. Yes, it's true that you have not been asked to play her conspicuously difficult part, but you may as well have been. You are clearly, that is, *as qualified* as each and every dancer you encounter. The spirit of a hospice party is in this way de facto democratic. Each person is created equally flawed, equally mortal.

Another way to get at my point is to consider Narcissus—but not the whole of Narcissus—just Narcissus in his brief maturity, *before* death but *after* all the love drama, all the hope. The Tony's dancer is—or she and you, together, are—Narcissus in the calm blind pulse of inparticularity's most decisive triumph: facelessness. The beauty that got the ball rolling has not been lost, but it has been transformed by the naïve effort to take possession of it. Beauty, when at first it arose, caused breathlessness, in which the other was made conspicuous as an other, a substance powerfully distinct from the substance of the self. The very air—unbreathed—confirmed this distinction. But then the air was taken away, and your face became the face of an other, and again (and this time quite literally) you can't breathe. Breathlessness, which at first compelled you into a kind of anxious hope about the otherness of the other, turns back in on itself, back on *you*, the always already achieved face. My sense is that breathlessness, relieved of that anxious hope, feels something like a comfort. The dance, relieved of the I-you chasm, becomes the dance of this more mature kind of breathlessness. Such a dance is yours as much as it is the dancer's; she dances not *for* you—she dances *of* you, or of your potential, your grotesque and beautiful energy.

And as far as this energy goes—well, I drink diet soda and coffee all day, take whatever pills I can get my hands on, eat a bag of processed sugar every night, never exercise, never eat vegetables, drink too much, lay on the couch for hours and hours staring at the television. The Tony's dancer, well, I don't know how *she* gets from morning to night, but I do know that she *has* managed it, and that she has managed it only barely. And it's this *barely* that amazes—it's this barely that justifies the whole celebration. It's this barely that heartens me, forgives me, and makes me feel obligated to do my part, to be my region of the party. It's this barely that says: *look at us—it is against all odds that we are upright and alive today!* And if the doctors have noticed that we are alive . . . and if the doctors—sensing the danger that exists for those who are alive—have proceeded to give orders *that we should not get out of this bed*, well, then we have disobeyed doctors' orders. We have gotten up from the bed and we are dancing. That's an interesting moment, if you've ever seen it, or if you've ever been it. More than interesting—it's the whole fucking ball of wax. It reminds me of an Aztec poem called "I Might Die in this Battle." This poem, to my mind, should be written in permanent marker on a stall at Tony's. Perhaps it will be.

You are slow,
my heart,
afraid.

Afraid to stand
where God is glad.

College

Joe Wenderoth

I remember I had a plastic cup
with too much bourbon and not enough ice
and I was tripping a little bit too hard,
and so I thought I had better try to *say* something,
try to get a ride home,
or find a door I could lock.
It was at this point,
or perhaps one moment beyond this point,
that the spotlight hit me—
and I was center-stage,
and I was *no one*—
I was not a part of the production on any level.
I froze.
I felt the dumb luck of my face
withstanding the delicate silence
of an audience that can't be acted out
and can't be made to understand
that this is not an act.

Wedding Vow

for Kevin and Britney

cleave you
unto this here
promise of nothing
but

whither you might lodge
brained singing
in the eat
of a brief mount

Joe Wenderoth

Against Zoning

in my mind it's full nude all the time
and never the same dancers

Which is how Henry Miller saved my life, scout's honor, the whole fucking Milleresque truth, which I pass on to women everywhere—stay away from squares and get enough sleep, even if it's in a dangerous spot.

(Kraman, page 125)

The Cookies of Fortune

Nancy Willard

THE NIGHT BEFORE MY LAST CLASS OF THE YEAR, I AM SITTING AT the dining room table with a pair of tweezers in my right hand and a fortune cookie in my left, extracting the fortune like a nerve in a bad tooth. In the college catalogue, the class is called English 217: Verse Writing. On dark winter mornings, the students arrive with coffee cups in their hands, and a single glance tells me who has stayed up too late studying for an exam or writing a paper.

Not until I stood on the other side of the desk did I realize that in the eternal present of the classroom the teacher sees every whisper, every frown, every struggle to overcome the effects of an all-nighter. On the last day, I bring in a pot of tea, a stack of paper cups, and fortune cookies. My students are mostly sophomores and juniors; they are the most promising group of poets I've ever taught, and miraculously they all seem to like each other.

I've fallen in love with ten of them.

What fortunes can my ten young poets hope for? In the last three weeks before the end of the semester, two of them learned their parents were getting a divorce, one was told she had a new stepmother, one fretted over a younger brother with a serious illness.

I come from a long line of women who believed it was unwise to walk under a ladder, break a mirror, or open an umbrella in the house. When my mother spilled salt on the dinner table, she threw a pinch of it into the fire or over her left shoulder. Once a year, my great-grandmother would go down to the river near her farm to fill a bottle with "holy water," which had to be dipped from a running stream before sunrise on Easter morning.

I knew what those women would say. *Why leave their fortunes to chance?*

So I buy a box of fortune cookies. Extracting the fortunes gives me a queasy feeling, as if I were taking the tongues of oracles. When the cookies are empty and look as innocent as snails, I insert the neatly typed fortunes destined for them: lines from my students' poems. "The world is a dictionary of smells not easily indexed." "Even an outspoken lump has its place." I've learned to dream in either light or dark." "What can be old that sings?"

On the last day of class, my students are startled to find that their fortunes come not from the stars but from themselves. They go out into a violent world with good fortunes in their pockets: the blessings they gave each other.

Auction

Nancy Willard

This steel box—who has the heart to open it?
Nobody? We will open it slowly.
What am I offered for this small flag,

and for this jawbone planted with teeth,
and for this finger, the print on its pad intact,
and for these candles, molded from footsteps

and prayers in procession, what am I offered?
And for this comb, clouded with hair and dust
starting its journey through the galaxy

to our first home in the stars,
and for the last words of the dead,
and for the waves that carried them, through air

poisoned with grief, into the ears of the living,
what am I offered? What am I offered for their absence
from the expensive real estate of your hearts?

What is it worth? In whose currency will you pay
for the soft evidence of these lives, these papers,
these lists and letters that escaped the fire,

and a man's left shoe found in the street,
and one cell from a hair that carries his name in code,
and for the roofless space in corridors

picked clean of lives, and for the light streaming
through a bombed house with no lock and no door,
what will you give me for this lot?

Going once, going twice, are you all done?
I'll throw in the key to the house for nothing.
Friends, tell me, who has the heart to open it?

The Beginners

Rebecca Wolff

1. Early June

I AM STANDING THERE IN MY USUAL SPOT BEHIND THE COUNTER at the Top Hat Café, looking down, thinking about evil, buttering toast. *Last night I dreamt about the Fourth of July. Perhaps that will be the day that I die—this Fourth of July? If not this year then maybe the next, or maybe in forty-two years.* And I am forced to decide whether I would be ready to die by then or not; or indeed, ever. I gauge my own reaction to the news of my impending death on a day when fireworks are the only identifiable landmark for miles around, when you picture a black night sky and small similes of stars against it, from the perspective of a craned neck and an open mouth, soundlessly *oohing* and *aahing*. I can see it all so clearly. I am fifteen years old.

Is it evil, I wonder, as I stack the toast, cut it into halves and arrange the halves on a small plate, to act consistently with one's wishes, even though one knows that among the consequences of these actions is pain and sorrow for those around one? Or is it evil to wish for things that will cause pain and sorrow. Or are these the same thing. Or is it evil . . . does evil contain . . . is evil *bigger* than any one person's actions, or thoughts, or wishes? Evil as a floating contingency of being, like a hat that lands on one's head. If that were so, then that would seem to exonerate one from any kind of personal responsibility.

****

The worst dream I ever had involved a house and a field. I was outside the house, under a big sky. It was all in Technicolor blues and greens. I had gone to this house to help save a friend—my "best friend," represented by a sort of grinning scarecrow figure—from persecution. He was accused of having committed a murder with an axe. The body of the dream consisted of the straw man chasing me over rutted roads and into a field, finally catching up with me where I was halted at a tall, wooden, electrified fence. All this under a wide, solidly blue sky. At the fence my friend revealed to me a truism. "Your best friend is your worst enemy," he said, through a toothy grin, and then proceeded to outline the punishment I was to endure for my crime.

With nothing in sight except the brilliant deep-blue sky at all edges of the horizon, my horribly grinning best friend tells me that I am to begin eating myself alive, immediately, starting with the tips of the fingers of my right hand, and that this will be a Sisyphean task, as no sooner will I finish eating myself than my innards will be all outside, and I will be turned inside out, and I must then begin all over again, and eat until I am outside-in again, and then begin again, *ad infinitum*, or *ad nauseum*.

But this, even, is not the full brunt of the punishment. This is just the flesh of the sentence; the skeleton, when revealed to me, is what terrifies me most, what causes me to wake up in a state of such horror and disgust that I can still recall it, although I dreamed this dream many, many years ago.

"Your sentence," the scarecrow says to me, "is to enact, over and over, the contents of the worst nightmare I have ever had: me, your best friend. And that is it; that's the worst one I've ever had. Now I will stand here and watch you eat yourself, as I have seen it only in my dreams, heretofore. Forever after, you will be the subject of this nightmare, not me."

That first day, in the café, I am amazed that I did not notice their entrance, the Motherwells, Raquel and Theo, a good-looking young couple. I was ringing up a check at the register when I heard a distinctive voice cutting through the general hum. "Theo," said the rich, low voice, "this toast is as dry as a witch's tit." And then laughter that was at once nervous and uncontrolled, like that of a child who has stayed up past her bedtime and is running on the energy of a new hour. I looked up in the direction of our one table in the window, which at certain times of day is too bright with sun, and saw her there with a man, or tall boy maybe (Theo is younger than she, slender, though built strongly.) His feathery hair was an ashy, dirty blond, and he wore loose shorts made of a fabric woven in Guatemala, or some other far-off land, and tennis shoes and a T-shirt. He seemed at ease in our homely setting. They were sitting with a newspaper—it did not look to be our local *Valley Republican*—on the table between them and some plates of eggs with bright yellow yolks, as yet unbroken, and toast, and coffee. Perhaps that was the very toast I had buttered, preoccupied as I was. Danielle, the other girl, must have served them quickly.

I had been working at the Top Hat, after school some days and on weekends, since the day I turned thirteen and my father suggested it. "Ginger, I think you're old enough now to earn your own pocket money," he said, and I went right down and got myself a job, first as a dishwasher, then as cashier, then to take orders and serve, and now I was entrusted with the ultimate responsibility: I could open and close the place. I was good at all of this, but especially at serving the patrons. I had known the Top Hat menu backwards and forwards since I was a little child, when my mother would bring me in after school for milkshakes and french-fries. Often I knew what customers would order before they opened their mouths.

It was not just for the extra twenty-five dollars a week that my parents had urged me to apply to Mr. Penrose for a job; I believe that they were already concerned, even at my tender age, that I was not sufficiently engaged in the life of our small community, its comings and goings. I never knew, for example, who was who's best friend in school, or who was having a birthday party that weekend. I simply didn't care—as long as I had Cherry, I had no need to bother with it. Cherry did all the caring for both of us.

But my parents were always prodding me to put down my book and go find the other kids—why didn't I walk over to the village green, where they often gathered after school, and attach myself to whatever warm bodies I could find? Any hijinks I might engage in, my parents seemed to think, must be better—healthier, more productive, more life-affirming—than sprawling endlessly on my belly in a patch of sun on the short-haired carpet in the living room with a stack of library books at my side, one in front of my face, shelling and chewing pistachio nuts. I think they thought I was lonely.

I was an indiscriminate reader, and regularly plundered the stacks of the Agnes Grey Town Library (a handsome stone structure erected with monies donated by said dowager lady) for obsolete Hollywood biographies, racy novels of early women's liberation whose heroines neglected their children and "screwed" their gynecologists, whole series of masculinity-charged spy novels featuring recurring protagonists with names like "Jim Prodder," men who concentrated as much energy on their sexual technique (he could peel a grape using only his teeth and tongue!) as on espionage, *anything* by Jane Austen, whose sharp eye for the materiality of romantic longing I found instructive as well as entertaining; anything, for that matter, that said "novel" on the cover and promised to feature a family, or a doomed love affair, or a failed life, or a dark secret, or a sexual awakening, or a path to crisis littered with coincidence.

And the Top Hat offered another outlet for my wide-ranging tastes: its owner, my boss, Mr. Penrose, kept a constantly updated collection of pornographic magazines in a stack in the cupboard under the employee-bathroom sink, and I often sat quietly with one of these in my lap—sometimes during my break, sometimes for an hour or so after closing the café at night. These clandestine reading periods left me feeling feverish, with knots in my intestines, but they also gave me a heady introduction to a power that might someday be mine, one not like the more circumscribed, esoteric powers I honed in my solitude; this was a power that could only be exercised in the presence of another.

The tall woman at the table in the window squinted as a shaft of sunlight found her in her seat. She scooted her chair to evade illumination, and in moving caught my eye in its fixed gaze, which she held as she stood up and came toward the counter, carrying her plate of toast cut into halves and stacked. The man watched her intently, as though she were a slow-moving missile. I inserted two fresh slices of whole-wheat bread in the toaster before she could speak. She leaned her side against the counter and, with nothing of consequence left to be said, asked my name.

"Ginger?" she repeated after me. "Well, that's fitting. I always admired Ginger on Gilligan's Island, who was so glamorous even after being shipwrecked for years. I hope I haven't embarrassed you, I know how redheads hate to have attention called . . . " she trailed off and turned sharply to look back at the man I assumed was her husband.

I studied her closely. After all, it's not every day that you see someone new in my town, especially not someone youthful. She looked rich, somehow, I thought, despite the nonchalance of her attire. Perhaps it was the total confidence she seemed to have in her worthiness of my attention. I figured they must be travelers who had stopped for the night and were having breakfast before getting back on the road. Every so often in summer and fall we get run-off tourists from one of the more accessible towns: families, mostly, looking for a cheap motel or a quick meal. I felt emboldened by her forthrightness and so I asked her, directly, to name their destination.

"Actually," she replied, glancing again around to where Theo sat, now leafing through the paper, "we've just bought a house. We're your newest neighbors. We're the Motherwells, Raquel and Theo." She said the name Motherwell as though it felt funny coming out of her mouth—the way a king might come and tell you his name was Commoner. Commoner the King. "It's next to the high school, out on Rt. 7. You could come by, after school, if you'd like. I'll draw you a map. We've been here for two weeks already and haven't had a single visitor."

I was surprised both at the invitation—*what had I done to deserve it?*—and at how long these new people had been in Wick without being remarked upon, but more sharply I was disappointed that she'd guessed, or—even worse—*assumed*, that I attended the high school. I liked to think of myself as ageless.

Raquel told me, one day, when so much had already happened, when I had looked at her face so often I could hardly even see it anymore, that someone had once told her that she had a muddy, brown aura. A chance encounter with a psychic healer from Copenhagen in a bar in Portugal. The woman clasped Raquel's becalmed face between her two smooth hands, then gently released it as though to send her away, to push her off like a little boat from the shore. And when Raquel told me this she laughed, but I could see the brown webbing fall over her face, restricting the motion of her jaw, her mouth filling with the dusty stuff.

I left the café that day by six-thirty, as usual, after giving the counter and tables a final wipe-down and separating the bills in the register into rubber-banded denominations, then stashing them in the little safe in the stockroom, switching off the lights, and locking first the front door, from inside, then the back door, behind me. I could indeed be trusted.

My bike was where I'd left it, where I always left it, propped against the fence where the trash cans were lined up, lids ajar, fat orphans eager for gruel. As I rode home I thought about the newcomers. As far as I could remember, no one had *ever* moved to Wick. But was that possible? I supposed some had moved away and then scurried back—my own father, for example, years before my birth—but that didn't really count. That was like a trick question on a math test: What's two plus two minus two.

Did this mean that I had never before met anybody I hadn't known my whole life? I guessed so, unless you counted newborn natives, who came bawling to the town and were duly presented in their swaddling clothes.

So these were my first adults.

When you stand in front of a mirror with someone you must see yourself together, and decide how it feels. You must acknowledge that you stand in some relation to each other, be it that of tailor to customer, sister to brother, mother to the bride, or that of two naked people who have just fornicated and now must look again, harder this time perhaps, at their partner, in the upright position. It is meant to be an emotional moment, usually: tearful mother smoothes bride's hair. Lovers' eyes are infused with renewed desire and they return to bed.

Raquel was twenty-seven, but she could have been nineteen, or thirty-five. Her face was long, her eyes green and narrowed like canoes. Nobody ever knows what you mean when you say that eyes are green. We tend to picture emeralds, stoplights saying "go," or grass the green of meadows and clearings (two of her favorite words). In this instance understand green like moss, like lichen, like the forest floor at the deep end of summer, about to turn brown. An enviable green, rather than the green of envy. Now you can picture her clearly, gazing into the mirror as one might gaze up at the sky, unaware of the identity of her observer but always appreciative of a compliment. Yet never equipped to respond appropriately.

Her hair was brown. She was tall, as tall as Theo almost. I remember once we were passing in front of the large mirror upstairs in her back bedroom when she caught sight of our reflection. "Look at how scrawny you are, Ginger," she said, and her arm slid around my waist and held me there. We had just been examining the wallpaper, which was very old and patterned with small bouquets of cornflowers, realistically represented, against an unrealistic ivory ground.

"It's possible that you haven't hit the full flush of puberty yet; but more likely it's just the way you are: string-bean, willowy, all those words that mean you'll never have to go through the anguish us more 'womanly' women do." She held her fingers up and wriggled them, to indicate quotation marks. I caught myself staring at the shapes of her round breasts beneath her T-shirt.

We stood still in front of the mirror and I saw that she was uncomfortable in the silence. She was trying to think of something to say.

I like the idea of auras: an organic byproduct of our living. A gentle, benevolent example of the baffling reserve of potentially real phenomena that we mostly cannot entertain as real, in order to live comfortably. Auras are organic, ghosts are supernatural, the mind is a combustion engine of perception, routinely creating and destroying and creating anew what matters—our hearths, our tongues. Who can dare to navigate these waters and still call herself a useful member of society? It takes all of your breath away. It cleanses your palate of its taste for that which is comfortable: ordinary knowledge, ordinary society, ordinary love.

But if comfort is not your highest priority, then you might live as Raquel did.

****

At home I went up to my room and sat down to begin my homework, and to wait for my mother to call us to the table—me from my desk, my father from his chair in front of the television, where he watched the nightly news and dozed. I never found that I had much to say to my father, but I knew the things he would like for me to say, and these I happily said. He seemed perfect to me, or at least perfected: complete, unassailable. I knew he loved me—I could feel it emanating at short range from his armchair, from his place at the dinner table or the kitchen counter, where we ate breakfast, and even sometimes from his cluttered workspace at the print shop, where he laid out a flyer for a sale at the shoe store.

I heard my mother's call from downstairs. We had lamb chops that night, and so I know we also had small green peas and mashed potatoes and mint jelly. Frozen peas, reconstituted potatoes from a box, jelly from a vacuum-sealed jar; these are the ends by which we come by our means. What more could we ask? That our mothers and fathers go out and slaughter the lamb? Pick the peas from the vine? Dig the potatoes out of the earth like old gold? That our mothers' mothers might send us, every year at Christmas, jars of mint they had grown in the window box and jellied themselves? My mother hated to cook—"didn't care about food"; "would just as soon have gone without"—though she never said this out loud, only muttered it under her breath as she stripped the yellow fat from raw chicken breasts, or sliced a bitter cucumber expertly against her pink thumb into the salad bowl. I am grateful that she saw the necessity of feeding her growing daughter as long as she did.

That night, after dinner, I had difficulty concentrating on my homework. There was a French exam to prepare for, a short essay to finish for my English class, and a final project for History, but none of it took solid form in my mind in the way that it must if I were to attend to it. I thought about calling Cherry, which I did most nights, and sometimes simply to distract myself from more tedious tasks, but I had a strange feeling that what I really wanted to do was to stay even more alone than usual; not to extend myself at all—not to write a word or to say a word, not to move even—not to disturb the silence of my little room, with the desk lamp throwing a small bright circle on notebooks and assignment sheets, and all else dim in the dusky blue shadow finding its way through the curtained windows. Spring was dying a winsome death outside. I could hear crickets rubbing their legs together in the yard, and someone's dog barking down the road. It all felt static, and I felt suspended within that stasis, but then strangely at the same time I was restless. It seemed as though I ought to go outside and disrupt the stillness—perhaps ride my bike down to the video store and rent a movie to watch, something my mother would like, a big bowl of popcorn between us on the couch? This was one of the ways that I communicated with her. But it was too late already for that; even in the time that I had taken to think of this anodyne, darkness had fallen completely and I found that I had locked my door, and was lying on my back on my bed, and had taken down my pants and spread my legs and with my index and middle fingers was gently seeking something I had only previously read about.

2. Late May

Cherry's mom gives us sandwiches and milk at the big kitchen table; she asks me about summer plans and I tell her the usual: longer hours at the café. "When are you going to start helping your folks out at the print shop?" she asks, turning around from where she stands, scrubbing potatoes at the sink, and Cherry says that she thinks I should find a boyfriend soon, and maybe *he* could help my parents out at the print shop. "Like going into the family business, y'know?" Increasingly, Cherry's thoughts turn to boys, and boyfriends; she even goes so far as to talk about husbands, and babies.

I cannot think like this. I use my allotted visions of the future to puzzle out smaller states of being; more internal movements; shifts in understanding. Will I always be this person that I am? Will my powers expand, or contract? Are the fleeting, unbidden visions that I have of myself in the future—striding on a street somewhere, with tall buildings shadowing me; crouching, blind, in a damp basement, imprisoned; burdened with odorous goods in an outdoor market—are these premonitions, or inventions? What is the difference?

Cherry and I go outside after lunch and meander around the green; kids from school are parked on the grass near the general store, smoking and waiting for nothing to happen. "Why don't we see what they're doing?" Cherry wonders, hesitantly; I suggest that instead we go over to the mill, and begin our summer properly. And this is what we do. I have that power.

We walk past the church, heading down toward Main Street, and Cherry tells me—I can't believe what I'm hearing—that she is thinking of quitting her job at the library and getting one at the drugstore. Perhaps, she says, she'll go to the community college in Springfield after she graduates and learn to be a pharmacist. She's been talking to Mandy Ensler, who works at Cobb Drug—we are passing it now, and stop briefly to look in the window at a display of toilet paper and foot powder on sale—and who says that it's a good job, and decent pay. You get a big discount on cosmetics and any other thing you might need to buy at the drugstore—like foot powder?, I ask myself. She says that the library is dull, and musty, and that she's always being corrected in her shelving by one of the old ladies who have worked there for a hundred years. We follow the curve of Main Street as the business district ends and we are on our way out of the town center, toward the mill.

This is absurd, this idea, and I tell her so. She is destined for better things than doling out tablets and capsules and directions on how to take them, with food or on an empty stomach or at bedtime. This is just the sort of employment—the sort of existence, no less—that we have always scorned. Can you imagine, we say to each other, and I say to myself, when I am alone, what that would be like, to be that person, to suffer that circumscription, to see the limits of your life in every direction at all times? At least at the library she is surrounded by books, which are limitless, if not unquantifiable, and I have heard that there is a science to shelving—called "library science"; I will ask my mother about this. My mother attended a large university in another state altogether and is often surprisingly knowledgeable about some things.

The mill is inactive; its many small windows have been dark and, mostly, broken, for three-quarters of a century. Cherry and I have had the luxury, all our lives, of whiling away hour upon hour just watching the play of the day's changing light, filtered through surrounding foliage, upon the old blasted red brick, and playing our own game as we watch.

Now it comes into view, and I have the same syrupy feeling of warm anticipation tingling in my arms and legs, in the pit of my stomach, as I often do when I sit down on the shag-carpeted lid of the employee-bathroom toilet to read one of Mr. Penrose's magazines. The promise of our game is that rich. We don't speak as we climb over the reflective guardrail, warm to the touch in the spring sunlight, and down the slope of the dry riverbank to our usual spot. Clean, dry smells rise up from the riverbed.

This day turned out to contain an ending, rather than the beginning I had anticipated.

The mill cast its two o'clock shadow, and we lay just out of its reach. I wanted to play Castle, as we always did, but Cherry had a different idea: "Let's talk about boys," she said, "instead." The cool rooms of the castle filled with dust at her careless words; its two-foot-thick stone walls trembled. I lay looking up at the imperturbable blue of the sky.

"All right," she said, rising on one elbow, "if you won't talk about boys, let's talk about Randy Thibodeau. He's really more like a man. Did you notice that he kept looking at me when Terry was sitting right there? Now Terry hates me, and I haven't done anything."

So this is how it's going to be, I thought. There is a way to grow up, I'm sure of it, that does not require of us this abject absorption … in what? In the hypothetical thought processes of a boy—or man—we don't know from Adam? In charting his actions and pondering his motives and interpreting his every glance? But I did the best I could, under the circumstances: I met Cherry halfway, mentioning the young couple I had seen at the Top Hat. I told Cherry she would undoubtedly find the man handsome, the woman pretty. Immediately I was pressed to make a full description—hair, height, coloring, build. Again I did my best, which proved good enough. By the time I had finished elaborating on Theo's sandy hair, his long arms, his dirty feet in their leather sandals, Raquel's statuesque figure and strangely inert, catlike, dolorous expression, Cherry was suitably thrilled at the prospect of the visit that we—really I—had been invited to make.

When Cherry and I were small we used to brew potions from cigarette butts we picked up in the playing field, under the bleachers where the high school kids dropped them. Butts and pine needles and hydrogen peroxide, with a toadstool thrown in if we came across one in our travels. We would never have called ourselves *witches* but it was certainly witches' spells we hoped to cast: We lifted them from an old book with a green marbleized cover I had found at the library, entitled simply *Spells*. I have never been able to find it again—they probably took it out of circulation. It was very professional sounding, though. The ingredients it called for were an intriguing mixture of commonplaces—things we might have on hand, like water from a hundred-year-old well, or a twig with a fork at the end; even leaves from a hemlock tree—and things that we could only just bring ourselves to timidly covet: mandrake root; the fatty layer of a stillborn babe; a frog with two heads. Often we made substitutions of other noxious substances. The spell we wished most would work was one entitled "To Make Oneself Invisible, and Walk amongst the People." Our dealings with the book tapered off substantially after my mother noticed that I was growing what she called "superstitious." My brother Jack had leaked to her a secret I had stupidly shared with him: I had been followed home from the mill, where we were practicing our spells, by something that transformed itself into a particularly large green leaf, its pale, veiny underside pressed against my bedroom window, when I turned to confront it.

But the mill was the closest we had ever come to true magic. That we had never seen its real interior was certainly part of its power, of the spell it cast over us, or that we cast over it.

For to us it was a castle, and we were princesses who had been abandoned long ago by our royal families when the kingdom was captured by neighboring armies and all the people fled. Only Cherry and I remained, in the vast, dark, desolate castle, but within its walls, its dank, serpentine hallways, its tiny rooms into which light filtered only through meager, slitted windows punched in the thick stone, we thrived like glowing white mushrooms. We prospered, foraging crows' eggs from the nests in the turret, coming to appreciate the crunchiness of mice roasted in the huge, man-sized fireplace, meant to heat whole rooms in the bitter winter.

But it was always summer in the castle, and we could be comfortable draped only in a few scarves, spending the days just brushing each others' hair into glorious coronets, or whispering reassurances that, although surely our parents, the royal family, would never return, eventually we would find our way out into the surrounding countryside and locate some other survivors of the scourge—perhaps some of the more lowly townsfolk, those whose company we tended to favor anyway, such as Tim-Tom the Tailor, or Merrykin the Midwife, or Jangler the Jewelry Maker. For though we had been born princesses, we did not relish the high station, the isolation thrust upon us by our noble birthright. . . . I startled. Cherry had flipped over and sat up with an abrupt, almost violent force. I sat erect too and the spell was broken. Her knees up, elbows propped, clasping her face between her palms, she cast her eyes down at the grass and spoke with a deliberation that made time stop.

"Ginger, I said I didn't feel like playing Castle. It just seems kind of stupid to me now." This was clearly painful for her. She was not accustomed to having to point anything out to me. "I mean, I feel like I'm too old for it. I think some of the kids from school saw us the other day, and heard what we were saying, and I just felt like such a baby. I was really embarrassed! I can see how maybe since you're only fifteen . . ." Cherry's lovely, open face had a dull cast to it, like a mirror over which a veil had been thrown.

I was surprised, to say the least. We'd been playing our game since we were little, and it had never seemed stupid to me, not once. How could something so transporting be stupid? "Stupid" was for Barbie dolls, sure, and for make-up kits with ugly colors, given to one by one's well-intentioned but misguided mother, and bra catalogs, and endless discussions of Randy Thibodeau. "Stupid" was for this world, not any other we might create.

Playing Castle, however, was just one of many techniques I had for removing myself from the tedium of our earthly kingdom as it had been constructed for us by our parents, our schooling, and the routes we must take between the two. If Cherry didn't want to play anymore, that was all right by me, really, and I told her so. I would find another game.

The relief on her face was more painful to me than her admission had been, as I could see from its depth that she must have been wishing for an end for quite a while. "It's time to go home anyway," she said, and I could not argue with her.

Literary Agency

Rebecca Wolff

Coretta Scott
King has died, the other
day. Dream

unrealized. Lost
and found, lost again, bathos
my motivation

my Elysian
dream. The place
inside

untutored, in-
corruptible,
without relation. That's

something to hold onto,
an uncontingency
dressing the wound. That's

sad and just "what it is."
It is what it is.
That's what I say

when I can't bear the news.

My Daughter

Some kind of reprehensible Sharon Olds poem about her sexuality, in its infancy, her vulva, "jewellike, Orchidean, [she would find some perfectly monstrous word for the slick, pearly tunnel and its fluttery, shuttered, open, violable, everyday, vulnerable, needing-of-my-care guileless portal]"

I do spend too much time thinking about how beautiful she is

She (my daughter, not Sharon Olds, the subject of this poem) laughs in the middle of a swallow and a thick trickle—a "rivulet"—of creamy hind-milk leaks out of the corner of her lips, unphotographable. I stuff my breast [limpid, floppy, miraculous] back in her mouth

to silence it.

Rebecca Wolff

Only Rhubarb

Rhubarb connect

A li'l ole
drainage ditch

could I put anything down
wholly deprivation?

Outside of the context of

hot man in the corner

centipede tricorner

Michelin fraction

Abattoir denim minus

The tissue it's not

Worth the time spent

Reading harsh

Determination, furrowed brow is what determination

Looks like

The Reductions

Let's go out and buy something. In the sun.

No, let's stay home and make something, the sun floods the room. It could be green, on paper. It could be money. That's the way to create new matter.

That's how I detach boats from moorings—my boat, my mooring—the harbor shallow at low tide

the skiff propelled over buffeting sand flats on

sheer
sonic puissance.

Rebecca Wolff

Who Can I Ask for an Honest Assessment?

The skin, its elasticity
Correction to the loss
its random fashioning
by homely
accident

Out of the vagina
gently spasming
a fresh vessel
all intact
The form, taking shape

And timorous
and gloomy
loafing
for deterioration

at the cellular level the decay
is not special
it's not even visible

but zoom out
to see
success

in failure

Open City Index (Issues 1–22)

Baumbach, Nico. "Guilty Pleasure" (story). *Open City* 14 (2001–2002): 39–58.

Beal, Daphne. "Eternal Bliss" (story). *Open City* 12 (2001): 171–190.

Beatty, Paul. "All Aboard" (poem). *Open City* 3 (1995): 245–247.

Becker, Priscilla. "Blue Statuary," "Instrumental" (poems). *Open City* 18 (2003–2004): 151–152.

Becker, Priscilla. "Recurrence of Childhood Paralysis," "Blue Statuary" (poems). *Open City* 19 (2004): 33–34.

Becker, Priscilla. "Typochondria" (essay). *Open City* 22 (2006): 9–12.

Beckman, Joshua and Tomaz Salamun, trans., "VI," "VII" (poems) by Tomaz Salamun. *Open City* 15 (2002): 155–157.

Beckman, Joshua and Matthew Rohrer. "Still Life with Woodpecker," "The Book of Houseplants" (poems). *Open City* 19 (2004): 177–178.

Belcourt, Louise. "Snake, World Drawings" (drawings). *Open City* 14 (2001–2002): 59–67.

Bellamy, Dodie. "From *Cunt-Ups*" (poems). *Open City* 14 (2001–2002):155–157.

Beller, Thomas. "Vas *Is* Dat?" (story). *Open City* 10 (2000): 51–88.

Bellows, Nathaniel. "At the House on the Lake," "A Certain Dirge," "An Attempt" (poems). *Open City* 16 (2002–2003): 69–73.

Bergman, Alicia. "Visit" (story). *Open City* 10 (2000): 125–134.

Berman, David. "Snow," "Moon" (poems). *Open City* 4 (1996): 45–48.

Berman, David. "Now, II," "A Letter From Isaac Asimov to His Wife, Janet, Written on His Deathbed" (poems). *Open City* 7 (1999): 56–59.

Berman, David. "Classic Water & Other Poems" (poems). *Open City* 5 (1997): 21–26.

Bernard, April. "Praise Psalm of the City Dweller," "Psalm of the Apartment Dweller," "Psalm of the Card Readers" (poems). *Open City* 2 (1993): 47–49.

Berne, Betsy. "Francesca Woodman Remembered" (story). *Open City* 3 (1995): 229–234.

Berrigan, Anselm. "'Something like ten million …'" (poem). *Open City* 14 (2001–2002): 159–161.

Bey, Hakim. "Sumerian Economics" (essay). *Open City* 14 (2001–2002): 195–199.

Bialosky, Jill. "Virgin Snow," "Landscape with Child," "Raping the Nest" (poems). *Open City* 12 (2001): 37–42.

Bialosky, Jill. "Demon Lover" (poem). *Open City* 17 (2003): 149.

Bingham, Robert. "From *Lightning on the Sun*" (novel excerpt). *Open City* 10 (2000): 33–50.

Bingham, Robert. "The Crossing Guard" (story). *Open City* 16 (2002–2003): 29–38.

Blake, Rachel. "Elephants" (story). *Open City* 18 (2003–2004): 195–209.

Blash, M. "Ghost Drawings" (drawings). *Open City* 21 (2005–2006): 131–136.

Blaustein, Noah. "Freezing the Shore My Father's Three Thousand Photographs of Point Dume & Paradise Cove" (poem). *Open City* 21 (2005–2006): 13–14.

Bolus, Julia. "Clasp" (poem). *Open City* 17 (2003): 155–156.

Bomer, Paula. "The Mother of His Children" (story). *Open City* 12 (2001): 27–36.

Borland, Polly. "Britain Today" (photographs). *Open City* 4 (1996): 181–185; front and back covers.

Bourbeau, Heather. "The Urban Forester," "The Lighting Designer" (poems). *Open City* 21 (2005–2006): 137–140.

Bove, Emmanuel. "Night Departure" (story). *Open City* 2 (1993): 43–46.

Bowes, David. Illustrations for Carlo McCormick's "The Getaway." *Open City* 3 (1995): 150–154.

Bowers, William. "It Takes a Nation of Millions to Hold Us Back" (story). *Open City* 17 (2003): 67–69.

Bowles, Paul. "17 Quai Voltaire" (story). *Open City* 20 (2005): 223–229.

Bowman, Catherine. "I Want to Be Your Shoebox," "Road Trip" (poems). *Open City* 18 (2003–2004): 75–79.

Boyers, Peg. "Transition: Inheriting Maps" (poem). *Open City* 17 (2003): 163–165

Bradley, George. "Frug Macabre" (poem). *Open City* 4 (1996): 223–237.

Branca, Alba Arikha. "Yellow Slippers" (story). *Open City* 3 (1995): 81–88.

Branca, Alba. "A Friend from London" (story). *Open City* 9 (1999): 43–52.

Brannon, Matthew. "The Unread Unreadable Master of Overviolence" (bookmark). *Open City* 16 (2002–2003): 119–120.

Bridges, Margaret Park. "Looking Out" (story). *Open City* 6 (1998): 47–59.

Broun, Bill. "Heart Machine Time" (story). *Open City* 11 (2000): 111–118.

Bao, Quang. "Date" (poem). *Open City* 8 (1999): 137–140.

Brown, Jason. "North" (story). *Open City* 19 (2004): 1–19.

Brown, Lee Ann. "Discalmer" (introduction). *Open City* 14 (2001–2002): 137–139.

Brownstein, Michael. "The Art of Diplomacy" (story). *Open City* 4 (1996): 153–161.

Brownstein, Michael. "From *The World on Fire*" (poetry). *Open City* 14 (2001–2002): 201–218.

Broyard, Bliss. "Snowed In" (story). *Open City* 7 (1999): 22–42.

Brumbaugh, Sam. "Safari Eyes" (story). *Open City* 12 (2001): 49–64.

Bunn, David. "Book Worms" (card catalog art project). *Open City* 16 (2002–2003): 43–57.

Burton, Jeff. "Untitled #87 (chandelier)" (photograph). *Open City* 7 (1999): front cover.

Butler, Robert Olen. "Three Pieces of *Severance*" (stories). *Open City* 19 (2004): 189–191.

Carter, Emily. "Glory Goes and Gets Some" (story). *Open City* 4 (1996): 125–128.

Carter, Emily. "Hampden City" (story). *Open City* 7 (1999): 43–45.

Cattelan, Maurizio. "Choose Your Destination, Have a Museum-Paid Vacation" (postcard). *Open City* 9 (1999): 39–42.

Cavendish, Lucy. "Portrait of an Artist's Studio" (drawings). *Open City* 11 (2000): 101–110.

Chamandy, Susan. "Hannibal Had Elephants with Him" (story). *Open City* 18 (2003–2004): 33–54.

Chan, Paul. "Self-Portrait as a Font" (drawings, text). *Open City* 15 (2002): 111–118.

Chancellor, Alexander. "The Special Relationship" (story). *Open City* 9 (1999): 189–206.

Charles, Bryan. "Dollar Movies" (story). *Open City* 19 (2004): 41–49.

Chase, Heather. "My First Facelift" (story). *Open City* 4 (1996): 23–44.

Chester, Alfred. "Moroccan Letters" (story). *Open City* 3 (1995): 195–219.

Chester, Craig. "Why the Long Face?" (story). *Open City* 14 (2001–2002): 109–127.

Chung, Brian Carey. "Still Life," "Traveling with the Lost" (poems). *Open City* 21 (2005–2006): 1153–156.

Clark, Joseph. "Nature Freak" (story). *Open City* 21 (2005–2006): 121–130.

Clements, Marcelle. "Reliable Alchemy" (story). *Open City* 17 (2003): 239–241.

Cohen, Elizabeth. "X-Ray of my Spine" (poem). *Open City* 2 (1993): 61–62.

Cohen, Marcel. "From *Letter to Antonio Saura*" (story). *Open City* 17 (2003): 217–225.

Cole, Lewis. "Push It Out" (story). *Open City* 12 (2001): 205–256.

Connolly, Cyril. "Happy Deathbeds" (story). *Open City* 4 (1996): 53–78.

Cooper, Elisha. Illustrations for Erik Hedegaard's "The La-Z-Boy Position." *Open City* 4 (1996): 117–121.

Corn, Alfred. "Ultra" (poem). *Open City* 20 (2005): 195.

Coultas, Brenda. "To Write It Down" (poem). *Open City* 14 (2001-2002): 185–186.

Cravens, Curtis. Photographs. *Open City* 2 (1993): 71–74.

Creed, Martin. "Work No. 202" (photograph). *Open City* 9 (1999): front cover.

Creevy, Caitlin O'Connor. "Girl Games" (story). *Open City* 8 (1999): 27–44.

Culley, Peter. "House Is a Feeling" (poem). *Open City* 14 (2001–2002): 173–177.

Cunningham, Michael. "The Slap of Love" (story). *Open City* 6 (1998): 175–196.

Curry, Crystal. "The Corporeal Other" (poem). *Open City* 18 (2003–2004): 187.

Curtis, Rebecca. "The Dictator Was Very Pleased," "The Government Eggs" (poems). *Open City* 20 (2005): 143–144.

Cvijanovic, Adam. "Icepaper #3" (paintings). *Open City* 11 (2000): 53–61.

Ellison, Lori. Drawing. *Open City* 17 (2003): back cover.

Ellman, Juliana. "Interior, Exterior, Portrait, Still-Life, Landscape" (drawings). *Open City* 19 (2004): 73–83.

Elsayed, Dahlia. "Black and Blue" (story). *Open City* 2 (1993): 29–35.

Elsayed, Dahlia. "Paterson Falls" (story). *Open City* 9 (1999): 153–158.

Engel, Terry. "Sky Blue Ford" (story). *Open City* 3 (1995): 115–128.

Eno, Will. "The Short Story of My Family" (story). *Open City* 13 (2001): 79–86.

Epstein, Daniel Mark. "The Jealous Man" (poem). *Open City* 17 (2003): 135–136.

Erian, Alicia. "Troika" (story). *Open City* 15 (2002): 27–42.

Erian, Alicia. "The Grant" (story). *Open City* 19 (2004): 109–117.

Eurydice. "History Malfunctions" (story). *Open City* 3 (1995): 161–164.

Faison, Ann. Drawings. *Open City* 12 (2001): 197–202.

Fattaruso, Paul. "Breakfast," "It Is I," "On the Stroke and Death of My Grandfather" (poems). *Open City* 20 (2005): 217–221.

Fawkes, Martin, trans., "Rehearsal for a Deserted City" (story) by Giuseppe O. Longo. *Open City* 15 (2002): 95–103.

Fernández de Villa-Urrutia, Rafael. "The First Visit to the Louvre: Fragments of an Improbable Dialogue" (story), trans. Jean Claude Abreu and Jorge Jauregui. *Open City* 16 (2002–2003): 177–181.

Field, Edward. Epilogue for Alfred Chester's "Moroccan Letters." *Open City* 3 (1995): 219.

Fitschen, David A. "Drive" (tour diaries). *Open City* 21 (2005–2006): 167–191.

Fitzgerald, Jack. "A Drop in the Bucket" (story). *Open City* 17 (2003): 99–104.

Fleming, Paul and Elke Siegel, trans., "December 24, 1999–January 1, 2000" (story) by Tim Staffel. *Open City* 12 (2001): 95–118.

Floethe, Victoria. "Object" (story). *Open City* 21 (2005–2006): 107–118.

Fluharty, Matthew. "To Weldon Kees" (poem). *Open City* 19 (2004): 107.

Flynn, Nick. "Bee Poems" (poems). *Open City* 5 (1997): 69–72.

Foley, Sylvia. "Dogfight" (story). *Open City* 4 (1996): 135–144.

Foo, Josie. "Waiting" (story); "Garlanded Driftwood" (poem). *Open City* 1 (1992): 16–18.

Forché, Carolyn. "Refuge," "Prayer" (poems). *Open City* 17 (2003): 139–140.

Ford, Ford Madox. "Fun—It's Heaven!" (story). *Open City* 12 (2001): 305–310.

Foreman, Richard. "Eddie Goes to Poetry City" (excerpted story, drawings). *Open City* 2 (1993): 63–70.

Fox, Jason. "Models and Monsters" (paintings, drawings). *Open City* 17 (2003): 51–58.

Francis, Juliana. "The Baddest Natashas" (play). *Open City* 13 (2001): 149–172.

Greene, Daniel. "Paul's Universe Blue," "Mother, Worcester, 1953," "Learning to Stand" (poems). *Open City* 15 (2002): 43–47.

Grennan, Eamon. "Glimpse" (poem). *Open City* 17 (2003): 161.

Grove, Elizabeth. "Enough About Me" (story). *Open City* 14 (2001–2002): 97–108.

Hakansson, Henrik. "Incomplete Proposals 1999–" (drawings). *Open City* 12 (2001): 89–94.

Hall, Marcellus. "As Luke Would Have It" (drawings, text). *Open City* 18 (2003–2004): 177–184.

Hanrahan, Catherine. "The Outer-Space Room" (story). *Open City* 18 (2003-2004): 99–114.

Harris, Evan. "Hope from the Third Person" (story). *Open City* 16 (2002–2003): 107–118.

Harris, Zach. "8" (drawings). *Open City* 19 (2004): 169–175.

Harrison, Jim. "Saving the Daylight," "Adding It Up," "Easter Morning," "Endgames" (poems). *Open City* 19 (2004): 20–26.

Hart, JoeAnn. "Sawdust" (story). *Open City* 21 (2005–2006): 97–105.

Harvey, Ellen. "Friends and Their Knickers" (paintings). *Open City* 6 (1998): 133–144.

Harvey, Matthea. "Sergio Valente, Sergio Valente, How You Look Tells the World How You Feel," "To Zanzibar By Motorcar" (poems). *Open City* 18 (2003–2004): 97–98.

Haug, James. "Everything's Jake" (poem). *Open City* 18 (2003–2004): 193.

Hauser, Thomas. "Schmetterlinge und Butterblumen" (drawings). *Open City* 12 (2001): 131–136.

Hayashi, Toru. "Equivocal Landscape" (drawings). *Open City* 12 (2001): 43–48.

Hayes, Michael. "Police Blotter." *Open City* 8 (1999): 107–110.

Healey, Steve. "The Asshole of the Immanent," "Tilt" (poems). *Open City* 15 (2002): 77–80.

Healy, Tom. "What the Right Hand Knows" (poem). *Open City* 17 (2003): 113–114.

Heeman, Christoph. "Pencil Drawings" (drawings). *Open City* 17 (2003): 91–98.

Hendriks, Martijn. "Swerve" (story). *Open City* 21 (2005–2006): 31–34.

Henry, Brian. "I Lost My Tooth on the Way to Plymouth (Rock)," "Intro to Lit" (poems). *Open City* 18 (2003–2004): 139–140.

Henry, Max and Sam Samore. "Hobo Deluxe, A Cinema of Poetry" (photographs and text). *Open City* 12 (2001): 257–270.

Henry, Peter. "Thrift" (poem). *Open City* 7 (1999): 136.

Hedegaard, Erik. "The La-Z-Boy Position" (story). *Open City* 4 (1996): 117–121.

Heyd, Suzanne. "Mouth Door I," "Mouth Door II" (poems). *Open City* 20 (2005): 175–179.

Kaplan, Janet. "The List" (poem). *Open City* 19 (2004): 71.

Kay, Hellin. "Moscow & New York, Coming & Going" (photographs, story). *Open City* 15 (2002): 81–92.

Katchadourian, Nina. "Selections from *The Sorted Books Project*" (photographs). *Open City* 16 (2002–2003): 143–153.

Kazanas, Luisa. "Drawings" (drawings). *Open City* 13 (2001): 139–146.

Kean, Steve. Paintings. *Open City* 4 (1996): 129–133.

Kenealy, Ryan. "Yellow and Maroon" (story). *Open City* 7 (1999): 60–70.

Kenealy, Ryan. "Resuscitation of the Shih Tzu" (story). *Open City* 16 (2002–2003): 89–96.

Kenealy, Ryan. "God's New Math" (story). *Open City* 20 (2005): 209–216.

Kennedy, Hunter. "Nice Cool Beds" (story). *Open City* 6 (1998): 162–174.

Kennedy, Hunter. "When Is It That You Feel Good?" (poem). *Open City* 9 (1999): 117–118.

Kennedy, Hunter. "Kitty Hawk" (story). *Open City* 12 (2001): 137–150.

Kharms, Daniil. "Case P-81210, Vol. 2, 1st Edition," "From Kharms's Journal," "A Humorous Division of the World in Half (Second Half)," "Blue Notebook No. 10" (poems). *Open City* 8 (1999): 130–136.

Kidd, Chip. Photographs. *Open City* 3 (1995): 129–133.

Kilimnick, Karen. "Untitled (Acid Is Groovy)" (photographs). *Open City* 9 (1999): 181–186; back cover.

Kim, Suji Kwock. "Aubade Ending with Lines from the Japanese" (poem). *Open City* 17 (2003): 117–118.

Kimball, Michael. "The Birds, the Light, Eating Breakfast, Getting Dressed, and How I Tried to Make It More of a Morning for My Wife" (story). *Open City* 20 (2005): 197–199.

Kinder, Chuck. "The Girl with No Face" (story). *Open City* 17 (2003): 31–38.

Kirby, Matthew. "The Lower Brudeckers" (story). *Open City* 22 (2006): 23–26.

Kirk, Joanna. "Clara" (drawings). *Open City* 11 (2000): 173–184.

Kleiman, Moe. "Tomorrow We Will Meet the Enemy" (poem). *Open City* 15 (2002): 119–120.

Klink, Joanna. "Lodestar" (poem). *Open City* 17 (2003): 109–110.

Knox, Jennifer L. "While Some Elegant Dancers Perched on Wires High Above a Dark, Dark Farm" (poem). *Open City* 19 (2004): 129–130.

Koolhaas, Rem, with Harvard Project on the City. "Pearl River Delta, China" (photographs, graphs, text). *Open City* 6 (1998): 60–76.

Koons, Jeff. Photographs. *Open City* 1 (1992): 24–25.

Körmeling, John. "Drawings" (drawings). *Open City* 14 (2001–2002): 129–136.

Kotzen, Kip. "Skate Dogs" (story). *Open City* 2 (1993): 50–53.

Lindbloom, Eric. "Ideas of Order at Key West" (photographs). *Open City* 6 (1998): 155–161.

Lipsyte, Sam. "Shed" (story). *Open City* 3 (1995): 226–227.

Lipsyte, Sam. "Old Soul" (story). *Open City* 7 (1999): 79–84.

Lipsyte, Sam. "Cremains" (story). *Open City* 9 (1999): 167–176.

Lipsyte, Sam. "The Special Cases Lounge" (novel excerpt). *Open City* 13 (2001): 27–40.

Lipsyte, Sam. "Nate's Pain Is Now" (story). *Open City* 22 (2006): 1–8.

Longo, Giuseppe O. "In Zenoburg" (story), trans. David Mendel. *Open City* 12 (2001): 153–160.

Longo, Giuseppe O. "Rehearsal for a Deserted City" (story), trans. Martin Fawkes. *Open City* 15 (2002): 95–103.

Longo, Giuseppe O. "Braised Beef for Three" (story), trans. David Mendel. *Open City* 19 (2004): 135–148.

Lopate, Phillip. "Tea at the Plaza" (essay). *Open City* 21 (2005–2006): 15–20.

Macklin, Elizabeth. "The House Style," "A Qualifier of Superlatives" (poems) by Kirmen Uribe. *Open City* 7 (1999): 107–111.

Macklin, Elizabeth, trans., "The River," "Visit" (poems). *Open City* 17 (2003): 131–134.

Madoo, Ceres. "Drawings" (drawings). *Open City* 20 (2005): 149–154.

Malone, Billy. "Tanasitease" (drawings). *Open City* 21 (2005–2006): 91–96.

Malkmus, Steve. "Bennington College Rap" (poem). *Open City* 7 (1999): 46.

Mamet, David. "Boulder Purey" (poem). *Open City* 3 (1995): 187–188.

Manrique, Jaime. "Twilight at the Equator" (story). *Open City* 2 (1993): 130–134.

Marinovich, Matt. "My Public Places" (story). *Open City* 13 (2001): 67–70.

Marshall, Chan. "Fever Skies" (poem). *Open City* 9 (1999): 187.

Martin, Cameron. "Planes" (paintings). *Open City* 15 (2002): 49–57.

Martin, Cameron, curator. "Interior, Exterior, Portrait, Still-Life, Landscape" (drawings, prints). *Open City* 19 (2004): 73–83.

Marton, Ana. Photographs, text. *Open City* 5 (1997): 141–150.

Marx, Pearson. "Lost Dog" (story). *Open City* 3 (1995): 143–150.

Masini, Donna. "3 Card Monte" (poem). *Open City* 17 (2003): 145–146.

Matthews, Richard. "Hudson" (poem). *Open City* 17 (2003): 107–108.

Maurer United Architects. "Façade" (photographs, images). *Open City* 15 (2002): 189– 196.

Maxwell, Richard. "A-1 Rolling Steak House" (play). *Open City* 13 (2001): 181–187.

McCabe, Patrick. "The Call" (story). *Open City* 3 (1995): 95–103.

McCormick, Carlo. "The Getaway" (story, drawings). *Open City* 3 (1995): 151–154.

McCracken, Chad. "Postcolonial Fat Man," "Second Grade" (poems). *Open City* 19 (2004): 165–167.

McCurtin, William. "Sometimes Skateboarding Is Like Dancing with Criminals" (drawings). *Open City* 20 (2005): 201–208.

McGuane, Thomas. "Bees" (story). *Open City* 4 (1996): 215–222.

McIntyre, Vestal. "Octo" (story). *Open City* 11 (2000): 27–50.

McIntyre, Vestal. "The Trailer at the End of the Driveway" (essay). *Open City* 22 (2006): 1–7.

McKenna, Evie. "Directions to My House" (photographs). *Open City* 12 (2001): 65–72.

McNally, John. "The First of Your Last Chances" (story). *Open City* 11 (2000): 125–140.

McNally, Sean. "Handsome Pants" (story). *Open City* 6 (1998): 131–132.

McPhee, Martha. "Waiting" (story). *Open City* 2 (1993): 109–118.

Mead, Stu. "Devil Milk" and "Untitled" (drawings). *Open City* 17 (2003): 177–185 and front cover.

Means, David. "What They Did" (story). *Open City* 6 (1998): 77–82.

Mehmedinovic, Semezdin. "Hotel Room," "Precautionary Manifesto" (poems), trans. Ammiel Alcaly. *Open City* 17 (2003): 141–142.

Mehta, Diane. "Rezoning in Brooklyn" (poem). *Open City* 7 (1999): 71–72.

Mendel, David, trans., "In Zenoburg" (story) by Giuseppe O. Longo. *Open City* 12 (2001): 153–160.

Mendel, David, trans., "Braised Beef for Three" (story) by Giuseppe O. Longo. *Open City* 19 (2004): 135–148.

Merlis, Jim. "One Man's Theory" (story). *Open City* 10 (2000): 171–182.

Metres, Philip and Tatiana Tulchinsky, trans., "This Is Me" (poem) by Lev Rubinshtein. *Open City* 15 (2002): 121–134.

Michels, Victoria Kohn. "At the Nightingale-Bamford School for Girls" (poem). *Open City* 4 (1996): 166–167.

Middlebrook, Jason. "APL #1 Polar Bear" (drawing). *Open City* 18 (2003–2004): front and back covers.

Milford, Kate. Photographs. *Open City* 2 (1993): 54–56.

Milford, Matthew. "Civil Servants" (paintings, text). *Open City* 7 (1999): 47–55.

Miller, Greg. "Intercessor" (poem). *Open City* 11 (2000): 51.

Miller, Jane. "From *A Palace of Pearls*" (poem). *Open City* 17 (2003): 157–160.

Miller, Matt. "Driver" (poem). *Open City* 12 (2001): 169–170.

Miller, Matt. "Chimera" (poem). *Open City* 21 (2005–2006): 119–120.

Miller, Stephen Paul. "When Listening to the Eighteen-and-a-Half Minute Tape Gap as Electronic Music" (poem). *Open City* 4 (1996): 162.

M.I.M.E. Photographs. *Open City* 9 (1999): 207–218.

Mobilio, Albert. "Adhesiveness: There Was This Guy" (story). *Open City* 5 (1997): 55–56.

Moody, Rick. "Dead Man Writes," "Domesticity," "Immortality," "Two Sonnets for Stacey" (poems). *Open City* 6 (1998): 83–88.

Moore, Honor. "She Remembers," "The Heron" (poems). *Open City* 13 (2001): 71–78.

Moore, Honor. "In Place of an Introduction" (assemblage). *Open City* 17 (2003): 105–106.

Moore, Honor. "Homage," "Hotel Brindisi," "Tango" (poems). *Open City* 20 (2005): 77–80.

Mortensen, Viggo. "From *Hole in the Sun*" (photographs). *Open City* 18 (2003–2004): 141–150.

Mullen, Harryette. "Unacknowledged Legislator," "Headlines," "Bumper to Bumper" (poems). *Open City* 14 (2001–2002): 141–143.

Munch, Edvard. "Passages from the Journals of Edvard Munch" (text, drawings). *Open City* 9 (1999): 233–250.

Münch, Christopher. Photographs, text. *Open City* 3 (1995): 89–94.

Mycue, Edward. "But the Fifties Really Take Me Home" (poem). *Open City* 11 (2000): 171–172.

Nadin, Peter. Paintings. *Open City* 4 (1996): 147–152.

Myles, Eileen. "Ooh" (poem). *Open City* 17 (2003): 143.

Myles, Eileen. "The Inferno" (story). *Open City* 18 (2003–2004): 67–74.

Nachumi, Ben. "Spring Cabin," "Crows," "Spring Cabin,' "Dream House" (poems). *Open City* 21 (2005–2006): 71–76.

Nakanishi, Nadine. "Seriidevüf" (drawings). *Open City* 19 (2004): 122–128.

Nelson, Cynthia. "go ahead and sing your weird arias," "the adoration piles of spring," "i almost get killed" (poems). *Open City* 14 (2001–2002): 169–171.

Nelson, Maggie. "The Poem I Was Working on Before September 11, 2001" (poem). *Open City* 14 (2001–2002): 179–183.

Nester, Daniel. "After Schubert's Sad Cycle of Songs" (poem). *Open City* 15 (2002): 165–168.

Nevers, Mark. "Untitled" (poem). *Open City* 20 (2005): 121.

Newirth, Mike. "Semiprecious" (story). *Open City* 18 (2003–2004): 87–96.

Nutt, David. "Melancholera" (story) *Open City* 21 (2005–2006): 53–69.

O'Brien, Geoffrey. "Roof Garden" (poem). *Open City* 3 (1995): 134.

O'Brien, Geoffrey. "The Blasphemers" (story). *Open City* 5 (1997): 43–54.

O'Brien, Geoffrey. "House Detective" (poem). *Open City* 8 (1999): 120.

O'Brien, Geoffrey. "The Browser's Ecstasy" (story). *Open City* 10 (2000): 195–202.

Pitts-Gonzalez, Leland. "The Blue Dot" (story). *Open City* 22 (2006): 71–86.

Poirier, Mark Jude. "Happy Pills" (story). *Open City* 17 (2003): 39–50.

Polito, Robert. "The Last Rock Critic" (story). *Open City* 1 (1992): 71–78.

Polito, Robert. Introduction to "Incident in God's Country." *Open City* 4 (1996): 167–168.

Polito, Robert. "Please Refrain from Talking During the Movie" (poem). *Open City* 17 (2003): 111–112.

Poor, Maggie. "Frog Pond" (story). *Open City* 4 (1996): 163–165.

Porter, Sarah. "The Blood of Familiar Objects" (story). *Open City* 14 (2001–2002): 25–31.

Primack, Gretchen. "It Is Green" (poem). *Open City* 18 (2003–2004): 153–154.

Pritchard, Melissa. "Virgin Blue" (story). *Open City* 11 (2000): 155–170.

Puckette, Elliot. "Silhouettes." *Open City* 8 (1999): 173–181.

Purdy, James. "Geraldine" (story). *Open City* 6 (1998): 145–154.

Quinones, Paul. "Peter Gek" (story). *Open City* 15 (2002): 105–107.

Raffel, Dawn. "Seven Spells" (story). *Open City* 19 (2004): 181–185.

Raskin, Jimmy. Art project. *Open City* 2 (1993): 57–60.

Raskin, Jimmy. "The Diagram and the Poet" (text, image). *Open City* 7 (1999): 120–126.

Reagan, Siobhan. "Ambassadors" (story). *Open City* 5 (1997): 27–34.

Reagan, Siobhan. "Neck, 17.5" (story). *Open City* 11 (2000): 61–68.

Redel, Victoria. "The Palace of Weep" (poem). *Open City* 17 (2003): 153–154.

Reed, John. "Pop Mythologies" (story). *Open City* 2 (1993): 97–100.

Reising, Andrea. "LaSalle" (poem). *Open City* 11 (2000): 153–154.

Resen, Laura. Photographs. *Open City* 11 (2000): 145–152.

Reynolds, Rebecca. "Casper" (poem). *Open City* 15 (2002): 93–94.

von Rezzori, Gregor. "On the Cliff" (story). *Open City* 11 (2000): 199–240.

Ricketts, Margaret. "Devil's Grass" (poem). *Open City* 11 (2000): 119.

Ritchie, Matthew. "$CaCO_2$" (drawings). *Open City* 6 (1998): 89–96.

Robbins, David. "Springtime" (photographs). *Open City* 8 (1999): 96–105.

Roberts, Anthony. "Wonders," "Two at Night," "Before Daybreak," "Beside the Orkhorn" (poems). *Open City* 20 (2005): 137–148.

Robertson, Thomas, and Rock Rofihe. "Four Round Windows" (drawings, text). *Open City* 19 (2004): 213–222.

Robinson, Lewis. "The Diver" (story). *Open City* 16 (2002–2003): 161–175.

Rofihe, Rick. "Eidetic," "'Feeling Marlene'" (stories). *Open City* 16 (2002–2003): 227–231.

Schwartz, Delmore. "T. S. Eliot's Squint" (story). *Open City* 5 (1997): 152–157.

Selby, Hubert. "La Vie en Rose" (story). *Open City* 1 (1992): 35–38.

Selwyn, Robert. "Journey" (paintings). *Open City* 21 (2005–2006): 157–165.

Serra, Richard. Paintings. *Open City* 2 (1993): 101–108.

Serra, Shelter. "Drawings (from Dynamo Series)" (drawings). *Open City* 20 (2005): 69–76.

Shapiro, Deborah. "Happens All the Time" (story). *Open City* 16 (2002–2003): 63–67.

Shapiro, Harriet. "The Omelette Pan" (story). *Open City* 18 (2003–2004): 189–191.

Shapiro, Harvey. "Where I Am Now," "History," "How Charley Shaver Died" (poems). *Open City* 8 (1999): 23–25.

Shapiro, Harvey. "Places," "Epitaphs," "Cape Ann," "Confusion at the Wheel" (poems). *Open City* 11 (2000): 185–188.

Shapiro, Harvey. "One Day," "Night in the Hamptons" (poems). *Open City* 19 (2004): 209–211.

Shattuck, Jessica. "Winners" (story). *Open City* 21 (2005–2006): 1–12.

Shaw, Sam. "Peg" (story). *Open City* 20 (2005): 97–111.

Sherman, Rachel. "Keeping Time" (story). *Open City* 20 (2005): 81–91.

Sherman, Rachel. "Two Stories; Single Family; Scenic View" (story). *Open City* 21 (2005–2006): 77–88.

Shirazi, Kamrun. "Shirazi's Problem" (chess maneuvers). *Open City* 2 (1993): 128–129.

Shields, David. "Sports" (story). *Open City* 2 (1993): 119–120.

Shirazi, Said. "The Truce" (story). *Open City* 9 (1999): 107–116.

Shope, Nina. "Platform" (story). *Open City* 19 (2004): 55–61.

Siegel, Elke and Paul Fleming, trans., "December 24, 1999–January 1, 2000" (story) by Tim Staffel. *Open City* 12 (2001): 95–118.

Sigler, Jeremy. "Inner Lumber," "Obscuritea" (poems). *Open City* 20 (2005): 137–141.

Sirowitz, Hal. "Chicken Pox Story and Others" (poems, drawings). *Open City* 7 (1999): 73–77.

Skinner, Jeffrey. "Winn-Dixie," "Survey Says," "Video Vault" (poems). *Open City* 8 (1999): 69–74.

Sledge, Michael. "The Birdlady of Houston" (story). *Open City* 16 (2002–2003): 211–221.

Smith, Charlie. "A Selection Process," "Agents of the Moving Company," "Evasive Action" (poems). *Open City* 6 (1998): 43–46.

Smith, Lee. Two untitled poems. *Open City* 3 (1995): 224–225.

Smith, Lee. "The Balsawood Man" (story). *Open City* 10 (2000): 203–206.

Smith, Molly. "untitled (underlie)" (drawings). *Open City* 21 (2005–2006): 41–48.

Smith, Peter Nolan. "Why I Miss Junkies" (story). *Open City* 13 (2001): 115–129.

Swartz, Julianne. "Loci" and "Beach with Car, Long Island" (photographs). *Open City* 13 (2001): 26, 40, 56, 78, 130, 188, 236; front and back cover.

Talbot, Toby. "Gone" (story). *Open City* 13 (2001): 95–109.

Talen, Bill. "Free Us From This Freedom: A Reverend Billy Sermon/Rant" (play). *Open City* 13 (2001): 173–180.

Taussig, Michael. "My Cocaine Museum" (essay). *Open City* 11 (2000): 69–86.

Tel, Jonathan. "The Myth of the Frequent Flier" (story). *Open City* 18 (2003–2004): 219–224.

Thomas, Cannon. "Dubrovnik" (story). *Open City* 16 (2002–2003): 75–88.

Thompson, Jim. "Incident in God's Country" (story). *Open City* 4 (1996): 169–180.

Thomson, Mungo. "Notes and Memoranda" (drawings). *Open City* 12 (2001): 311–320.

Thomson, Mungo, curator. Art projects. *Open City* 16 (2002–2003).

Thorpe, Helen. "Killed on the Beat" (story). *Open City* 5 (1997): 118–136.

Torn, Anthony. "Flaubert in Egypt" (poem). *Open City* 1 (1992): 21–22.

Torn, Jonathan. "Arson" (story). *Open City* 1 (1992): 10–12.

Torn, Tony. "Hand of Dust," "Farmers: 3 A.M.," "To Mazatlan" (poems). *Open City* 10 (2000): 225–230.

Tosches, Nick. "My Kind of Loving" (poem). *Open City* 4 (1996): 23.

Tosches, Nick. "*L'uccisore e la Farfalla*," "*Ex Tenebris, Apricus*," "I'm in Love with Your Knees," "A Cigarette with God" (poems). *Open City* 13 (2001): 45–55.

Tosches, Nick. "Proust and the Rat" (story). *Open City* 16 (2002–2003): 223–226.

Tosches, Nick. "Gynæcology" (poem). *Open City* 18 (2003–2004): 165–166.

Tosches, Nick. "The Lectern at Helicarnassus" (poem). *Open City* 21 (2005–2006): 165.

Toulouse, Sophie. "Sexy Clowns" (photographs). *Open City* 17 (2003): 201–208.

Tower, Jon.P hotographs, drawings, and text. *Open City* 1 (1992): 79–86.

Trubek, Anne and Laura Larson. "Genius Loci" (photographs, text). Open City 7 (1999): 85–94.

Tulchinsky, Tatiana and Paul Metres, trans., "This Is Me" (poem) by Lev Rubinshtein. *Open City* 15 (2002): 121–134.

Uklanski, Piotr. "Queens" (photograph). *Open City* 8 (1999): front and back covers.

Uribe, Kirmen. "The River," "Visit" (poems) trans. Elizabeth Macklin. *Open City* 17 (2003): 131–134.

Vapnyar, Lara. "Mistress" (story). *Open City* 15 (2002): 135–153.

Vapnyar, Lara. "There Are Jews in My House" (story). *Open City* 17 (2003): 243–273.

Vicente, Esteban. Paintings. *Open City* 3 (1995): 75–80.

Vicuña, Cecilia. "The Brilliance of Orifices," "Mother of Pearl," "The Anatomy of Paper" (poems), trans. Rosa Alcalá. *Open City* 14 (2001–2002): 151–154.

Walker, Wendy. "Sophie in the Catacombs" (story). *Open City* 19 (2004): 131–132.

Wallace, David Foster. "Nothing Happened" (story). *Open City* 5 (1997): 63–68.

Walls, Jack. "Hi-fi" (story). *Open City* 13 (2001): 237–252.

Walser, Alissa. "Given" (story), trans. Elizabeth Gaffney. *Open City* 8 (1999): 141–150.

Walsh, J. Patrick III. "It's time to go out on your own." (drawings). *Open City* 19 (2004): 35–40.

Wareham, Dean. "Swedish Fish," "Orange Peel," "Weird and Woozy," "Romantica" (song lyrics). *Open City* 15 (2002): 197–200.

Webb, Charles H. "Vic" (poem). *Open City* 4 (1996): 134.

Weber, Paolina. Two Untitled Poems. *Open City* 3 (1995): 72–74.

Weber, Paolina. "Tape" (poems). *Open City* 9 (1999): 95–106.

Wefali, Amine. "Westchester Burning" (story). *Open City* 15 (2002): 59–75

Weiner, Cynthia. "Amends" (story). *Open City* 17 (2003): 71–89.

Welsh, Irvine. "Eurotrash" (story). *Open City* 3 (1995): 165–186.

Welsh, Irvine. "The Rosewell Incident" (story). *Open City* 5 (1997): 103–114.

Wenthe, William. "Against Witness" (poem). *Open City* 6 (1998): 115.

Wenthe, William. "Against Witness" (poem). *Open City* 12 (2001): 273.

Wenthe, William. "Shopping in Artesia" (poem). *Open City* 19 (2004): 63.

Wetzsteon, Rachel. "Largo," "Gusts" (poems). *Open City* 12 (2001): 285–286.

Weyland, Jocko. "Burrito" (story). *Open City* 6 (1998): 27–36.

Weyland, Jocko. "Swimmer Without a Cause" (story). *Open City* 10 (2000): 231–238.

Weyland, Jocko. "The Elk and the Skateboarder" (story). *Open City* 15 (2002): 169–187.

Weyland, Jocko. "Vietnam Is Number One" (story). *Open City* 22 (2006): 27–37.

Wheeler, Susan. "Barry Lyndon in Spring Lake, 1985" (poem). *Open City* 17 (2003): 115–116.

Williams, C. K. "The Clause" (poem). *Open City* 17 (2003): 129–130.

Williams, Diane. "*Coronation* and Other Stories" (stories). *Open City* 1 (1992): 4–9.

Willis, Elizabeth. "Ferns, Mosses, Flags" (poem). *Open City* 17 (2003): 147.

Willis, Elizabeth. "Devil Bush," "Of Which I Shall Have Occasion to Speak Again" (poems). *Open City* 21 (2005–2006): 29–30.

Wilson, Tim. "Private Beach Bitches" (story). *Open City* 16 (2002–2003): 193–199.

Winer, Jody. "Mrs. Sherlock Holmes States Her Case," "How to Arrive at a Motel" (poems). *Open City* 11 (2000): 141–144.

Wolff, Rebecca. "Chinatown, Oh" (poem). *Open City* 5 (1997): 35–37.

Wolff, Rebecca. "Mom Gets Laid" (poem). *Open City* 9 (1999): 177–180.

Woodman, Francesca. Untitled photographs. *Open City* 3 (1995): 229–234 and back cover.

Wormwood, Rick. "Burt and I" (story). *Open City* 9 (1999): 129–140.

Woychuk-Mlinac, Ava. "Why?" (poem). *Open City* 19 (2004): 179.

Yankelevich, Matvei, trans., "Who By Fire" (story) by Victor Pelevin. *Open City* 7 (1999): 95–106.

Yankelevich, M. E. Introduction to Daniil Kharms. *Open City* 8 (1999): 127–129.

Yankelevich, Matvei. "The Green Bench" (poem). *Open City* 19 (2004): 149–150.

Yas, Joanna. "Boardwalk" (story). *Open City* 10 (2000): 95–102.

Yates, Richard. "Uncertain Times" (unfinished novel). *Open City* 3 (1995): 35–71.

Yau, John. "Forbidden Entries" (story). *Open City* 2 (1993): 75–76.

Young, Kevin. "Encore," "Sorrow Song," "Saxophone Solo," "Muzak" (poems). *Open City* 16 (2002–2003): 121–127.

Zaitzeff, Amine. "Westchester Burning" (story). *Open City* 8 (1999): 45–68.

Zapruder, Matthew. "The Pajamaist" (poem). *Open City* 21 (2005–2006): 35–39.

Zumas, Leni. "Dragons May Be the Way Forward" (story). *Open City* 22 (2006): 15–22.

Zwahlen, Christian. "I Want You to Follow Me Home" (story). *Open City* 19 (2004): 27–32.